404

The Surgeon

The Surgeon

by W. C. Heinz

Doubleday & Company, Inc.
Garden City, New York

To the many skilled surgeons

Author's Note

This book, which the publisher has decided to call a novel, was not intended to be a fictional portrayal of a surgeon of our time. Rather, it was to be a factual narrative, but early in the research it became obvious that for this effort to obtain its objectives it would have to go beyond the beginnings and experiences of any one man. What those objectives were I shall leave to the reader, but he should know that the professional characters portrayed are composites, and that only those giants of the past, such as Osler, Billroth, Liston, and Evarts Graham are identified by name. Although the surgical cases dealt with are true, the names, occupations, and other identifying characteristics of the patients have been changed to insure privacy.

Because of the anonymity which the medical profession prefers to impose upon its members I am unable to thank by name those dozen men who gave so freely of their knowledge, patience, and understanding. They know that I am in their debt.

The Surgeon

"Good morning, Dr. Carter," the voice of the woman on the phone was saying. "It is now 6:45."

He had been lying there only half asleep in the heavy gray darkness, half waiting for the phone to ring. When it had rung he had picked it up quickly, before it could ring a second time, he had sat up and swung his legs out from under the covers, and now he was sitting on the side of the bed and, with his feet, finding first one slipper and then the other.

"At 8 o'clock, Doctor," the woman's voice was saying, "you're at Mercy Hospital for a pneumonectomy. At 1 o'clock you're at University Hospital for a conference. At 2 o'clock you have a mitral stenosis there. At 5 o'clock you're at your office to see patients until 7. At 8:30 you're at the Academy for a meeting of the Medical Society. That's all."

"Thank you," he said, softly.

"You're welcome, Doctor," the woman's voice said.

He sat there for a moment, listening to his wife breathing evenly in the other bed by the heavy-draped windows, and then he bent over and pulled the phone plug out of the wall jack. He stood up and, carrying the phone, he went out and closed the door softly behind him and walked down the dark hall toward the light of the lamp on the table in the foyer.

Good morning, Doctor, he was saying to himself, hearing the voice again. For twenty years they have been awakening me like this and, unless I have passed them on the street or, perhaps, in a restaurant, I have never even seen them.

In the foyer he put the phone on the table and plugged it in. Then he went into the guest bathroom.

For twenty years, he was still thinking, theirs are the first voices I hear each day and I have no idea what they look like and I am seldom even conscious of the difference in one voice from another. The only one I could ever distinguish was that one with the English accent and I suppose I remember her because she sounded so cultured. In fact, I do not even know where that switchboard is they call from, because Carrie pays the bill, whatever it is, from the office, and every Valentine's Day, instead of Christmas, she sends them that perfume.

"But what do you want to send them?" she said once. "Mink stoles?"

"I don't know," he said. "I just wonder how they can use up the perfume everybody else sends them on Christmas by the fourteenth of February."

"Oh, for John's sake!" she said. "If that's all you have to think about, why don't you at least look at your mail?"

When he came out of the bathroom he walked to the kitchen and went to the range. He lifted the percolator off one of the back burners and onto a front one, and he could tell from the weight of it that there was enough water in it. He took the top off and saw the fresh coffee grounds and fitted the top back on. Then he turned the gas up under it and, hearing it ignite, he saw the flare of the blue flame and turned it down just enough so that it would not boil over while he shaved.

What this is going to come down to with this Mr. Scheller this morning, he was thinking, the razor in his right hand and starting to shave the lather from the left side of his face, is about five minutes in the three hours or so it is going to take me to do this thing, if the cancer hasn't spread too far already and if I do it at all. Actually, I can win it in three and a half minutes, or four, but I have those five minutes if I need them, and I lost before because that polyethylene tube slipped. It slipped because it was a first try and I did not flare the flange at the end of it enough, and by the time I had reclamped and recovered I had used up my time. And that, he thought then, is just a professional euphemism, because what I had really used up was my patient's time, not my time but that little Brazilian lawyer's time, the time of that little, dark-haired, dark-eyed Roberto Leon who came into my office so dynamic and decisive and, when I told him what had to be done, said: "I have confidence." I will never forget it, or him, and it was his time.

As he started to shave the right side of his face he shifted the razor into his left hand, but he did it automatically, without thinking and without remembering. He had begun to develop the dexterity of his left hand in his third year in medical school, so what ambidexterity he possessed was really born of boredom in Parasitical Diseases.

The course lecture was right after lunch when, as he knew by then, the distribution of his twelve pints of blood would be primarily devoted to supplying his digestive organs rather than his brain, which would be slightly ischemic, or sluggish. Because he went reluctantly, he was always one of the last to file in. He would sit in the back, rather than walk down the tiered, curved rows of the old amphitheater, and down at the bottom, backed against the blackboard, that tall, thin, and tired old Westby —Millard Fillmore Westby—would clear his catarrh and begin. He was one of those mumblers who talk to the floor, so what you saw, as you looked down at him from above, was his long and narrow bald head.

The steam radiators were under the low, curved windows, high in the back, and near the top of the high room the temperature must have been in the 80s. On clear days in winter the sun's rays would cut across the room on sharp, slanting planes, and in them the dust would settle slowly and somewhere along the back a steam valve would open and a radiator would hiss.

One day, because the subject was schistosomiasis, which is a disease prevalent in Egypt and the Orient and contracted by wading in infested water, and because he had already decided that he wanted to be a surgeon and would probably never go to Egypt or the Orient anyway, he began to equate the dexterity of his left hand with that of his right. To remain awake he began to write his notes with his left hand, his notebook on the desk arm of the seat to his left, and by the end of the course he could write as legibly, if not as neatly, with his left hand as with his right.

Sometime during that period he began to shave with his left hand and to brush his teeth with it too. Ambidexterity is not an absolute essential in surgery but it is an asset. It increases your speed and smooths out your moves and, if you can do it, you use your left hand almost as much as your right when you work in a right chest, as he would do this day.

So the first thing for me to check on, he was thinking, still shaving, is that they have that polyethylene tubing in three sizes soaking in that germicide. The diameter of the superior vena cava, which is the main vein that drains the blood from the upper half of the body to the right atrium of the heart, varies with the individual, but you can eye-match it for size when you get in there. You can eye-match it, or sight-measure it, or whatever you want to call it, if you have to, meaning if the cancer has spread from the right lung to the pericardium, the covering over the heart, and to the superior vena cava.

He realized then, as he had realized many times over the past eighteen months, that what he was hoping to find, when he opened that chest this day, was something that no sane and decent human being could wish upon another. During those past eighteen months, though, when he could find time, he had perfected his procedure in the dog lab, and now he had four live animals to prove that he could do this, if he had to, upon a human.

Besides, he said to himself now as he had before, my waiting for this and my desire to find it and to defeat it, will have nothing to do with whether this man, this Mr. Scheller, has it or not. Besides, for twenty years I have been seeing this about once every two years and, like all the rest of us, I have been closing them and leaving them to die within days or, at the most, weeks. That is ten cases for me alone in twenty years, and if I find this today I know I can do it and I can cure this man, and that will be the end of all this for all time. Certainly, he thought, it is not wrong for me to wish this for this day.

When he finished shaving he went to the window in the guest room and looked across the seventy-five feet of the court toward the opposite wing of apartments and then down at the grass plot with the rhododendrons and laurels. The air had that gray-gauze quality of early morning city air before the day has a chance to assert its character through the smoke and the dust and the fog.

If it has any character, he thought, starting to dress. A man shouldn't live in a city like this. He should live in the suburbs of a city of about 150,000 where a good clear day has a chance. It takes about 150,000 in population to support a thoracic surgeon, but the trouble with me is that, when I started, the thoracic giants were either in the universities or the big cities and I had to be with the best. I had to learn from the best and then you learn and the first thing you know you are one of the best and you're fifty-two and the big city has you. What it all comes down to, when you think of it, is that a man goes where his kind of work is, whether he's a fruit picker or a bridge builder or a chest surgeon or whatever he is.

He was dressing from the mahogany valet stand that they sent him air freight, special handling, from Costa Rica after he went down there to deliver that paper on "The Management of Chest Injuries" and to do that lobectomy for tuberculosis. He had admired one just like it in that little Juan's house on the hillside outside San José, deriving an actual pleasure sensation from the look and the feel of the hand-turned and hand-polished mahogany across the top where it represents the cervical region and the shoulder girdle in the human anatomy.

Then that little Juan says nothing and never lets on and just sends it, he thought, and he's a good little surgeon, too. If I had to describe him I would call him quick, rather than fast. He does everything quickly, and his only fault is that he doesn't know change of pace and his operations have an almost frenetic quality about them. That could be putting it a little strongly, because it doesn't make one bit of difference in the final result, but the operations that are pleasing to watch and to do are the ones that have the smoothness and the easy natural rhythms of a fine piece of music.

Maybe that's just a North American temperament talking, and you don't get that every day, anyway. A man operates according to his personality, and the Central and Latin Americans are different, and so is their music. That could be the answer right there.

He left his tie and his coat on the stand and he walked to the kitchen. He could smell the heavy-bodied, soft, head-filling aroma of the coffee, and he turned the gas off under the percolator and went to the counter and came back, carrying the cup on the saucer. He started to pour the coffee, the steam following it but coming up off it, into the cup, and he saw from the color in the bottom of the white cup that it would be strong enough. He filled the cup almost to the top and then he carried it to the table and put it down and walked out to the foyer and to the front door.

Opening the door, he bent over and picked up the folded copy of the newspaper. As he walked back he opened the paper and read the headline:

RUSSIA EXPLODES 2 MORE;
K LAUGHS OFF THE BIG ONE

Damn, he thought, feeling the depression come, as he had felt it come many times in the past year or so. I am feeling good today because I know I can do this thing, and I can cure a man. It makes me feel that I am important, which every man must feel, but after I have worked at my best for three tough hours and saved a life these idiots talk about dropping bombs that will take millions of lives, and what satisfaction does that leave me or any man who is doing his job in our time?

He was seated now at the table and he put the paper down. He tried the coffee, black, felt the cup too hot against his lips, and took just one small sip. Then, without looking at the headline again, he opened the paper to the sports page and found Red Smith's column on the left and folded the paper and started to read.

"Men who have heretofore," he read, "looked upon wealth with admiration, if not downright tenderness, choked on their rock Cornish hen in Twenty-One yesterday, when one of their number got up on his hind legs and put the knock on $302,365. Even the Chambertin turned pale.

"Assembled at lunch were some of the owners and trainers of horses that will endeavor to extract this sum from . . ."

When he heard the white wall phone ring he reached over with his left hand and took it down. He took another sip of the coffee and put the phone to his ear.

"Yes?" he said.

"Dr. Carter?" the feminine voice said, and he recognized it. "Sally Wheeler."

"Well," he said. "Sarah. How's my gal Sal?"

"Terrible," she said.

"Oh, come on," he said. "It's too early in the day for that."

"It's not too early for me," she said. "We're in a real jam here, and I called to say that your 8 o'clock case, your Mr. Scheller, has to be moved back."

"To when?"

"I'm hoping for 9:30 or 10."

"How about another room?"

"Not this morning."

"What's going on?" he said. "What kind of a schedule have you got?"

"The schedule's not the problem," she said, "but we had a real free-for-all last night. Don't even ask me about it."

"I won't."

"We got two out of an auto crack-up. We had a stabbing, two Caesareans—and I'm just giving you the hit shows. The girls I have on call I had in here all night, and one of them is having her period. You know that one who has dysmenorrhea?"

"Yes," he said, although he had no idea about whom she was talking.

"You know, the one who fainted the other day. Well, even she came in, but she spent most of her time flat on her back in the nurses' lounge. Anyway, three of our major instrument kits are just now being cleaned and they have to be autoclaved and set up. Dr. Berkman and the great Jaffrey are also delayed, but I thought I'd call you first."

"You're my gal," he said.

"Listen," she said. "That reminds me. Your young friend Stanczyk has been on an emergency in Room Three since 6 o'clock. The way he's calling for blood he's not enjoying himself."

"What's he doing?"

"A sub-total gastrectomy, but what I started to say is that he's got your room, so if he ever gets out of there you'll follow him."

"All right, Sal," he said. "I'll see you."

"Listen," she said. "Another morning like this and you'll see me, but as a cardiac patient."

"You'll handle it," he said.

"Stop flattering me," she said. "Good-bye."

She certainly will handle it, he thought, when he had hung up. He had been waiting for this morning and this operation for eighteen months. He could drink his coffee now, however, and feel neither annoyance nor frustration, because years ago he had come to accept that few days, even as few operations, go exactly as you foresee them, and because, for as long as he had known her, Sarah Wheeler had had that quieting influence upon him that only the really competent can impart to others.

"We've got this operating-room supervisor," he was telling someone, not another doctor, not long ago, "who used to be a great scrub nurse. You ask me if a surgeon ever gets nervous. Well, in my first year of residency, about 3 A.M., this emergency case came in, a woman out of an auto accident, and I had to relieve the pressure on the brain. I'd assisted on this kind of thing and I knew what I had to do, but when you do it your first time you're nervous as hell. After all, it's just you with the assistant resident and the intern and the scrub nurse and the anesthetist, and you're the boss.

"Anyway, I was sweating right through my scrub suit, but you have a tendency to hold your hand out and this gal I'm telling you about, this Sally Wheeler, was slapping the right instrument in there every time. When I wasn't so sure what I wanted next, she had it in there. She wasn't much older than I was but she'd been around those operating rooms while I was just going through med school.

"A good scrub nurse," he had told whoever it was, "is like a good caddy. A good caddy may not be able to make the shots himself but he knows his course. You finish a shot and walk up to your ball and stick out your hand and the club he gives you is the one you'd better use."

Sally's no great intellect and she's a little too flip for some people sometimes, he was thinking now, walking to the range and pouring another cup of coffee, but somebody should have married her. She's about fifty-three now and carries too much weight and those varicose veins forced her out of the operating room, but about twenty-five years ago somebody finishing up his residency would have been a lot better off with Sally than marrying social standing or intellectual stimulation or whatever those losers married. The trouble is, women like Sally don't want that kind anyway.

He walked back to the table and sat down. Then he took the phone off the hook and dialed the hospital and, while he waited for the answer, he took another drink of coffee.

"Mercy Hospital."

"Good morning," he said. "This is Dr. Carter. Do you think you can find our eminent thoracic surgical resident, Dr. James Bronson?"

"Yes sir, Doctor. I'll try. . . . I'm ringing. . . . Just a moment. . . . Here he is."

"Hello?"

"James? Matt Carter."

"Good morning, Doctor."

"You know my 8 o'clock has been delayed?"

"Yes, sir."

"How's everything else?"

"Yes and no."

"What's the trouble?"

"I have a question about Benjamin Davies."

And I know what your question is, he thought. You want to know why I'm taking him off the morphine.

"Shoot," he said.

"His night nurse called me, and said the sedation is wearing off and the patient is starting to complain. I checked the orders you left last night, and I see you don't want him to have any more morphine. It seems to me that the pain will increase and I'm wondering if you want to revise the orders."

"No," he said, "and I'll tell you why. You and I know this man is terminal, and he hasn't got more than about thirty-six hours, at the most, to go. When Bob Robinson and I operated on him originally a couple of years ago he forbade me to tell his wife it was a cancer. I went along with this, and now I have to pay the price."

"That's not right," Bronson said.

"I've never met his wife. When we operated on him he told her it was for an old football injury and, as far as I know, she never came to the hospital. When he checked in a couple of days ago she was with him but I was operating and Bob Robinson saw her. Since then the grown daughter has arrived in town but I've had him heavily doped up all the time and they're complaining. When they come in to see him, if he's awake at all, he doesn't recognize them, and they want to talk to him."

"I see."

"Now they called last evening to say they'd be in at 9 o'clock this morning, and that's the reason for the orders to take him off the morphine. We know his physical and mental state is such that there won't be much of a conversation, but this is a husband and a father and this is going to be the last chance these people will have to see any resemblance to the man they knew. After all, they're going on living, so I'm allowing them this."

"I understand."

"As a matter of fact, when they see him and find out he's having pain they're going to come running to me to ask me to put him back on the drug. He won't be off for long."

"I see."

"You'll soon find out that for every patient you treat you've got to treat two or three or four relatives."

"I've found that out already."

"Just remember that, about four thousand years ago, when the patient died they cut off the surgeon's hands. They later amended that custom so that, when the surgeon failed, he was given to the patient's relatives to do whatever they wanted with him."

"Then things are improving?"

"We sometimes wonder. How's Mrs. Kirk?"

"She's doing all right. She had some nausea."

"That's expected. Did they change her position from her back to her right side?"

"Yes, sir."

"Do you know why?"

"I have an idea."

"That's to reduce any chance of pneumonia."

"She's a very fine woman."

"And she's got two nice girls and, I understand, a fine husband. We're not going to tell her that I just opened and closed her chest without being able to do anything for her, but I've got to tell her husband. He'll be in this morning, and I've got a little time now with this delay. Tell the nurse to call me if I'm not on the floor while he's there, and if I'm not in the O.R."

"Yes, sir."

"How's Bernie Waterman?"

"Fine. He had a good night, and he says he's hungry."

"You may not believe it, but in about three weeks or a month I'll buy that kid a steak, and he'll be able to eat it."

"I believe it, Doctor."

"All right. If you have no problems, I'll be over in an hour."

That Bronson is all right, he thought, finishing his coffee. He's conscientious and he's a learner and I'll open his eyes today if we get to that vena cava problem. I'd really like Stan to see it but Sally says he's having trouble and he'll work his way out of it but this won't be the day for him to watch me. This will be one of those days when he'll be doubting how good he is and right now he's at that stage where he suffers a little by comparing himself to me.

That's what happens when you like some kid and you take him under your wing. While he's interning or in his residency he thinks you're a god. He may dream it, but he never quite dares say to himself that he will be as good as, or better than, you. Then he's out two years and start-

ing to move, and one day it comes to him that maybe he *can* be you.
Now he's lost a god, and when he looks at the man he's found he forgets
that you've got twenty years to his two. This man, toward whom he feels
a challenge for the first time, is too much for him, and this is when he
needs you as much as he ever has. This is no time to dazzle him, because
as much as you have enjoyed it you can never be a god again anyway, and
he doesn't need that any more.

It is like Pete Church and me, he thought. When I came back after
five years and watched him again that first day doing that lobectomy I
thought: "He's slipping. He's not what he used to be." The truth was
he was better than he had ever been, but while I had been moving forward whole yards at a time his progress was in inches, as it must be after
so many years and when about all that there is left for you to do is to
refine your techniques. It was only the gap between us that had nar-
rowed.

Of course this Mr. Scheller's vena cava may be free of the cancer,
anyway, he thought. He had rinsed the cup and saucer at the sink and
left them on the drainboard and he was walking back to the guest room.
You can't really be certain about a thing like this from the X rays, but
after you have looked at enough of them you can almost sense it. If I
get shut out again I hope it's because this vena cava is clean and not
because the cancer has spread to the diaphragm and it's hopeless and
I've got another Mrs. Kirk.

So how will I tell Mrs. Kirk's husband? How will I tell him that in
five months or six he will be left alone with two little kids? He will look
at me and force a smile and say: "Well, Doctor, what did you find?" I'll
look back at him and somehow I'll tell him, although I don't know
exactly how I will do it because I have never learned it in twenty years
and I never will.

When he finished dressing he went out and closed the door behind
him. He rang for the elevator and looked at his watch and saw it was
7:40.

II

"Good morning, John," he said to the doorman.

"Good mornin', Doctor," big John said, handing him the car keys.
"It's still across the street where you're leavin' it last night."

"That's all right. How's your health?"

They were standing on the sidewalk, under the awning. Big John, in his uniform overcoat, seemed bigger than ever.

"I'm not for complainin'."

Any day now big John would tie one on. About twice a year he tries to challenge single-handed the combined inventories of Schenley and National Distillers and then his son, the cop, comes into the office on his way home from the precinct and he says: "Dad's got that bronchitis again, Doctor. Will you write out that prescription and send a note to the superintendent saying you're treating him and he'll be back to work in a couple of days?"

"So what kind of a day are we going to have?" he said now, feeling the chill.

Across the street, in the park, the two black oaks near the fence still held some of their jagged, dried, rust-brown leaves. Beyond them the single-pointed, almost ovate, light brown leaves of the big gray beech would cling, most of them, into the winter and beyond it, but the maples and the plane trees were already bare.

"I'll not be predictin' the weather, Doctor. There's too much smoke and fog every day now."

"That's right."

"Now you're a doctor, and you'll be knowin' this better than I, but I think it's them Bolsheviks explodin' their bombs that's makin' this."

"You may know as much about it as I do," he said.

"I'll be goin' home now and to bed, anyway," big John said.

"Good."

He drove the Mercedes down the half-block to the dead end and swung it around the concrete stanchion and came back past the apartment house. At the corner, as he passed under the traffic light, it changed from green to yellow, so he turned left, knowing that he could pick up three green lights going south before he turned west again and, if he timed it right, pick up three more green lights before he would have to stop.

Near the first corner, in the gray dampness, a middle-aged woman in a green coat with the fur collar held tight around her throat and her hair in curlers was curbing a black cocker spaniel. At the bus stop on the next corner two teen-age girls, their stacked books cradled in their crossed arms, were talking and laughing, and on the one-way street the traffic, mostly trucks and taxis, the taxis cruising empty or heading back to the garage, moved easily and with a shushing sound.

It is all right, he thought, knowing again the sensation that is not nervousness, but the starting small, spreading feeling of excitement. When he was younger and just beginning and still insecure, every operation would be prefaced by anticipation and tension. He would lie in bed the night before and play it over and over, trying to imagine every complication that he could possibly run into and trying always to think one step ahead. What, he would ask himself, if I run into this? Now he was fifty-two and had opened more than three thousand chests, and he had it all so beautifully systemized that each move was almost a reflex. It is never boring, because no two are exactly alike, but now, in most of them, the tension is gone and so is almost all of the exhilaration, and now you just refine and refine and refine.

"My God, Matt!" Bob Robinson said to him one day, assisting and watching him dissect around the aorta, which is the great artery. "How simple can you make it?"

Rob will be a little anxious today, he thought. We've got those four dogs, living, but he won't really be convinced until we succeed in a human. Thinking this, he could see the superior vena cava, thin-walled and showing the dark blue of the de-oxygenated blood it is returning to the heart and, where it crosses it, he could see the right pulmonary artery, thicker-walled than the vena cava and pink, and both of them about the size of a man's thumb.

Sally won't have that jam cleared away before 10:30, he thought now. He turned right then and, finding no parking space in front of his office, he drove halfway down the block before he found one. After he had backed in he walked back and through the arcade and around the fish pool, dry now and its bottom covered with damp leaves, and he unlocked the door and went in.

He walked through the heavy, close air of the darkened waiting room and through Carrie's office and into his own. He turned on the lamp on the end table beside the sofa and the hanging light over his desk and saw the stack of opened mail, where he had left it the night before, with Carrie's note, scrawled on a piece of memo paper, lying on top: "Will you PLEASE look at these!"

Paper work, he thought. If there is anything you don't want to put your mind to when you would rather be operating it is paper work. You don't want to put your mind to it after you have been operating, either. In fact, you don't ever want to put your mind to it, if you can help it.

He sat down and picked up the first letter. It was written on notebook paper, white with light blue lines, the rectangular folds still showing, the writing in blue ink level with the lines, but labored and awkward.

Dear D.R. I don't know who else to turn to for help. D.R. as you no Wm. Siler was cut off the Welfare last June. Just as soon as you said he was able to work they cut him off. D.R. he have look high and low for a job and he just can't find one and you have been so good for him I am wondering if you know a job. . . .

What she sees in that sob I don't know, he thought. Maybe he's the first and only man she ever had, but he's got the intelligence of a ten-year-old and it is all you can do to get an answer out of him or to get him to look at you. In a stolen car, too, he remembered, and he plants it on top of a fire hydrant and the intern who rode the ambulance said there was water and oil everywhere. Multiple broken bones, and then four years later he comes in with that traumatic aneurism, that dilation, of the aorta.

Today we'd bypass an aneurism like that with the artificial heart pump, but on that Siler we made a temporary shunt with that cow's carotid artery from that kosher slaughter house. That rabbi was a nice little man and they always cut the carotids at the angle at the jaw so he preserved the length we needed for the shunt instead of cutting it at the origin in the chest the way they do in the commercial stock yards. You might almost say that was another example of the wisdom of the rabbinical laws, and then we took that aorta from that marine killed in that three-car wreck and preserved it by freeze-drying and gas-sterilized it and grafted it onto that aorta of our Mr. Siler.

What this skinny, sandy-haired, squint-eyed Siler doesn't know is that he's walking around today with about two inches of the aorta of a U.S. marine in him. Then he uses a mail drop to get $65 a month from welfare but he moves in with her and she gets another $65. That's $130 and then she does daily cleaning at different places but not enough in any one place to get on social security and lose that welfare, and Carrie can handle this.

"You answer," he wrote in pencil at the top of the letter. Then he underlined the "you," and put the letter aside. He picked up the next one, and saw the letterhead of The American Association for Thoracic Surgery.

This is to confirm acceptance of your paper entitled 'Radical Pneumonectomy for Carcinoma of the Lung' for presentation on the scientific program of The American Association for Thoracic Surgery. Your paper will be presented on April 17. The exact order of presentation has not been decided as yet, but . . .

He put that on top of the first letter. He picked up a letter typed on single-sheet male personal stationery, and when he did not recognize the engraved name and the suburban address, he looked down at the bottom and saw the signature "Vi Landers." The i was dotted with a small circle.

This is the second one in about ten days, he thought, and I will bet you dear Vi has lost again. I remember him now, the name on the letterhead, a benign tumor in the upper lobe of the right lung about a month ago, a retired real estate broker in his late fifties and free game for dear Vi.

"Dear Dr. Carter:" he started to read. "I am writing this while my patient is taking a nap, because it is getting so that he watches everything I do, and there are some things I think you should know. . . ."

I'll bet, he thought. I'll bet he's got a wife somewhere, or you've overestimated his economic resources or his married daughter doesn't like you or he eats onion sandwiches before he goes to bed.

In the first place, the patient is fine. He has no more pain, his blood pressure is normal and his appetite has improved. Except for his nap he is up all day (and into the night) and he really has no more need for me. That is, I should say he has no more need for my nursing services. He needs me to cook for him and clean house and do the shopping and run errands.

As you may recall, when I came out here with him, my understanding was that he had a maid who came in for four hours daily. Since I have been here, however, she has come only on Thursdays, so you can imagine what I have been spending most of my time doing.

I think you should also know that everything else is not as it appeared, either, and that is why I am writing this. Last evening, to my great surprise, he suggested that we go out to dinner. We did, and he had two bourbons before we left and another at dinner. When we came home he talked more freely than he has before, and after I gave him his sleeping pill he told me that the bank owns this place and just about everything else.

I immediately thought of you, because you know how I respect you, and after what you have done for him I wouldn't want you to be stuck for your bill. Please, however, do not write me or call me about this, as he sorts all the mail and overhears any conversations I have on the phone.

As you know, we will be in for his check-up next Thursday at 4 P.M., anyway. At that time, will you please make it plain to him that he has no more need for me? I'm sure you will, and I hope all else goes well with you.

Your good friend,
Vi Landers

My good friend, he thought. If we weren't short of private-duty nurses, like everything else, I'd lose my good friend quick. My good friend must be about forty-one or forty-two now, and she'll never pick a winner. She's got a nice body, or used to have, and about fifteen years ago it was interns and then residents and then young doctors and now patients. You're trying to speed a patient's recovery and she's holding it down. You're trying to get him to believe in himself, and she's trying to get him to depend on her.

"Have you billed this yet?" he wrote in pencil at the top of the letter, and then he encircled the letterhead.

He picked up a postcard and glanced at the aerial photo of the modern white concrete and glass hotel on the beach. Turning it over, he saw the Miami, Florida, postmark and he read the scrawled writing: "Down here to give Father some of this wonderful sunshine. He's feeling fine and we both send you our thanks again. Best, Isabel Damon."

She's the one, he thought, who came in here after the operation complaining that Father had lost so much weight that his gums shrank and now they had to get him new dentures and could I please take something off the bill? So I tell Carrie to take $200 off, and they're nice people and appreciate everything I did for Father and now they want me to know they're thinking of me while they're having their good time in Miami. They forget it's my money they're having this good time on, but Carrie won't forget. Carrie just drops it in here, but she'll hit me with it.

The next letter was on pale yellow folded stationery, with a small purple orchid in the upper left-hand corner. Although it had been lying open for probably twenty-four hours a slight odor of perfume still came off it, and he recognized the handwriting in the purple ink.

My dear Doctor Carter—I bet you'll be surprised to hear from me again so soon. I know you're busy (you always are!) but I imagine you like to take a few moments off and relax and read letters from friends (I should say patients, but I consider myself your friend.)

I am feeling much better since you reassured me, and I hope Dr. Berman won't mind waiting for my money. I got a bill from him for $40 (!) I didn't think it would be that much as this very young doctor, maybe a student, got to practice on me so I thought maybe it wouldn't cost so much. Anyway . . .

Why do I get hooked by all these neurotics? he thought, putting the letter on top of the other three he had read. You feel sorry for people, and they abuse it. This kind of stuff is all right for Jaffrey, who needs these hypochondriacs as much as they need him, but I don't have to be involved with every . . .

He heard the outside door open and close. He looked at his watch and saw it was 8:35, too early for Carrie, and then she walked in.

"What are *you* doing here?" she said, looking at him and making a show of surprise.

"What are *you* doing here?" he said.

"Listen, I've got work to catch up, but you have an 8 o'clock."

"Delayed."

"Mr. Scheller?"

"Right."

"Not poor Mr. Scheller. You know we had to postpone him once because we couldn't get him a bed. What's the matter over there?"

"They've got a traffic jam. I'll do him at 10 or 10:30."

"Well, at least you're looking at the mail. Honestly, some of it has been lying there since . . ."

"I'm not looking at it any more. I've retired."

"Oh, for John's sake, Matt."

"I'll go over it when I get back."

"You can't. You and Rob are going to be crazy from 5 o'clock on. You've got the biggest patient load in weeks."

"Never mind. Call what's-his-name over at University and tell him I can't make the conference at 1. I'm delayed."

"You know you have a mitral there at 2."

"That reminds me," he said. "See if you can get Mrs. Scheller on the phone, or her son. Tell them I'll be doing him around 10 or 10:30, so if they can get over there, they can see him for a while now."

"Honestly," he heard her saying, walking to her desk and talking to herself. "Poor Mr. Scheller. That place is getting worse all the time."

You can't buy them like Carrie, he thought. She and Rob and I get on one another's nerves once in a while, but she's right about the mail and she's right with the patients. They come in here feeling sorry for themselves and she mothers them, and I'll bet she gets Christmas cards from some we cured ten years ago. She's therapeutic. Mother Carrie.

"Good morning," he heard her saying, and he knew she was talking with the answering service. "Well, that's because I'm full of vim today. What have you got? All right. That's all?

"Matt," she said, hanging up. "Dr. Fineman has been trying to reach you. He's waiting for your call."

"Who?"

"Dr. Fineman."

"Call him," he said, "and look up his first name."

"It's Harry," she said, dialing. "Hello, Dr. Fineman? Dr. Carter's office. Dr. Carter will talk with you now."

"Hello, Harry?" he said, feeling the split-second guilt from the familiarity he knew that Fineman, whom he had never seen, would expect. "How are you?"

"Good," Fineman said. "You?"

"Okay. What's your problem?"

"I've got a woman," Fineman said, "the wife of an attorney, and last night she was eating a hamburger, and a piece of meat or a sliver of bone got caught in her throat. She says it's been making her cough, so it must be in her trachea or bronchi. She called me at 8 this morning, so I've been trying to get you. Have you got time to take care of her?"

"I'll make time," he said. "I'd better bronchoscope her. I've got a friend whose eighty-two-year-old mother, a couple of months ago, did something like this with a chicken bone. She neglected it, and the bone perforated into the mediastinum and she died."

"But don't tell this woman that. She's the nervous type, and it'll scare her to death."

"Of course not. I'm telling *you*. When did she eat last?"

"Last night. The hamburger."

"Then we can bronchoscope her right away. How long will it take her to get to Mercy?"

"She can be there in a half-hour. She can take a cab."

"Okay. What's her name?"

"Louise Brower. She's fifty-three."

"All right. Hold a minute, and I'll turn you back to Miss McKeen, and she'll book her into the hospital."

He put his hand over the mouthpiece of the phone.

"Carrie? Pick up Dr. Fineman on three. He's got a woman with a piece of meat stuck somewhere and I'm bronchoscoping her. She'll be at the hospital in a half-hour."

"How in heaven's name are you going to do her this morning?" Carrie said. "You've got Mr. Scheller."

"They won't be ready for him yet. I can do this in ten minutes. Pick up three."

So the first thing he tells me is that she's a woman, he thought, and the second thing he tells me in a nice offhand manner is that her husband is a lawyer. The shysters have us all scared, and now he's clear and I've got the ball. I'd do this woman, whatever her name is, anyway. I'd do her if her husband were a bank robber, but it's something the way they always let you know now if there's a lawyer in the family or somewhere in the shrubbery. The shysters have us on the defensive and the shame of it all is that every day now you have to order a lot of unnecessary tests. You overload the labs, which are too busy anyway, just to play it safe on the legal side and the public gets stuck with rising hospital costs. Too many insurance companies are settling out of court, too, and that's another reason we're all stuck with rising rates.

"I've got a woman swallowed a piece of meat or a bone the wrong way," he heard Carrie saying, talking to the hospital. "She'll be there in a half-hour. Mrs. Louise Brower. B-r-o-w-e-r. No, give her a private room, if you've got one. She'll be out by late afternoon."

"A general anesthetic," he said, walking out to Carrie's desk. "Pentothal."

"Pentothal," Carrie said, into the phone. "Okay."

"I'll go over now," he said, when she had hung up. "I'll call you later."

"Wait a minute," she said. "Are you and Marion going to that dinner party tonight?"

"What?" he said, and then remembering, "I forgot. I should go to the Academy. I missed the last meeting."

"I know."

"I could go to the Academy, and pick Marion up at the party about 10:30."

"Didn't she talk to you about it last night?"

"No. I got home late and she was still asleep this morning. Call her about 10, and see what she thinks."

"I know what she thinks. She's been to the last two alone. She thinks she hasn't got a husband."

"Is it formal?"

"Yes, and that's why I want to know. Your two shirts are still at the laundry, and if you're going to dress here, I'll have to go out and buy you another one."

"Do that, and call Marion and tell her I'll see her there at 8 o'clock."

"Pick her up at home."

"All right. Good-bye."

"One other thing," Carrie said, but the phone was ringing, and she picked it up. "Dr. Carter's office."

As he opened the door to the court the postman was about to push the bell. He said hello to him and took the mail, holding it in both hands, and closed the door again with his shoulder. He carried the mail back into Carrie's office, a dozen or more flat envelopes and a couple fat with samples of sedatives or antacid pills for which he had no use, glossy brochures from equipment houses, at least one of them a new one putting the last of its economic resources into this advertising, a square cardboard box with samples of a new suture material, a copy of *Newsweek*, a copy of *Life*.

"That's all right, Mrs. Mossman," she was saying on the phone but shaking her head at him. "Dr. Carter or Dr. Robinson will be able to see you on Friday. I'm putting you down for 4:30. All right?"

"Enjoy yourself," he said, turning.

"Listen, Matt," she said, hanging up the phone. "One more thing."

"I'll call you," he said.

One more thing, he thought, walking to the car, and then another. Maybe I am really starting to get old, but the only place I get any peace these days is in the operating room. That's the way it should be, I suppose, because that's the only place where I really have something to contribute anyway. The O.R. has become my only sanctuary, and I don't know how those general practitioners and internists can stand it without it. Nothing can get at you in the O.R., nothing or nobody. It is really an only sanctuary.

8:58 A.M.

III

The receptionist saw him as soon as he came through the door, and smiled at him.

"Good morning," he said. "How's everything?"

"Just fine."

In the doctors' lounge he pushed the light button next to his name. He looked at his watch and saw it was 8:58, and signed in on the registry. He was starting toward the elevators when he became aware of the lighted coffee shop and heard the low sound from it coming out of the open glass door. He walked in and sat down at the counter.

"Hello, Doctor."

"Why, Mac!" he said, seeing her two stools away. "I didn't expect to see you here."

Mary MacGowan was in her street clothes, a dark blue coat over her shoulders, her overnight bag at the foot of the stool. She was all of five feet, one inch, and about a hundred pounds, about fifty years old now, her hair going all gray but her complexion still smooth and young.

"I know," she said, smiling. "I didn't expect to be here."

"I saw you on the 4 to midnight with my Mrs. Kirk," he said, sitting down next to her.

"That's right. She's a lovely lady."

"She is."

"I'm sorry about her. I'm sorry you couldn't do something for her."

"I'm sorry, too. That kind make you feel so helpless."

"Not you, Doctor. You should never feel that way."

"You know her husband is that TV newscaster."

"I know. I watch him when I'm home."

The Puerto Rican counter girl was wiping the counter in front of him with a paper napkin.

"Coffee, black," he said to her, "and a piece of coffee cake. Mac?"

"No, thank you. I have to be going."

"So you did a double shift?"

"They're short-handed again, so I had your Mr. Davies on the midnight to 8."

"How was he when you came off duty?"

"He was sleeping again. He was restless about 6 and complained of a little discomfort but I noted you didn't want him to have any more morphine. Dr. Bronson said he'd checked with you about that."

"That's right. The patient's family is coming in, and they want him alert. He'll be all right for a while."

"Both his wife and his daughter called this morning," she said. "They seemed very disturbed."

"They can't accept it," he said. "How are your two kids?"

"Fine. Annie's finishing up business college, and John made the dean's list again last semester."

"He'll be an engineer before you know it."

"In one more year."

"What will you do when you haven't any more educations to pay for? Buy another duplex?"

"Not on your life," she said, standing up. "You know what I'm going to do right now?"

"You're going home and sleep until 3."

"I'm going home and leave this," she said, picking up the overnight case, "and I'm going to take my tool box and take a bus up to the apartments and replace a fuse."

"You're kidding."

"No, I'm not. You won't believe this, but last night one of my tenants—this woman married to an oaf—called the Private Duty Office and insisted on talking to me. They called me off Mrs. Kirk and I phoned her back. She said: 'Mrs. MacGowan, you've got to come up here right away and fix the lights. They won't light in the living room or the dining room.' I said: 'Then it's a fuse. Have your husband go down in the basement and the new fuses are right on top of the fuse box.' You know what she said?"

"I might guess."

"She said: 'My husband doesn't know how to change a fuse, and he's afraid of being electrocuted.' He must be six feet two and weighs over two hundred pounds, and that's God's truth."

"I believe you," he said and then, thinking the rest to himself: and that one you married must have been like that and the kindest thing he ever did was leave you and the two kids.

"The God's truth," she was repeating.

"So you really have a tool box now?" he said.

"I do. Two dollars and fifty-eight cents from Sears, Roebuck. Now I've even learned how to rewire a lamp and change a washer in a faucet."

"Good. The next time I need a plumber at the office I'll call you. Last month it took us two days to get one."

"Anytime," she said, smiling, "but right now I'm about to fall asleep on my feet. I'll be back for Mrs. Kirk at 4."

"You're the best, Mac," he said, "and thanks for everything."

And she really is the best, he thought, having his coffee and cake. She may fall asleep on her feet, but if she does it won't be while she's on duty. You won't walk in and find her asleep in the chair like I did dear old Vi Landers, my good friend.

It had happened about five years before. The patient was in terminal condition. He was an old Italian landscape gardener with no money but with his grown kids all kicking in to give Pop the best, including private nursing around the clock. It was about 7:15 in the morning, and dear old Vi was sitting by the window, her head down and asleep.

When he took the patient's wrist to feel for the pulse, there was none.

He pressed the back of the hand with his thumb and, when he released the pressure, the thumb mark stayed white and he quietly picked up dear old Vi's stethoscope and put it over the heart and then took it off and put it on the foot of the bed.

"Why, good morning, Doctor," she said, obviously thinking he had just walked in.

"Good morning," he said. "How's the patient?"

"He seems to be quite comfortable," she said.

"I know," he said. "Has he had any liquid lately?"

"Not for several hours."

"Try to get him to take some right now," he said.

She took the water glass with the bent glass tube in it. She put her right arm behind the patient's back, lifting him.

"Now," she said to him, "it's time . . ."

Still holding him she turned, and she looked like the old man had just slapped her across the face.

"Why!" she said. "He's dead!"

"I know," he said, and he made the notation on the chart, with the time, and walked out.

Damn, he had thought then, they are paying for nurses because they did not want the old man ever to be alone again. He went easily and it made no difference to him, but he was alone.

Now he stood up at the counter and picked up his check and paid the cashier. In the hall he pushed the button for the elevator and waited.

"Good morning, Doctor," the elevator boy said. "O.R.?"

"Yes," he said. "Good morning."

The elevator stopped at the second floor. A young Negro girl in the green uniform of a ward maid was waiting for it, and she started to get in.

"You going down?" the elevator boy said.

"No," she said, surprised and hesitating. "I'm going up."

"So am I," the elevator boy said, laughing. "Get in."

"Honest," the girl said, getting in. "That all you got to do?"

"You know me," the elevator boy said.

"I know you all right," the girl said. "That's the last time you'll do that to me. Now, if it's not too much bother, would you mind letting me off on seven?"

"Anything you want," the elevator boy said, still enjoying it. "O.R., Doctor."

When he got off he walked across to the glassed-in nurses' station. There was just the faintest, light, sweet-sharp odor of ether in the air, but he had long ago become insensitive to it, unaware of it even on his person when they were using it almost exclusively and, hours later, he would come home and his wife would detect it immediately.

"How's my gal Sal now?" he said, when she turned from showing the other nurse something in the schedule book.

"Do you really want to know?" Sarah Wheeler said, looking up at him over the tops of her glasses, and then standing up.

"You'll handle it," he said.

"I don't think we can get you into Room Three until about 11:30."

"Stan is still having trouble?"

"He's on his fourth pint of O-Negative. After last night the blood bank may be hollering for help."

"He'll work his way out of it," he said. "Have you seen my invaluable associate?"

"I called him after I called you, but I haven't seen him."

"Dr. Robinson was here a while ago," the other nurse said. "He said to tell you he's seeing patients."

"Thanks," he said, and then to Sarah Wheeler: "I suppose I'll have to do my bronchoscopy down in Emergency."

"Unless you want to do it out on Walker Avenue," she said.

"It's too cold out there, and they'd give me a parking ticket. I've got two already that Carrie has to answer."

"I got one myself the other day."

"While I think of it," he said, "I want to be sure they've got the polyethylene tubing in three sizes in my kit today."

"If you called for it, it'll be there. You know we're efficiency plus."

"I'll be down on Four seeing patients for about twenty minutes," he said. "Then I'll be down in Emergency."

"Enjoy yourself," she said. "I'm leaving on my yacht for the Bahamas."

On the way down the stairs he took out the slip of memo paper on which, the evening before at the office, he had written down the names while he and Bob Robinson had divided up their rounds. Rob had put his in his little black book, carefully writing down, after each cancer case: "Patient knows. Wife doesn't." Or: "Patient, no. Wife, no. Son, yes."

"God, Matt," Rob had said to him, going over the in-hospital cases about a month after he had joined him. "I don't know how you can keep them all straight."

"Keep what straight?" he had said.

"Who we're telling what. I walked in this afternoon to see that case we did four days ago, that Mr. Isaacson with the cancer of the left lung . . ."

"We told him because he asked, and he took it all right."

"I know, but I thought his wife knew."

"No."

"That's what I found out. She walked me out in the hall and started to question me about his recovery and I said: 'Well, you have to remember he had a cancer . . .'"

"What happened?"

"She went into hysterics. I had to get a nurse, and it took me about ten minutes to get her back to normal. I finally got her to listen and I told her we got it all out."

"We did."

"But I don't know how you remember who knows what."

"I may have a fair memory. I don't know. As long as I'm treating them I remember them, but if a patient I cured five or six years ago walks up to me on the street, I won't have the vaguest idea who he is. He'll be walking around with my big incision on him, but I won't recognize him. If I saw his chest X rays again I could tell you everything about him—occupation, family, everything—but his face means nothing. You'll get like that."

"I'll have to start keeping a little notebook," Rob had said, and then: "but I don't like it."

"None of us like it," he said, "but we have to face it. Curing a difficult surgical problem is a pleasure, and that's why we chose surgery. Treating a difficult mental or emotional problem, unless you're a psychiatrist, is, to put it succinctly, a pain, but it has to be done."

"I know, but I'm no good at lying."

"I wasn't either, but today I'm one of the world's biggest liars. For a long time I was ashamed of myself. I used to hate myself, but you get over it. I don't mean you'll ever enjoy it."

"You can bet I won't."

"You worry too much about it. In the time you've been around, how many patients have come right out and asked you if they had cancer?"

"Damn few."

"You'll find that ninety per cent never ask the question. If they ask, you're morally obligated to give them the truth, eventually, but you can see it coming, and if the time isn't right you can take the play away until it is."

"Have you ever had a situation where the patient said: 'Tell me, but don't tell my wife,' and then the wife says: 'Tell me, but don't tell my husband'?"

"Yes, I've had that, too. Somebody in the family, close to the patient, if not the patient, has to know. You figure out who it is, remembering it's the patient that you're treating."

He had gotten up then, and gone out to the small refrigerator in the back room and poured a bourbon for Rob and a vodka for himself.

"A few years ago," he said when he came back, "I had a case that proved to me that I was right. He was an intellectual—a college professor —who came into town to see me on a Thanksgiving vacation. When I examined him he talked pleasantly enough, but I knew he was scared. He had a fast pulse, he was perspiring, and his skin was cold.

"Anyway, the next day I bronchoscoped him and when the biopsy report came back I called his wife at the hospital. She'd been in the office with him, an intelligent woman, and I told her it was cancer. She said on the phone: 'Well, we've always been very close, and I think he should be told.' I said: 'All right, but when I examined your husband and again while they prepared him for the bronchoscopy, I found him apprehensive. Let me tell him in my own way in my own time.' She agreed.

"The next morning I read about it in the paper. He was dead. He'd jumped out of the window of their hotel room. Later on I found out that about 11 o'clock that night, after she'd talked to me, she had said to him: 'The doctor wasn't sure you should be told right away, but you have cancer.' When she went into the bathroom a few minutes later, he went out the window."

"Damn," Rob had said.

"I'd have told him, because she wanted him told, that the tumor was not large, that it was easily removable, that there was small operative risk and a high prospect of cure. All that would have been the truth, too."

"I read a paper not long ago by somebody who doesn't hold with this. He says he tells them, at least ninety or ninety-five per cent of them."

"I know, I've read those papers and listened to them on panels, and they may be right. If they are, they're treating a different race of human beings than I am. They say that they tell their patients, and their patients thank them. If we're honest men, it's easier to tell the truth than to lie. Also, we all like to be thanked, but after you've told a patient you couldn't get all the cancer out and he thanks you for being so honest and goes home, something happens to him. He lies there at night, 'the only one awake in the house, and in his mind, if not in fact, you've pronounced the death sentence on him. Then he begins to feel pain, either real or imagined, and this now is not the same man you told three weeks or three months before, and who thanked you. This is a different man and, whether he'd admit it or not, I'll bet he wouldn't thank you again."

Now, walking down the stairs and looking at the list on the memo paper in his hand, he saw there were six names on it, and he realized that he couldn't see more than three or four before the bronchoscopy. Coming out of the stairwell onto the floor he walked to the nurses' station and saw two of the newer ones sitting and talking with their backs to the desk.

"—and then," one of them was saying, "Jackie Cooper gets this chance to take this temporary assignment in Hawaii. He wants to go, but he doesn't dare tell her, so . . ."

"Oh, hello, Doctor," the other one said.

"Hello," he said. "Did he go to Hawaii?"

"Who?" the one who had been listening said.

"Jackie Cooper."

"Oh," the first one, the talker, said, "that was just a television show, Doctor."

"But did he go?"

"Yes, sir."

"Good. How are all my chest patients?"

"No complaints, Doctor."

"All right, but now I'm going to have to check up on you. See if I've got the rooms right."

"Yes, sir," the listener said.

"Benjamin Davies, 410."

"That's right," the listener said, referring to her list.

"Grace Cowan, 415, and Lynn Cummings, 417."

"Correct."

"Mrs. Elizabeth Kirk, 412. Anthony Trusco, 414; and Bernard Waterman, 418."

"All correct."

"Now I'd better look at Mr. Benjamin Davies' chart first."

The talker went to the chart rack and took it out and handed it to him. He scanned it quickly and saw that the temperature was 101, the respiration was 36, and the pulse 110.

His respiration is rapid because it hurts him to breath deeply, he thought, and his pulse is fast because of the pain. Morphine will bring his respiration back to about 24 and his pulse down to 90. At least the blood pressure is 130 over 85, which is normal for a man his age, but it doesn't mean a damn thing when Benjamin Davies is dying.

IV

Although, if anyone had asked him now, he could not have told him exactly when it had been, he had first seen Benjamin Davies twenty-seven months before. Benjamin Davies's secretary had called and talked to Carrie McKeen and said that Mr. Davies was sending some X rays over by messenger and that he wanted Dr. Carter to look at them and call him. In fact, Mr. Davies hoped Dr. Carter would be able to call him the next morning, as on the next afternoon he would be leaving town for two days.

"Good God, Matt!" Bob Robinson had said to him, after he had slapped the plates up under the clips on the light panel in the office, "this guy inhaled a golf ball!"

That is exactly what it looked like. The shadow in the root of the right lung was the size of a golf ball, and as perfectly round. The rest of the right lung was clear, but in the upper lobe of the left lung there was another and smaller shadow.

"I'd say your golf ball was benign," he said, "except for one thing."

"The other lung?"

"That's right. When you see a single tumor as round and clean and self-contained as this, the chances are nine out of ten that it's benign. If that's a tumor in the other lung as well, your odds go the other way."

"How long has he been walking around with this?" Rob said, still looking at the plates and fascinated.

"I don't know. I've never seen anything on him before."

"You can almost read the Top-Flite trade mark on it," Rob said.

The next morning Carrie called Benjamin Davies. She never got through to Mr. Davies, but Mr. Davies's secretary said that Mr. Davies would be in to see Dr. Carter three days later, at 6:15 in the evening.

At exactly 6:15 on that evening Benjamin Davies appeared, and Rob did the preliminary examination: chief complaint, present illness, past history, marital history, family history, systemic review from the texture of his hair—graying black, dry, coarse—to the reflexes of his knees—right: normal; left: torn medial meniscus ligament but normal reflex in the quadriceps, the muscles that run down along the front of the thigh.

"For John's sake, Matt!" Carrie said, when he finally arrived in the office. "Get in with Mr. Davies. You're the one he wants, and I don't think he takes to Rob."

By the time he had changed into his white smock and walked into the examination room, Rob had just about finished with the work-up on Benjamin Davies, and Benjamin Davies was standing there with his trousers back on, but still stripped to the waist. Benjamin Davies was fifty-nine years old, six feet one inch, 220 pounds and not much of it fat.

"Good evening," he had said, shaking hands with Benjamin Davies. "I'm Matt Carter."

He has the look of class, he thought, Harvard or Yale, Class of '22 or '23.

"I thought I had an appointment with you," Benjamin Davies said, big and looking right at him.

"You did. I'm sorry to be late. I had an extended operation and I had several hospital patients to check on before I could get over here."

"All you doctors are alike, aren't you?"

"I don't know about that, but Dr. Robinson is as fully capable as I am of conducting an examination."

He had taken the work-up sheets from Rob, and was checking through them.

"How are you feeling?"

"Not badly."

"That's not why you came in to see me."

"I came in because of those damned X rays. What's that in my lung?"

"We're not sure. Do you play golf?"

"Yes. Why?"

"Dr. Robinson and I think you may have inhaled a golf ball."

"Whatever it is, are you going to take it out?"

"Someone has got to take it out. Do you have any pain now?"

"Not right now. Once in a while in my chest, here, for the last month or so."

"Any pain up here in the right shoulder?"

"Once in a while, in the back."

"Have you been coughing up anything?"

"About six weeks ago I spit up quite a lot of phlegm."

"What color was it?"

"Rather odd. Sort of dark blue, not the color of blood. Then it disappeared."

"But then it recurred?"

"Yes, but the second time it cleared up quicker."

"And now it recurs more often?"

"That's right. The other day it happened at a conference, and I had to get rid of it in my handkerchief. It's damned embarrassing and a nuisance."

"Does the phlegm have a metallic taste?"

"That's right. It does."

"Now I don't think I know your doctor. What has he told you?"

"He recommended you. He's the doctor who handles my employees at the plant. Except for a banged-up knee I've never needed a doctor in my life."

"Where did you play football?"

"Princeton. How did you know?"

"You've got what we call a running-guard knee. You pulled out of the line once and turned and the knee went."

"That's exactly the way it happened. My last year. That's amazing."

"That's the way they usually happen with linemen, unless they get clipped."

"Do you think it's cancer, Doctor?"

"I don't know," he said, stalling him. "We can't tell from X rays, or just a general physical examination."

"How can you find out?"

"Well, we can put a bronchoscope down into your windpipe and take a small sample of that golf ball and the laboratory will be able to tell."

"How long does that take?"

"Oh, you'd be in the hospital for a half a day, and it would be a couple of days before we got the lab report. On the other hand, it's got to come out, no matter what it is."

"Why?"

"It will probably continue to grow, and you'll have increasing pain. It's already a fairly sizable growth."

"Then there's no need for me to go in for a test? I can save time if I just have it taken out?"

"That's right."

"I'm opening up a new plant in the South. I want to get this thing out, and be done with it."

"What business are you in?"

"Plastics. This will be my third plant, and I've got to be down there next week."

"How long will you be gone?"

"Four days or so. How long will I be in the hospital?"

"Oh, a couple of weeks."

"Why that long?"

"This is major surgery. Even after you're out you'll have to take it easy for a while."

"There's no reason why I can't handle some of my work at home, though, is there?"

"That depends on you. I just recommend that you have this done as soon as possible."

"Today's Thursday. How about a week from Monday?"

"Make it a week from Tuesday. I'll have my secretary book you in and call your office."

Benjamin Davies finished dressing then and left. He walked out as if he were leaving one business conference for another.

"How would you like to work for him?" Rob said.

"He may be all right. He probably does a great job for his stockholders."

"What do you think now?" Rob said.

"I think it's a cancer sitting on his right pulmonary artery."

"That's why he's been coughing up that blue blood," Rob said.

"The other lesion is so small and dense," he said, "that I'm inclined to think it may be an old TB scar he never knew he had."

The following Thursday afternoon Benjamin Davies's secretary called Dr. Matthew Carter's office, and spoke with Carrie McKeen. Later that afternoon Carrie McKeen relayed the message to Dr. Carter.

"Benjamin Davies wants to see you tomorrow morning. He's too busy to come over this afternoon or evening."

"I can't see him tomorrow morning. I think I'm operating all morning."

"You are. You have an 8 o'clock at Mercy, and an 11:30 at University, but he'll see you anywhere you say."

"Tell him to meet me outside the north entrance of Mercy tomorrow morning at 11 o'clock."

At 11:06 the next morning, when Dr. Matthew Carter came out of the north doors of Mercy Hospital into the flat, humid August heat, he saw a black Cadillac parked at the curb, a uniformed chauffeur standing beside it. In the back seat Benjamin Davies was sitting, and he tapped on the glass and the chauffeur opened the back door and Dr. Matthew Carter got into the air-conditioned Cadillac and sat down beside Benjamin Davies.

"Good morning," Benjamin Davies said.

"Good morning. How are you feeling?"

"About the same," Benjamin Davies said, putting some papers into a black leather attaché case on a small writing desk that folded down from the back of the front seat. "I've been giving this trouble of mine some thought, and I have some questions."

"Go ahead."

Benjamin Davies had in his hand a large, yellow, blue-lined note pad. He looked at it and then took out a pack of cigarettes.

"Smoke?" he said.

"No, thanks."

"First question," Benjamin Davies said, lighting a cigarette. "What do you think the chances are that I have cancer?"

"I don't know. It's impossible to put a figure on it, but in a man of your age we've got to consider it seriously. That's why you're going into the hospital."

"You're not answering my question, Doctor. You've handled enough cases so you can give me a pretty good estimate of the odds."

I have, he thought, and I can give you your pretty good estimate but I won't.

"Estimates are valueless in my business," he said, "so we don't think that way. We have to check everything out, and we've checked nothing on you except your X rays and the general state of your health."

"All right. Suppose, instead of surgery, I had radiation treatments?"

"Now you're trying to cross a bridge before you're there. We don't know anything about that tumor in your chest. That's why we're operating."

"But what about radiation? Suppose you find cancer. How effective would radiation be?"

"There's no law that governs that, either. I've had patients who have been cured that way. Some cancers are vulnerable to radiation, some aren't. We never know what we're fighting until we take a piece of it and examine it under the microscope."

"What about chemical treatment of cancer?" he said, looking at the yellow pad.

"In some cases they've had a very significant effect, but again we have to wait and see what this particular shadow is."

"What about hormones?"

"Hormones are used mostly for tumors of the endocrine glands—like the testicles, breast, ovaries and prostate."

"All right. Why do you think I might have cancer?"

"If you're talking about cause, we don't know the cause. What you're doing right now doesn't help you."

"What?"

"Smoking two or three packs of cigarettes a day."

"You believe in this cigarette scare? It hasn't been proven."

"Certain things have been proven. We know that tobacco tar is an irritant. We know that the death rate from lung cancer among heavy smokers is between twenty-five and thirty times as high as it is among non-smokers."

"But after thirty-five years I can't give up smoking, especially working the way I do."

"Try cigars."

"Why? They've got tobacco tar in them, too."

"You won't inhale them like you do cigarettes."

"What's the rate of survival from lung cancer?"

"After surgery?"

"Yes."

"Again we're dealing with variables," he said, sparring. "It depends on the individual case. Age of the patient makes a difference. So does the element of time—whether the disease is discovered early or late."

"What about my case?"

"We don't know that you've got cancer, but even if you have you've got a fine chance. Your age is in your favor, and so is your general health. You haven't had any complaints, up until the past six weeks, so although that tumor may be growing fairly rapidly we're catching it fairly early."

"All right," Benjamin Davies said, opening the attaché case and putting the pad into it. "If you're going to operate on Tuesday, I suppose you'll want me in here sometime Monday afternoon."

"We'll want you in here before 6 o'clock Sunday night."

"Why? This thing is complicating my schedule as is. I planned to work all this weekend."

"That's why I scheduled you for Tuesday, instead of Monday. If I were doing you on Monday you'd have to be checking in here today."

"What's the reason for that? Don't you people function on weekends?"

"Some of us do, but some of us don't. Hospital laboratory and clerical personnel, for example, like to go to the beach or play golf on weekends, too."

"That's not right."

"I agree with you."

"You people need a reorganization. You ought to have swing shifts in your laboratory and clerical departments."

"We do to a degree, but the problem is not organizational. It's economic. When a hospital gets some money, there are always ten other things to do with it."

"Suppose I come in Monday morning?"

"No. They have to get you started very early that morning."

"For what?"

"Well, they've got to cross-match your blood, do a urinalysis, take a cardiogram, make a number of other tests. Also, your X rays are now about a month old, and we want a new set."

"All right, Doctor," Benjamin Davies said, shaking hands. "I've had good reports on you from everybody. Thank you."

"You're quite welcome."

Benjamin Davies reached across and opened the door. The chauffeur standing on the sidewalk, opened it the rest of the way and Dr. Matthew Carter got out.

It could have been worse, he thought, walking to his own car and feeling the heavy heat pressing in upon him. He's done a little research, or had someone do it for him, and I thought he'd push me harder than he did. He's a realist and may be entitled to more than I told him. Anyone is entitled to all they can accept, but you're never quite sure how much that is and I'm glad he didn't try to nail me on that rate of survival. The trouble with rate of survival statistics is that they're based only on apparent cure after five years and disregard palliation. They disregard the relief of symptoms and the prolongation of life you can give a man you can't cure. They forget that if you give a sixty-year-old man just another four years you're giving him a third or maybe a half of what additional living he has a right to expect, but who wants to accept that? Everybody wants all of it, and I have cured them, completely cured them, and then had them go out in a plane crash or with coronaries or with cirrhosis or killed by a cab.

On Sunday evening, Benjamin Davies arrived in the hospital at 6:15. He had been preceded by three dozen long-stemmed red roses and a potted white azalea, and he was accompanied by his secretary and his chauffeur. The chauffeur was carrying nine individually wrapped one-pound boxes of candy, and the secretary gave one to the nursing supervisor and left another at the nurses' station. The rest she put in the closet in Benjamin Davies's room for the other shifts and the private duty nurses.

Although Dr. Robert Robinson had seen Benjamin Davies twice on Monday, Dr. Matthew Carter did not see him again until 7:55 on Tuesday morning when Benjamin Davies had been wheeled in his bed on and off the elevator and down the hall of the fifth floor to the door of the operating room. The wheeling had been done by a bald, middle-aged orderly who happened to be an ex-convict and who, in a few minutes, but unknown to Benjamin Davies, would shave Mr. Davies's chest and back.

"Good morning," Dr. Carter said to Benjamin Davies. "How are you feeling this morning?"

"As well as can be expected, I suppose. In the past twenty-four hours I've been poked by every doctor, intern, technician, and nurse in this place. How are you?"

"I'm fine. I've been looking at the results of your tests. You're going to do all right."

"How long will it take you in there?"

"Oh, a couple of hours."

"All right," Benjamin Davies said. "It's obvious I'm ready when you are."

"Good."

It took two hours and twenty minutes. The new set of X rays showed that the tumor in the right lung was now slightly larger than a golf ball and the shadow in the left lung, although still small, was more distinct. Because the large tumor in the right lung had penetrated the right pulmonary artery Dr. Carter had no choice but to perform a pneumonectomy, meaning he removed the entire right lung. He did this because he knew that as long as the small shadow in the other lung, now presumed also to be malignant, could be reduced, or at least controlled by radiation therapy, the breathing capacity of the left lung would be sufficient for the needs of Benjamin Davies.

After all, he reasoned, this man is not in the habit of running for trains and he doesn't take stairways two steps at a time. Although the right lung normally performs about sixty per cent of the pulmonary function, he will not even know that it is gone until I tell him, and telling this man at the right time and in the right way should be no problem.

Dr. Carter did not choose to tell Benjamin Davies until the fifth post-operative day. On the third post-operative day Benjamin Davies had asked him if the laboratory had made its report as yet, but Dr. Carter had answered in the negative and diverted him by inquiring about the presence of pain, his sleep problems, his elimination difficulties and his appetite. On the fourth day Dr. Robert Robinson, and not Dr. Carter, had visited Benjamin Davies and he, too, had professed ignorance, detecting not only some annoyance on the part of Mr. Davies but, it occurred to him later, some suspicion as well.

At 3:15 in the afternoon of the fifth day, which was a Sunday, Dr. Carter had found Benjamin Davies's private nurse visiting at the nurses' station. She informed him that Mr. Davies was dictating to his secretary, and when Dr. Carter entered the room he found Mr. Davies, in a mono-grammed maroon silk dressing gown over gray pajamas, sitting in one arm chair, and his secretary, a thin, bespectacled, stylishly dressed woman in her forties with a sheaf of papers in her lap and a notebook on her knee, sitting in the other.

"Good afternoon," Dr. Carter said.

"Oh," Benjamin Davies said. "Hello."

He introduced Dr. Carter to his secretary. He then told his secretary that he wouldn't be needing her any more that day, reminded her of a couple of details he wanted checked and told her to come back the next morning.

"I don't know whether you're starting a florist's shop or a lending library," Dr. Carter said after the secretary had left.

There were flowers on the bureau, on the bed table, and on the floor in one corner of the room. There were a half-dozen books, new in their dust jackets, on the bureau and several more on the window sill.

"Neither," Benjamin Davies said.

"How are you feeling today?"

"I'd feel a lot better," Benjamin Davies said, "if I knew when I could get out of here. I can't find out anything around this place."

"Well, maybe I can help you," Dr. Carter said. "What would you like to know?"

I know exactly what he wants to know, he thought. I could have told him the first day he came into the office, and he knows it, too.

"Did you get that report back from the lab yet?"

"Yes. We've got it."

"What did they find?"

"Well, they found you had a tumor. The X rays weren't lying."

"What was it?"

"It wasn't a golf ball."

"It was cancer, wasn't it?" Benjamin Davies said, looking right at him. "I know it was cancer."

"Yes. It was a carcinoma, but . . ."

"It was a cancer," Benjamin Davies said. "Cancer. Cancer. Don't evade it. Don't . . ."

"I'm not evading anything. I'm trying to tell you, and please listen to what I'm saying, that it was a cancer but we got it all out."

"You got it all out?" Benjamin Davies was saying, staring at him now, his face pale. "You got it all out? How do you know you got it all out? How does anybody know you got it all out? How do *I* know you got it all out? How . . ."

"Now listen to me," he said, and he was standing over Benjamin Davies, his hand on Benjamin Davies's shoulder. "We know we got it all out. Get hold of yourself now, and stop this!"

"How do you know you got it all out? How do you know? How do you know?"

"I know," he said. "Listen to me. It was completely contained in your lung, and I removed the lung. There's no more cancer . . ."

"My lung!" Benjamin Davies said, looking at him, and then looking down at his own chest. "My God, my lung!"

He put his right hand, open, over his right chest. Then he dropped his head in his hands and he started to sob, half crying, half talking, gasping, and starting to swallow air.

"Doctor?" the nurse said, coming into the room, hurrying.

"I need you. He's going into shock. Get me five grains of sodium amytal quick, and then we'll get him into bed."

"My God, my lung!" Benjamin Davies was saying, crying it, swallowing more air, then starting to belch, his skin cold and wet with sweat. "God . . . God . . ."

"Will you listen to me? Stop acting like a child! Listen to me for a minute!"

When the nurse came back they moved Benjamin Davies, holding him under the shoulders, into the bed. Benjamin Davies was still trying to talk, but now just sobs and air were coming.

"Let me have that syringe and crank the bed up. He may vomit."

"Yes, Doctor."

He took the syringe and, with Benjamin Davies still irrational and unaware of what was happening, and the nurse baring Benjamin Davies's left arm, he found the median cubital vein between the two condyles, the bony prominences of the elbow, and he inserted the needle and slowly injected the sedative.

"He'll be all right now for about four hours," he said, watching Benjamin Davies subside. "Let's keep him warm."

"Excuse me, Doctor," the nurse said, "but what happened?"

"He's been hounding Dr. Robinson and me for the last two or three days about his lab report."

"I know. He's been hounding all of us."

"I finally had to tell him he had carcinoma, and that I took his lung."

"You just wouldn't believe this would happen," the nurse said, shaking her head. "I mean, that a man like this would take it like that."

"Tell your relief nurse," he said, "to call me if he starts to act up again. On the way out I'll leave an order for a tranquilizer."

At the nurses' station he signed the order for a routine dose of twenty-five milligrams of thorazine three times a day. He tried to call Mrs. Benjamin Davies on the telephone but there was no answer. Then he saw two other patients and drove home.

"He had me boxed in," he was telling his wife. "When they ask the direct question you can't lie."

"Doesn't he have a family?"

"Yes, he has a wife and a married daughter who lives out of town. I've never seen either of them, but I spoke with his wife on the phone after the operation. I told her it was successful, and she asked no questions. I was hoping to see her with him this afternoon, but he had his secretary in there and he was running an office."

They were sitting in the living room. He was having a vodka and tonic before dinner.

"I would have had to tell him eventually anyway," he said, "because he's got a financial responsibility not only to his family but to his stockholders. If you lead a man like this to believe he's been completely cured this could be detrimental to the interests of his estate and of his business. In fact, you can get yourself into a nice legal jam that way."

"But if you got it all when you took out his lung he may be cured."

"I didn't get it all. It's started in his other lung, and he'll have to receive radiation treatments. That's another reason why he had to be told."

"Then it seems to me," his wife said, "that you did the only thing you could do. You shouldn't be sitting here blaming yourself."

"I'm not blaming myself, but I don't feel like celebrating the way I managed it."

If I'd had the chance over an extended period of time, he thought then, I might have prepared him a little better, but it wouldn't have made much difference. He was pretty sure of what he had and he knew more about the cure rate than he let on that day he didn't press me in his car. He didn't want to hear it then and he didn't want to hear it today, but the tip-off was that day in the car.

"I suspected him," he said, "but I guess I still read him wrong. He has all the outward mannerisms and the business-success history of a completely self-assured man. I should know by now that the ability to face life doesn't necessarily encompass the ability to face death."

"He was like a child," he said. "I hadn't felt any emotional involvement with him, because he wasn't a man you could get close to and, God knows, I don't seek that. I have too much of it with too many patients every day of my life, but when he broke down I went right out to

him as if he were a child. Standing over him, it came to me that he was
like a child that I had just struck and just hurt. You know what I mean."

From now on, he thought, lying in bed that night and trying to get to
sleep, we won't be treating just an organic disease. We'll be treating a
mental and emotional sickness, and you can call it the anaemia of hope.
What this Davies has got, the metastasis to the other lung, is exactly
what took Evarts Graham, and Evarts Graham did the first successful
removal of a lung in a human being on that obstetrician in 1933. That
obstetrician is still living, the last I heard, and Evarts Graham died in
1957 and the irony is that he himself died of cancer of the lung.

There is no doubt, he was thinking, moving into sleep now, that
Evarts deserved that "Father of Modern Chest Surgery" and he looked
the part, too. He must have been about six feet two and about 195
pounds and he stood straight and he was a scholar and you could see it.
He not only could operate but he could teach, too, and one of his tricks
was to find three different ways to say anything that he wanted you to
hang on to. It was funny the way he did that, and Marion noticed it the
first time she ever heard him when I took her to that meeting in Atlantic
City and she came out and said: "He's good, but he says everything
three times." It was the truth because he would say something like: "The
underlying lung was responsible for the pus in the pleural cavity." Then
he would say: "When you have the lung infected it will transgress the
visceral pleura and infect the pleural cavity." And a few minutes later
he would say: "It's a basic law of nature that if you have an infection of
an organ adjacent to a cavity the infection will extend into that cavity
unless controlled." It's funny how he would do that and I had never
noticed it until Marion spotted it the very first time.

When he entered Benjamin Davies's room at 7:40 the next morning,
the night nurse was sitting in the arm chair where Benjamin Davies had
been sitting the afternoon before. Benjamin Davies was in bed, two
pillows under his head, awake and staring at the opposite wall.

"Good morning, Doctor," the nurse said.

"Good morning. How are you?"

"Fine, Doctor."

"Good morning," he said to Benjamin Davies.

"Hello, Doctor," Benjamin Davies said.

"Why don't you take a ten-minute break?" he said to the nurse.

"Thank you, Doctor."

"How are you feeling?" he said to Benjamin Davies.

"I want to apologize, Doctor," Benjamin Davies said.

"There's no need to apologize. Anyone might have reacted the same way. I've forgotten about it, and you should forget about it, too."

"I shouldn't have acted that way. I knew it was cancer, but I didn't want to hear it."

"No one wants to hear it, but you're better off knowing."

"I don't have much of a chance, do I?"

"You've got a good chance. We got to you early."

"I know, but the national statistics on permanent cure of lung cancer is only seventeen per cent."

"Where did you get that?"

"I had some research done before I came in here."

"Your research isn't up to date and it's not complete."

"What do you mean?"

"Any good chest surgeon will have a permanent cure rate today of at least twenty-five per cent. Mine happens to be thirty-three per cent."

"Is that true?"

"Look. You and I understand each other now. We're not playing any more games. That thirty-three per cent happens to be the truth, and I happen to be proud of it."

"I don't mean to doubt you."

"I know, and I'll tell you something else. When a patient has this disease and knows it, he has a tendency, no matter what his chances are, of putting himself on the losing side. If a patient learns he has a ninety per cent chance of cure it's human nature for him to envision himself in the other ten per cent. I have I don't know how many patients who had just what you had and who are going about their work, having their fun and leading completely normal lives."

"I won't miss my lung?"

"Never. You wouldn't even know it was gone, if I hadn't told you."

"You're making me feel a little better, Doctor," Benjamin Davies said.

"Good."

It's not only I, he thought then, but it's also that thorazine. That thorazine gives them a feeling of well-being, and I might as well make the best of it right now while he's still on it.

"When do you think I might get out of here?" Benjamin Davies was saying.

"Well, we want to get you up on your feet more first. Maybe by the end of the week."

"That will be fine with me."

"We'll want you in here for a while every day, though."

"What for?"

Well, he thought, here I go.

"We want to give you some treatments. Now don't go jumping to any conclusions, but we're going to give you some radiation."

"What?" Benjamin Davies said. "I've got it in the other lung, too?"

"Now you're doing just what I told you not to do. You're jumping to conclusions. Your X rays show just a small shadow on the other lung. Because it's so extremely small we didn't even look at it, so we don't know what it is. It doesn't look anything like that other tumor, and whatever it is, we're going to knock it out with radiation therapy."

Benjamin Davies didn't say anything.

"Look. There's no reason to be concerned about this. We're just taking normal precautionary measures. You wouldn't want us to do otherwise. Besides, I've got you cured right now, and I want to be sure you boost my batting average. I told you I'm proud of it."

"All right, Doctor," Benjamin Davies said.

"Incidentally," he said, "I tried to reach your wife on the phone last night. Because you knew your problem, I thought that she should, too."

"She's been away at our country place over the weekend," Benjamin Davies said, "but I'd rather you wouldn't tell her, anyway."

"Whatever you say. That's up to you."

"My wife is excitable. She hasn't been too well herself these past few years and she knows nothing about these things. When I came in here I told her it was for something that developed from an old chest injury that I got in football. She hasn't any idea of what it was."

"All right. I'll remember that."

All things considered, he thought when he left him, I got away with it all right. If it weren't for those statistics I'd have gotten away with it even better, but you run into these statisticians every now and then and there's nothing you can say to talk them out of it. Their statistics become their cross, and that first one, whatever his name was, was the worst. I don't remember his name, but I'll never forget the man.

He was still in his residency then, and that first one was a retired life insurance executive. At 8 o'clock in the morning they had opened his chest for cancer of the lung and twenty minutes later they had found him inoperable and they had closed him again. At 8:55 he had started to come out from under the anesthesia in the recovery room.

"Do you know what time it is?" the nurse had said to him.

"I don't know," he had said.

"There's a clock on the wall there," she had said. "Can you read it?"

It is a standard procedure they use to test the patient's awareness.

"It's 8:55," he had said, and right then he had known it all. He had known it was an 8 o'clock operation and now he knew that they had merely opened and closed him and he had been dealing with life-expectancy charts and disease statistics all his working life.

Four days later he began to drink in his room. Three days after that he bled from an old ulcer, and after five transfusions they operated on him. They did a Billroth II, to close the duodenum and attach the stomach directly to the intestine, but the duodenum was so scarred that they couldn't close it completely so they put in a tube to bring out the bile and juices until the duodenum could heal.

The problem with such a tube is that, although it will be ninety-five per cent efficient, a small sinus track forms around it and the remainder of the drainage follows the outside of the tube as it would a wick, and digests the skin where the tube emerges.

So we used Philadelphia cream cheese, Dr. Matthew Carter was remembering now. We pasted the skin with Philadelphia cream cheese and we had to replace it every three or four hours. I'd get up at 6 o'clock and replace it and after every operation I'd run back and replace it again. I'd start my rounds with him and I'd finish my rounds with him and when I'd miss breakfast or my lunch I'd grab a package of Saltines and stop off and, while I was talking with him, I'd eat some of his stockpile of Philadelphia cream cheese.

He was really a nice old guy and that was an angel of a wife he had. She must have been about twenty-five years younger than he was and when he started to hemorrhage from that ulcer and we called her that night she said: "Let him go. He's an old man." But we gave him another eighteen months and he took most of it on that cruiser of his and he got in that deep-sea fishing he used to talk about all the time.

Benjamin Davies's wife can't be like that, he thought now, but it's too bad he can't lean on her. It's too bad I can't count on her for any help, either, but at least I've got him going my way right now.

For almost a month Benjamin Davies continued to go Dr. Matthew Carter's way. For three weeks, after leaving the hospital, he reappeared there five days a week and submitted to radiation. Suddenly, and without explanation, he kept no more appointments and when Dr. Carter, on several occasions, attempted to reach him by phone Benjamin Davies was out of town. Finally, Dr. Carter spoke on the phone with the plant doctor who had referred Benjamin Davies.

"You know he's a tough man to reason with," the plant doctor said. "He's been feeling like his old self again, but you know he's the type that can't accept it when something is wrong with his body. The idea of radiation therapy bothers him and one Saturday a couple of weeks ago he told me that he was discontinuing the treatment."

"We can't let him do that."

"I know it. I told him that, but I can't reason with him. He won't even see me any more. He's actually been out of town a lot, but I told him to go see you."

"If I can get him on the phone," Dr. Carter said, "I think I may be able to get him to come in. I'll try."

Dr. Carter tried, but never reached Benjamin Davies by phone. A letter he wrote to him brought no response, although the bill Carrie sent was promptly paid, and Dr. Carter heard nothing of Benjamin Davies again until two years and two months later when the plant doctor called and said he was sending Benjamin Davies into Mercy Hospital the next morning.

"He has a lot of pain constantly now," he said, "and he's coughing some blood. He's lost about twenty pounds and he doesn't want to see anybody. I don't suppose there's anything you, or anyone else can do for him now, but I'd like you to take him over again."

"Certainly," Dr. Carter said. "He's still my patient."

The next morning and afternoon Dr. Carter was operating at University Hospital. Dr. Robert Robinson saw Benjamin Davies.

"I was looking at a dead man, Matt," he said. "He's got no chance. I'll bet you it's all through him now. He was in such pain that all I could do was put him on morphine. If he's lucky he'll go in thirty-six hours."

"He may hang on longer. He's a pretty rugged guy. Was he clear mentally?"

"Only about the pain. His wife was all excited. She doesn't seem to know what's going on."

"She probably still doesn't know. At the time we did him she thought we were repairing an old football injury."

"You're kidding."

"I'll take him on the rest of the way," Dr. Carter said.

"You're welcome to that one," Dr. Robinson said.

The rest of the way stretched on through the next three days.

V

"Excuse me," he said now to the older woman. "Are you Mrs. Davies?"

He had seen the two of them walking up and down the hall. As he had approached Benjamin Davies's room they had paused by the door and were talking.

"Yes," she said.

"I'm Dr. Carter."

"Oh," she said, looking at him. "I'm glad you got here."

She was of medium height and carefully groomed and it was still apparent that she had once been quite beautiful. She had rather large brown eyes but the rest of her features were small and delicate. She was obviously extremely nervous and fatigued and may even have been crying.

"This is my daughter," she said.

"How do you do?" the daughter said.

She was a thirty-year-old model of her mother, perhaps an inch taller, but with the same precise, patrician features. She was wearing a mink coat over her shoulders and was carrying her mother's.

"Look, Doctor," the daughter said. "You've got to do something for Father."

"I am doing something for him. I——"

"It seems to me you're doing very little."

"You've got to help him," the mother said. "He's starting to feel pain now and he doesn't want to see us and I don't understand this."

"It seems to me," the daughter said, "that——"

"Excuse me," he said, "but I'm going to do something for your father right now. The first thing I'm going to do is to go in and see him and give him something for that discomfort. Then I'd like to talk with both of you."

"I'd certainly like to talk with *you*," the daughter said.

"You go down to the lounge, just two doors down from here, and I'll see you there in a few minutes. Is that all right?"

"At least that's something," the daughter said.

When he walked into the room the nurse was at the head of the bed, with her back to him, filling a water glass from the carafe. She turned when she heard him and nodded to him and moved aside.

"Good morning," he said to her.

He walked to the side of the bed and took Benjamin Davies's left hand. Benjamin Davies, much thinner than when he had seen him last, his cheeks hollow and his skin faintly yellow and pulling tight over the cheekbones, was lying on his back, slightly elevated.

"Oh," he said, opening his eyes. "It's you."

"You're having some pain?"

Finding the radial artery in the wrist with his middle and index fingers he felt the pulse, rapid.

"It's starting up again now," Benjamin Davies said slowly. "It's no use."

"I don't want to hear you talking like that," he said, still taking the pulse. "We're going to lick that pain, and you're going to start feeling much better."

"It's no use," Benjamin Davies said, his breathing rapid and shallow. "No use."

"I want you to listen to me," he said. "Are you listening to me?"

He knew that Benjamin Davies was starting to subside now into that semicomatose state. He knew that, with his chest function reduced by his disease, Benjamin Davies's blood was inadequately oxygenated and so he was beginning to experience cerebral anoxia, like an aviator without an oxygen mask at 18,000 feet. It is compassionate Nature's own anesthesia, and now he wanted to give Benjamin Davies, if he could, just that small gift of hope to take into it with him.

"Are you listening?" he said again. "Please listen to me."

"Yes," Benjamin Davies said.

"I want to tell you something, and I want you to understand me clearly. What you're going through now is the kind of crisis people used to go through in the old days of pneumonia. You've heard of that."

"Yes," Benjamin Davies said.

"The crisis occurs and then, suddenly, it's over. Your temperature will fall, your chest congestion will start to clear, you'll start to eat and you'll get your strength back. You can understand that."

"I'd like to believe you, Doctor," Benjamin Davies said.

"Of course you believe me. You know I'm a good doctor, and I've had other cases like yours and I know what I'm talking about. You're suffering now, but we're going to fix that pain in a moment and you're going to start feeling better."

"I hope so," Benjamin Davies said.

"Remember now. You know you don't get anything for nothing, but you've paid for your recovery through your suffering and now you'll start getting well. In fact, you and I will shoot a couple of rounds of golf next spring."

"I hope so."

"That's a date. Right now, though, the nurse is going to give you something for your pain, and I'll be back to see you later. All right?"

"Thank you," Benjamin Davies said.

"I'll see you later."

Thank Nature, he thought, turning from him. Thank sympathetic, pitying, compassionate Nature and that small seed of undying hope that is there to be nourished.

"Doctor?" the nurse said.

"Oh, yes," he said, and he motioned and she followed him out into the hall. "Give him a quarter-grain of morphine. He should have it every three hours."

"Would you mind writing that?"

"I'll do it right now," he said, walking toward the nurses' station.

"Will you have a chance to talk with his wife and daughter?"

"I'll do that right now, too."

"Thank goodness," the nurse said.

She found Benjamin Davies's chart on the rack and gave it to him. He opened the aluminum cover and wrote out the order on the first sheet, and handed it back to her.

"Excuse me, Doctor," one of the young nurses said.

It was the talker, the one who had been telling the other about Jackie Cooper and Hawaii.

"Yes?"

"A Dr. Morrison called for you."

"Who?"

"A Dr. Morrison. About Benjamin Davies. He left his number."

"Oh, yes," he said, and then to the private-duty nurse: "After you've taken care of Mr. Davies, would you mind calling this Dr. Morrison? Tell him I'll be tied up all day, but he can reach me if he wants to at my office early this evening. He knows the patient is terminal, so you can tell him, if he asks, that it's my opinion he has about twenty-four hours to go. Tell him we're keeping him doped up now and that I'm talking with the family."

"Yes, Doctor."

He walked back down the hall, past Benjamin Davies's room, and turned left into the small lounge. Mrs. Davies and her daughter were alone in the room, sitting in the left corner, the blond wood corner table between them. The daughter was leaning toward her mother and talking.

"Oh," Mrs. Davies said, seeing him and starting to stand up.

"Please stay seated," he said, and he pulled another chair over and, facing them, sat down.

"How is he now?" the daughter said.

"The nurse is giving him something that will relieve his pain."

"It's about time," the daughter said. "I don't know why she couldn't have done that sooner."

"Don't blame her," he said. "She was merely following my orders."

"Well, someone's to blame."

Yes, he thought, and it's you and your mother. I should come right out and say it.

"I don't think it's a matter of blaming anyone," he said. "Your father has been under sedation since he came in here, but both you and your mother have complained, first to the nurses and then to Dr. Robinson and then to me on the phone last night, that he was sleeping all the time."

"I just wanted to talk with him," Mrs. Davies said, "but——"

"After all," the daughter said, "I've come almost a thousand miles to see him, and I think I had a right to expect that he would recognize me and know that I was here."

It's what the psychiatrists call morbid guilt, he was thinking, the culpability of the young who stray too far from the nest, and now she wants to take it out on all of us.

"I agree that you had that right," he said, "and no harm has been done. We didn't take him off the sedation until early this morning, so when you saw him the pain was just beginning. Now we've taken care of that, and he's quite comfortable."

"But Doctor," Mrs. Davies said, "I don't understand any of this. I don't understand what's the matter with him."

"Well," he said, trying to find the right way, "as you can see, he's a very sick man. There isn't much we can do for him except to keep him comfortable."

That isn't any good, he was thinking. Tell them and get this over with.

"He has cancer," the daughter said. "Doesn't he?"

Thank you, he thought. Thank you very much.

"I'm afraid he has," he said.

"Oh, no!" Mrs. Davies said, looking at him and blinking and the tears coming into her eyes. "Oh, no, Doctor!"

"I told you," her daughter was saying to her. "I knew it right away, and I told you."

Mrs. Davies was crying now, her handkerchief to her face. Her daughter got up and sat down on the sofa beside her and put her right arm around her mother's shoulders.

"Please, Mrs. Davies," he said. "I'd like you to listen to me."

"But why weren't we told?" the daughter said, looking at him. "We should have been told this."

"Your father forbade me to tell you. He didn't want to worry your mother or you."

"Then he knows?"

"He's known for more than two years, since I operated on him."

"Oh, no!" Mrs. Davies was saying, crying. "It was just some injury he got in football. That's what he said."

"I know that's what he told you," he said.

"But what are you doing for him?" the daughter said.

"I'm afraid there isn't much we can do, except to see that he doesn't suffer."

"But someone should be able to help him," the daughter said. "Can't someone else help him?"

"I'm afraid not. You may, of course, call in anyone you want, but I'm afraid there's nothing anyone can do when the disease progresses to this point."

"This is terrible," the daughter said.

"I know it is," he said, and he reached over and took Mrs. Davies's hand. "I'm very sorry, and I'm concerned about you."

"But what's going to happen now?" the daughter said. "I mean, how long do you think it will be?"

"No physician is God," he said, "and I don't know. We don't believe it will be long, but we do know he's not suffering."

"Now please, Mother," the daughter was saying.

"Mrs. Davies," he said, "I'm going to send in a nurse to help you. Then I think you should go home and rest. You may come back later in the day, if you feel up to it."

"Please, Mother," the daughter was saying.

"I'm sorry," he said, releasing Mrs. Davies's hand and standing up. "I'm very sorry. I'll send the nurse."

"You've got to stop this, Mother," the daughter was saying.

He walked back to Benjamin Davies's room and opened the door.

The nurse saw him and he motioned to her and she came out into the hall.

"How is he?"

"He's all right now. He's sleeping."

"I'd like you to take a few minutes with his wife," he said. "She's pretty distraught, but I think she'll be all right. See if you can get her to go home."

"Certainly, Doctor," the nurse said.

"And don't forget to call that Dr. Morrison."

"I have his number right here."

"Good."

At the nurses' station the Jackie Cooper fan was talking on the telephone. When she saw him she said something final into the phone and hung up.

"I'd like you to call downstairs," he said, "and see if a Mrs. Louise Brower has checked in. B-r-o-w-e-r. I'll stop by again in a few minutes."

"Yes, Doctor."

"Thanks."

He reached into his pocket and took out the page of memo paper and looked at the list.

Mrs. Elizabeth Kirk, he thought, in 412. If her husband is here I might as well get that one over with, too.

"Before you make that call," he said, "can you just reach over there and hand me the chart of Mrs. Elizabeth Kirk?"

"Surely."

"Thank you."

The temperature is all right at 99.4, he thought. After all, it's less than twenty hours since I opened her. The pulse is fast at 96, but she has a good heart and I took nothing but the rib out, so her oxygenating power is not responsible. Probably the morphine was wearing off. Her respiration is a little rapid at 24 because it hurts her to breathe deeply right now so she breathes shallow, but at 120 over 80 her blood pressure is normal.

"Patient unable to keep fluids down because of nausea," he read, scanning the nurse's notes. "On complaint of pain Pantopon gr. ⅓ given." . . . "Patient sleeping quietly." . . . "Color good." . . . "Pulse strong." . . . "Patient's position changed from back to right side." . . . "Patient awake. Deep breathing and coughing encouraged."

"They're not answering at Admissions, Doctor," the nurse was saying. "I don't know what's wrong with them. Honestly, I sometimes wonder——"

"Try them in a few minutes," he said. "I'll be back."

Maybe I'll recognize this Roger Kirk when I see him, he thought, walking back down the hall, but I doubt it. Marion sees them all and she says he's the best in his business. She says the rest of these newscasters are just voice boxes; that their facial expressions never change whether they're telling you about fifty people being killed in a plane crash or about the Easter-egg-rolling on the White House lawn. Marion says that at least this Roger Kirk seems to be aware of what he's saying.

"Good morning," he said.

"Oh, hello," Roger Kirk said. He was sitting beside the bed, and he stood up.

"I'm Dr. Carter."

I recognize him now, he thought. Now I remember seeing him.

"I'm glad to meet you, Doctor," Roger Kirk said, smiling and shaking hands.

"It's nice to meet you. How's our patient?"

"She seems to be doing pretty well, Doctor."

"Good," he said, turning to Mrs. Kirk. "So you're enjoying your vacation?"

She was a rather petite blonde, with a square face and blue eyes. She was resting on her right side.

"Not exactly," she said, smiling back at him.

"I didn't hurt you too much, did I?" he said, taking her pulse and feeling it strong.

"I don't know. I don't feel much like moving around to see."

"You'll be up and moving around again in a couple of days. What we want you to do now is to breathe as deeply as you can and cough when you have to. That's the way you'll cleanse your lungs."

"I'll try."

"We also want to get you to drink something."

"I've tried that, but it didn't stay down."

"It will now, and we've got an excellent list of wines and spirits. There aren't any sparkling Burgundies or scotches or bourbons, but you can have orange juice or ginger ale or liquid Jellos in any flavor. You can even have a malted milk."

"It all sounds terrible."

"What you probably want to do is just take a nap."

"That's all I want to do. I feel dopey."

"You go right ahead and take your nap. The nurse will give you a little liquid later. You'll be able to keep it down, and it might even taste good to you."

"The nurse will be right back," Roger Kirk said. "She just went out for a couple of minutes."

"I'm back now, Doctor," the nurse said.

"Fine," he said, and then to Mrs. Kirk: "We're going to let you sleep now, and Dr. Robinson will be in to see you this afternoon."

"Thank you, Doctor," Mrs. Kirk said.

"Thank you for being such a good patient," he said.

"Do you have a moment?" Roger Kirk said.

"Certainly," he said, and then to the nurse: "I think she'll be ready for some liquids when she wakes up. Let's keep encouraging her on that deep breathing, too."

"Yes, Doctor."

Roger Kirk followed him to the door. He was in his mid-thirties, of slightly less than medium height but with a good, square, mannish jaw and live eyes and a facile expression. He was beautifully tailored in a conservative dark gray suit and wearing a tab-collared white shirt and a plain dark blue tie carefully knotted with the cleft just below the knot.

"My wife is an admirer of yours," he said to Roger Kirk, walking him down the hall toward the window at the end. They were passing the lounge and he glanced in and saw the nurse sitting where he had been sitting and Mrs. Benjamin Davies drinking a glass of water and her daughter still sitting next to her and watching her.

I'm having a great morning, he thought. I got up actually looking forward to that Mr. Scheller because I know I can do that vena cava and cure him, and I never will learn how to do this business well. It's impossible to do it well.

"That's always nice to hear," Roger Kirk was saying.

"Being a doctor's wife," he said, "she has a lot of time alone to read the books and watch the television that I can never find time for."

"I think you doctors lead the most demanding lives of our time."

"We're too busy, but I guess it's always been that way," he said stopping at the window and looking down at the street but registering nothing he saw outside.

I am always bringing them to this window, he had often thought, bringing them to the lounge sometimes but so often to this window or the ones above or below it. I have told so many at the window.

"I was sorry not to be here last evening," Roger Kirk was saying, "but I have to do those two news shows now."

"I know," he said. "Your wife would have been sleeping anyway."

"I would have been here, though," Roger Kirk said, and then: "What I'm anxious to know now is what you found. Did everything go as you hoped it would?"

"No," he said. "I'm sorry to say it didn't."

"Why? What happened?"

"Well, you'll probably remember that Dr. Robinson told you on the phone what we were hoping to do."

"That's right," Roger Kirk said, looking right at him.

"The X rays showed several small shadows in the right lung. As Dr. Robinson said, we were hoping to remove the lung, but when we made our incision and explored the adjacent areas we found the disease had spread too far. It had spread all over the pleura—that's the covering over the lung—and down onto the diaphragm, which is the partition that separates the chest from the abdomen."

"Then it's cancer?" Roger Kirk said, still looking at him.

"I'm afraid it is."

"Are you sure? Are you absolutely sure?"

"Yes, we're sure."

"I don't know what to say, Doctor," Roger Kirk said, his eyes starting to fill now.

"Of course you don't."

"You'll have to excuse me, Doctor."

"There's nothing to apologize for."

"But how could it be?" Roger Kirk was saying. "How could it be? She's only been coughing for about a month. Otherwise she feels fine, so how could it be? I just don't understand."

"I know, but we don't know the answer. Sometimes the disease is very fast-growing."

"Did you take any of it out?"

"Just a small biopsy to confirm the diagnosis. I made an incision only six inches long and removed part of the ninth rib in the back so we could look in there. She won't even know her rib is gone, but when we discovered that we couldn't remove all the disease, even on one side, we knew there was no point in submitting her to a larger operation on either side."

"She and I haven't talked about it," Roger Kirk said, looking out the window now, "but I know she thinks that whatever it was you got it out. I know she thinks the worst is over."

"It's better for her to think that right now."

"I don't know what to say. I don't know what I should tell her."

"It's not a decision you have to make right now."

"But isn't there anything else that can be done?" Roger Kirk said, facing him again. "Won't radiation treatments help her?"

"There's some hope there. X rays work sometimes. I've had cases in which they've been successful, but you should know that, the way her disease has spread, the odds are against her."

"But they do work sometimes? You have really had cases where X rays worked?"

"Yes," he said. "I've got a man, a fishing boat captain, who first came in nine years ago. He was thirty-five years old at the time and he's alive and well today at the age of forty-four."

He was a big, willowy, smooth-muscled blond, and when he had opened him for a tumor the size of a lemon in the upper lobe of the right lung, he had seen that the cancer had spread, whitish-pink and looking like a healing skin burn, to the mediastinum, which is the area between the lungs. He had closed his chest and sent him for radiation therapy, 6000 roentgens total dosage in twenty-five treatments over five weeks.

"Then it worked in his case?" Roger Kirk was saying.

It had worked beautifully. The first X-ray plates were so totally obscure he could distinguish no detail. At the end of a year, though, he could actually see the contraction of the lung tumor and six months later it was even more obvious. At that point the shrinkage hit its level, and it had held it after two years and then five and now nine.

"Yes," he said. "In that instance it worked, but his is an exceptional case. I tell you this because I respect your intelligence and your courage. I think you should know the whole truth."

"I want to know it," Roger Kirk said, looking out the window again, "but I don't want my wife to know it."

"If there's any way I can help I will."

"You see," Roger Kirk said, "my wife and I have been married twelve years now, and we've never had any secrets. When we were married we said we'd never lie to each other, and we never have."

"I understand."

"Now I'll have to lie to her. For the first time, I'll have to tell her lies."

"Let's say you'll have to put on an act. If you make up your mind to this let's say you'll have to be an actor, and you'll be a great one."

"I don't know whether I can do it."

"You'll do it."

"Then we've got our two daughters. They're still just kids, and they won't know what's happening. You know you think of a lot of things at a time like this, Doctor. Now she'll never see her children grow up."

"I met your children when Mrs. Kirk came to my office," he said. "They're great kids."

The older girl seemed to be about ten years old and the younger must have been seven or eight, and she had turned the office appointment into a day in town for her children. While he had been examining her, Carrie had been amusing the kids or they had been amusing Carrie, and after he had completed the examination and looked at the X rays and they had left, he had wished he had never seen the kids.

"But if you give her X-ray treatments," Roger Kirk was saying, "she'll know. Won't she?"

"Not necessarily. You see, we don't have to start her immediately. If the cell structure is going to be vulnerable to X rays it will be vulnerable later on, too. So we don't have to face that at the moment."

"When will we have to face it?"

"Well, she'll feel fine for a while. She won't notice any change, or have any pain, for a couple of months."

"At least we'll get through Christmas."

"Yes."

"When you have kids, you think of Christmas."

"I know."

"But then what?"

"Sometime after the New Year she'll probably start feeling some discomfort. When she does, you have her call me and I'll tell her it's neuritis. If you still feel then as you do now about not telling her, I'll simply explain that we're going to give her treatments for neuritis."

"And after the two months? I mean, supposing that the X-ray treatments aren't successful, will she have a month or two?"

"No. It will be longer than that."

"Can you tell me how long?"

"No physician is God," he heard himself saying again. "We don't know. The X rays may have a palliative effect. They may help for a while."

"If they don't, will she have four or five months from now?"

"She has six months at least, perhaps longer."

"Six months," Roger Kirk said.

"At least that."

"That isn't very much, is it?" Roger Kirk said, his eyes filling again.

"No."

"You know I've just thought of something else, Doctor. I don't like to bother you with all these things, and take your time."

"You're not bothering me, and I have all the time you need."

"We're just about to sign the papers for a new home. We're buying a bigger place, and now that I think of it I wish we weren't. If she goes, the kids and I won't live in it alone."

"I understand."

"She's very happy about it and buying a lot of things for it. You know how women are."

"Yes."

"I mean, I don't see how I can call it off now."

"Of course not."

"If I do, she'll know something is wrong, and she'll realize what it is."

"If the new home and all that goes with it are making her happy," he said, "and if you can afford it, I'm sure you'll want to go on with it."

"That's true. That's not a problem, really, and I shouldn't even have mentioned it."

"That's quite all right. Remember, I've painted a black picture here because I believe you want to know how I see it and what I think."

"I do, and I thank you for it."

"There's one thing that you shouldn't forget, though, and that's that we never know. There's always hope. They're searching and experimenting all the time on new treatments. Who knows? Tomorrow or next week or next month there may be a new drug. Some years ago a relative of mine died of pernicious anemia just five months before what we call the 'classic report' was published containing the cause and cure. This will happen some day with cancer, too. We just don't know when."

"I see."

"There's something else I want to tell you, too. I've found Mrs. Kirk to be an imaginative and impressionable woman. You know that, so you've made your decision not to tell her. It's going to be hard for you to lie, and you're going to want to free your conscience and tell her the truth. You must remember that you're doing by far the braver thing. You're carrying the burden alone, rather than to tell her and transfer to her shoulders all the terror and fears that her imagination would multiply.

"Remember, too," he said, "that you're not alone. There are many other husbands and wives who have had to do this, too, and some are doing it right now. When it gets to the more difficult stage, when it starts to bother her, she'll come to me and I'll give her drugs so she won't have any pain, and you and I will carry her along together."

"You're really being most kind, Doctor. I appreciate this."

"You and I understand each other, and we're going to share this together. We have the same problem in a way, because my conscience will bother me, too. Right now your wife thinks I'm a fine surgeon, but one day she'll say to me: 'I feel worse than before you operated on me.' Then I'll be tempted to tell her the truth. I'll want to say: 'But I'm not a bad surgeon, and no surgeon could have cured you.' Of course, I won't say that, and I tell you this only to show you that, in a way, I'm a small partner of yours."

"Thank you, Doctor," Roger Kirk said, shaking hands and fighting back the emotion. "Thanks very much."

"Mr. Kirk?" the voice behind them said.

They turned, and it was a black-haired, brown-eyed young man wearing a dark blue flannel gown over pajamas.

"Why, Rocco!" Roger Kirk said. "What are you doing here?"

"I had my appendix out," Rocco said.

"Oh, excuse me," Roger Kirk said. "This is Dr. Carter. This is Rocco DeVito. Rocco is one of our camera men."

"How are you, Doctor?" Rocco said, shaking hands. "Pleased to know you."

"I'm glad to know you."

"You know a doctor named Stanczyk?" Rocco said.

"Yes. I know him very well."

"He's a real good doctor, ain't he?"

"He certainly is."

"You know somethin'?" Rocco said, turning to Roger Kirk. "You know, I always figured to be a real good doctor you should be an old doctor—not too old, but kinda old. This guy—excuse me, I mean this doctor, I got—is kind of a young guy but he's great. The day before yesterday he takes my appendix out, and already I feel good enough to go home. Ain't that pretty good, Doc?"

"That's fine," he said. "Dr. Stanczyk is an excellent surgeon."

But I wonder how Stan is doing on that sub-total gastrectomy, he thought. I wonder when I'll finally be able to get Mr. Scheller in there, but I've still got that bronchoscopy, that Louise Brower, if she's here yet.

"So when are you coming back?" Roger Kirk was saying. "You know the show can't go on without you?"

"Yeah?" Rocco said. "Don't kid me. I watched it last night and it was great. Believe me, I got all this sick leave and I never use it in my life and I'm gonna take it."

"Good."

"What are you doin' in here?" Rocco said.

"Mrs. Kirk is here. Dr. Carter is caring for her."

"She all right?" Rocco said. "I mean, everything all right?"

"Fine," Roger Kirk said, smiling, "she's fine."

"Good," Rocco said. "I'm glad to hear that, and I didn't mean to interrupt."

"That's all right."

"Glad to meet you, Doc."

"Glad to meet you."

"Take care of yourself now, Rocco," Roger Kirk said. "I'll see you."

"Don't worry about this kid," Rocco said.

"Rocco's a good boy," Roger Kirk said, turning back, "but I don't want to take up any more of your time, Doctor."

"I'll walk you back to the room."

He's quite a man, he thought, walking away when he had left him. Roger Kirk is quite a man. It was something, the way he took that, and particularly when that Rocco walked up and he turned to him as if he didn't have a worry in the world. It was a great performance, and maybe he can do that because he's a performer. We're all performers and how I got started in this performance business I no longer know.

VII

His mother was the one who had started it all. She was thin and wiry, with high cheekbones and dark eyes and her black hair drawn straight back and parted in the middle, and when he and his brother teased her they called her "The Indian." Like their father she was deeply religious, and while she would be working around the house, standing at the stove and humming to herself or scrubbing the kitchen table until the wood was almost white, she would be casting her philosophy out.

"Be a healer," she would say. "Jesus was a healer, but if you can't be a minister and heal the soul, be a doctor and heal the body."

When a dust storm would start and they would see it moving slowly, ceaselessly toward them from the horizon like a great, gray-brown, whole-world-enveloping veil, she would call them into the house. They would stuff the cracks around the doors and windows with rags and newspapers and she would tie clean white cloths like bandit masks across the lower halves of their faces. They would stand by a window and watch for their father to come in, a dark, slow-moving, heroic shadow bent against the gray-brown universe.

"'All service ranks the same with God,'" she might say. "'With God, whose puppets, best and worst, are we; there is no last nor first.' A man named Robert Browning, a poet, wrote that."

After a while, when they would look at one another, they would laugh. On the white bandit masks there would be two growing dark smudges over the nostrils behind them, and when the storm had passed and she would start at once to clean the house she would always begin at the tops of the frames of the doors and windows and work down.

"God is everywhere," she would say often. "You don't see Him, but He sees you and everything you do, and He is with you always."

It bothered him that God was with him, always following him but never showing Himself. He was about seven years old at the time, and he envisioned God as a kindly, white-haired Old Man, and he devised a method, a trick, by which he would surprise God and see Him.

"Is little Matt all right?" the neighbor down the road asked his mother one day.

She had come in to visit. As his mother used to tell it, they had been sitting in the kitchen and talking for some time before the good woman mentioned it.

"Why yes," his mother said. "He seems well."

"I've been wondering," the neighbor said.

"Why? Has he been pestering you?"

"No, but there's something kind of strange about him lately."

"I haven't noticed anything. What's he doing?"

"I don't really know," the neighbor said. "The last few days I've watched him walking down the road past our place to school. He walks along and then suddenly he stops and he turns quick. Then he walks along and stops again and turns quick the other way. He seems to have some kind of a nervous jerk."

It was the trick he had devised. He had worked it out, lying in bed one night and thinking about God being with him always, but hiding always.

When nobody else is around and I'm alone with God, he had said to himself, I'll fool Him and I'll see Him. I'll say out loud: "Now I'm going to see God. I'm going to turn quick now and look this way and see Him." Then when He hears me say that, and He thinks that's what I'll do, I'll turn quick the other way. That's how I'll see Him.

When it was that he had stopped believing in God as a kindly white-haired Old Man, watching him always, he never knew. In college he read Spinoza, Diderot, Holbach, Huxley, and Darwin. At the fraternity-house bull sessions there was always some upperclassman who would stand up and defy God to strike him dead, giving Him thirty dramatic seconds in which to do it. In physics and chemistry, in biology and zoology, the devotion was all to scientism, the emphasis on provable certainty, and the rewards for accuracy of observation.

There was the amoeba, that microscopic animalcule perpetually changing shape but dead now on the slide, and the assignment was to draw it, magnified. He had squinted through the microscope with one eye, the other closed, his facial muscles tiring because he had not yet mastered the ability to keep both eyes open and to admit into his consciousness only that which the 'scope eye sees. He had drawn the amoeba in three dimensions because his mother had taught him, while he was still small, to paint and to draw and to use the principle of perspective.

The professor was Frog Ramsay. He was short and stocky, with long arms and large head and a shock of gray hair. He walked around the laboratory with his smock open, his hands clutched behind his back, stopping and looking and sometimes saying something and walking on.

"Oh, yes," he said, when he had stopped and looked at the amoeba in three dimensions. "Now would you mind standing up and letting me see for myself this unusual creature?"

He sat down on the stool and he bent his head and looked through the microscope. Then he stood up, his hands still behind his back.

"Young man," he said, "draw only what you see. That's all you know."

When he came home from college after his third year, the house shook with the reverberations of his revolt. He did not assail his mother but, torn and uncertain and trying to find the truth, he struck like a cornered, wounded animal at his father.

"But I challenge you," he said. "I challenge you to prove any of it."

"The proof is in the Bible," his father said.

"The Bible?" he said. "The Bible isn't the only book in the world. It isn't the authority for everything."

"If you believe this," his father said, "there is nothing I can do about it, but I don't have to hear it in my own house."

"You're a coward," he said. "You're afraid to discuss it, because you can't prove it. You can't prove any of it."

He was helping to drive the cattle to the water holes that summer, riding out with the others early each morning to sweep the valleys, each man taking an area alone. By the end of the day they would have assembled quite a herd, but after a day or two the cattle would have moved out again, trying to get to good grass, and they would have to bring them back.

It was noon and the temperature must have been 110. There was not a cloud in the sky and not a tree on the horizon and it was so clear that he could see a hundred miles. The jack rabbits slept in the shade of the soapweeds, and in this great, scorched, heat-welded, immobile universe nothing else moved. Only his horse moved, moving him, the only sound the clop-thock of its hooves against the stones. It moved more slowly now, for it had been working since sunup, and finally it stopped, starting to drop its head and he heard the last hoof sound die.

It was so still that he could feel the silence, and then it came. It came to his consciousness like a clap of sudden thunder, but not ceasing nor subsiding. It assaulted his ears, filling his head, filling this universe, the dry, grating, million-rattle, steady thunder sound of a million insects everywhere, always there.

So there must be a God, he thought, sitting there unmoving and assailed by the sound. Call it God or Force, but there is a Something and it is here and everywhere.

In Gross Anatomy, in his first year of medical school, examining every vessel that fed every muscle, isolating every nerve that activated it, dissecting every organ, he knew that the answer wasn't here and there must have been a Something that motivated and moved this man. Witnessing a complete autopsy, watching the emptying and then the careful, skilled, hidden, and disguised closure, it came to him that what they had removed would tell them why this now manikin-man died, but it would not tell them why he had hoped and feared and lived.

"You can't be a surgeon," he was to come to say many years later, "and not believe in some kind of supreme law. You can't witness the whole series of dynamic, immutable changes that is life from beginning to end without believing. I have seen death hundreds of times. I have seen brave men die and men you would call cowards die, and at the end there is no difference between them. There comes over all of them that same blessed euphoria, and only their survivors suffer. You may not want to call it God's numbing, as I have heard it called, but you can't deny it."

He did not come to medicine and then to surgery, however, to serve but to be served. It is merely, he recognized and admitted to himself, that what serves me is regarded, and not wrongly, as service and I am one of the fortunate.

"Tell me something, Doctor," he heard someone ask Peter Wakefield at a dinner party one night. "I'm curious to know why you became a surgeon."

Peter had come over from England to deliver two lectures, and he had been charming them all evening with his graciousness, his erudition, and his humor.

"My dear lady," he said, dropping his head, his pink chin overflowing his collar and Peter looking at her out of the tops of his blue eyes. "I became a surgeon for the same reason that my plumber became a plumber. There's really no difference, you know, except that I have more need for him than he, fortunate fellow, has for me."

On another evening it was not Peter but Carl Broeck from the Netherlands. They were talking about Carl's home town, which was Heerlen, and he was telling Carl how, when they went through there during the war, the Germans were running for the Siegfried Line and so the town was untouched and not left in ruins like the small towns in France and it reminded him of the suburb of any northern American city.

"It is a funny thing about that town," Carl said. "You know, I sometimes think that the reason I became a doctor was because of that town. In that town then, when I was a small boy, the most important man was the doctor. He was a big, impressive man, and we had then the telephones that you would crank and when the operator would answer you would say: 'Give me, please, number ten.' Or you would ask for number sixteen or twenty-nine, or whatever the number was. One day I watched the doctor when he cranked the phone. When the operator answered he said: 'My home.' That was all he said, but the operator knew who he was and she knew his number and when I heard this I said to myself that I wanted to be a doctor, too, and be important like this.

"I suppose," Carl said, "that, if I had grown up in a big city, the doctor might not have seemed so important. I suppose that, if I were growing up now, the doctor might not seem so important, either, because that is changing back home."

"It is changing here, too," he said to Carl then. "When I was in college I was important. I played football, and everyone knew me, and I hated to have it end. I used to see the football players graduate and disappear, selling bonds or insurance or going into some manufacturing plant. I couldn't imagine myself doing this.

"Of course, it happened that I was better in the sciences than I was in the arts, and one evening we were sitting around the fraternity house and the others were talking about what they were going to do when they graduated. One of them was going into a bank. Another was going into his father's business, whatever it was, and someone turned to me and said: 'Hey, Matt, what are you going to do?' I said: 'I'm going to be a doctor.'

"The moment I said it, I felt a change come over the room. They all looked at me, and I could see it in their faces. I hadn't done anything yet, except to make a statement, but already I was important.

"I suppose," he said, "that if I want to be absolutely honest about it, this and the need to prolong the academic association rather than face the necessity of making a living, is why I went to medical school."

"Of course," Carl said. "It is a perfectly natural thing."

VIII

"How about Mrs. Brower?" he said to the talker. "Mrs. Louise Brower. Has she checked in yet?"

The talker was on the phone again, but when she had seen him she had put her hand over the mouthpiece and looked up at him.

"No, Doctor. I finally got Admissions a minute ago, and they said they hadn't seen her yet."

"That's all right," he said, and he motioned to her to go back on the phone. Then he walked to the rack and took out the chart of Grace Cowan.

Grace Cowan was forty-one years of age, and she had first come into his office eight days before. She was unmarried, lived at what is considered a good address, had the outward manifestations of both wealth and sophistication, and was still a physically attractive woman. Aside from the fact that she drank too much and smoked too much she had treated herself well all her life, and there was an irregular shadow in the upper lobe of her left lung.

"Do you suppose it's cancer, Doctor?" she had said, openly.

"I can't say right now," he said. "That's what we've got to find out."

"But it wouldn't surprise you, would it?" she said.

"Nothing surprises me any more," he said.

"I'm sure that's true," she said. "Few things surprise even me any more."

He remembered the lines six days later, after he had stopped in to see her just before he operated. Her only relatives were her sister, about five years older and also looking as if she had once emerged from a Miss Somebody's finishing school and come out at the Cotillion. Her sister's husband was about fifty, impeccably groomed, slim, with classically even features and slightly wavy gray hair. He resembled the man you see flattering the bored, bare-shouldered woman in the full-page magazine color ads for whisky, perfume, cosmetics, or a deodorant, and his name was Warren Leeds.

"I'm feeling quite well right now, Doctor," Grace Cowan said.

"You'll be all right," he said. "There's no need for worry."

"I'm not the least bit worried," she said.

"Doctor," her sister said, "you will take good care of her?"

"Of course," he said, "and you mustn't worry."

"I mean, you'll really do your best?"

"Of course I will," he said, no longer struck by the absurdity that they think you might apply only partial effort.

"She's my only sister, and she means a great deal to me."

"Excuse me, Helen," Grace Cowan said, "but I'd like to talk with the doctor a moment alone."

She said it very nicely, and her sister and Warren Leeds walked out into the hall.

"You'll have to excuse my sister," Grace Cowan said. "She's like our mother was—the emotional type."

"I understand that."

"I have a couple of questions, Doctor," she said. "I'd like to know how much of a scar this is going to leave."

"Well, it will be a fairly extensive one."

The truth is, he thought, it will be the biggest one you ever saw, but what difference does it make at a time like this?

"I mean," she said, "how obvious will it be?"

"It will start below your left breast and extend in a C part way around the back. It's my brand—C for Carter—and at your bridge club, when they start bragging about their scars, you might even win first prize."

"The reason I'm asking," she said, "is that I do wear bathing suits and sometimes low back dresses."

"In cases like yours," he said, "I then make the incision a little lower."

"You can actually do that?"

"Yes, I've done it quite often."

It was the truth. You put the anterior, or front, end of the incision in the breast fold and keep it a couple of inches lower when you bring it around the side and up between the shoulder blades. That means you have to tunnel up under the skin in the back, and so you can call it a nuisance or, if it is important to the patient, a nicety.

"Then it won't show?"

"Not while you're wearing any reasonable costume. I don't think a bikini would hide it completely, and neither would a dress that's cut down in the back to your coccyx."

"Well, I had neither of those in mind," she said. "I'm a little beyond that age."

"Good," he said. "Then we'll hide it, and after six months it will hardly be visible anyway."

"I have just one more question."

"Go ahead."

"I have never had an operation before," she said, "but I've heard or read somewhere that, when a patient comes out of the anesthesia, they talk. I mean, I understand that they absolutely divulge their souls."

"That's not quite true," he said. "Some patients will talk briefly and rather rationally, but I have never known of anyone to reveal any secrets. You don't need to be concerned about that."

"I'm not concerned," she said. "I was just curious."

"Good. I'm going to leave you now, but I'll see you downstairs before they wheel you in."

"Thank you, Doctor."

In the hall he saw the sister and her husband.

"You may go in now," he said. "She seems in good spirits."

"She's taking this better than I am," her sister said.

"Why don't you go in, Helen?" her husband said. "I'll be there in a minute."

"Of course," she said, and then: "And please do your best, Doctor."

"You know I will."

"Doctor," Warren Leeds said, watching his wife walk into the room, "I want you to know how important my sister-in-law is."

"I know how important she is," he said, "to both your wife and you."

"It isn't just that, Doctor," Warren Leeds said. "You can't have any idea how important she is. What I'm going to tell you may shock you, but I want you to know."

Why, he's breaking up, he thought. The man in the ad is coming apart.

"I wish you'd tell me anything you think I should know," he said.

"You should know this, Doctor," Warren Leeds said. "Grace isn't just my sister-in-law. Grace and I are in love. We've been lovers for almost twenty years. That's how important she is to me."

"I see."

"Doesn't that shock you?" Warren Leeds said, but just glancing at him and looking away.

"No, it doesn't shock me," he said, but thinking that it did surprise him because this was the first one who had ever told him. "After all you're telling me because I'm a doctor."

"You're the only one in the world who knows now, Doctor, other than ourselves. Of course my wife doesn't know. She doesn't have the slightest suspicion. I think Grace and I have handled it very well."

Oh, you've handled it very well, all right, he was thinking. I'm glad you didn't say you've handled it beautifully.

"You see, I wanted you to know this, Doctor," Warren Leeds was saying, "because you simply must save her. You simply must."

"Now take hold of yourself," he said, looking right at him. "For any thoracic surgeon this is a reasonably routine operation. I don't expect any complications, and I'm going to cure her."

"But she has cancer, doesn't she?"

"I don't know that. We're going to find out this morning."

"But she's convinced she has cancer."

"Just a moment, Mr. Leeds," he said. "Just reason this out. I've devoted most of the past twenty years of my life to this disease and its cure by surgery, and I don't know for sure what your sister-in-law has. She can't possibly have any knowledge remotely comparable to mine."

"But it doesn't seem to bother her," Warren Leeds was saying. "I'm upset, but she isn't. I must say I don't understand how she can be like that."

"She's a courageous woman. It seems to me that out of respect for her courage you should face up to all the possibilities, too."

"Believe me, I'm trying. I haven't behaved like this with her, or in my wife's presence, either. I had to let down with someone, though, and that's why I've told you."

"And I respect your confidence. What I want you to understand, however, is that even if your worst fears are realized, and this is a cancer, I'm going to remove it. I do this every day of the week. Do you understand that?"

"I understand," Warren Leeds said, looking at him now. "I apologize for behaving badly."

"There's no apology necessary."

He'll be all right, he thought. The pieces of the man in the ad are coming back together again.

"I did behave badly, but I'm quite all right now."

"Then forget it," he said, shaking Warren Leeds' hand, "and don't worry. She'll be all right."

"Thank you, Doctor," Warren Leeds said, and then he turned and walked toward the room.

When he opened Grace Cowan, making the incision as low as possible and tunneling, as he had promised, he found the left lung cancerous and he removed it. There was no visible spread to any of the adjacent areas, however, and when he examined the lymph nodes, the depots at which a cancer stops if it spreads through the lymphatic channels, he saw that the nodes were small and the pigmentation was a normal black and not marked with small patches of white. He isolated and removed three of the nodes for immediate microscopic examination, and when the report from the pathologist was negative he knew that Grace Cowan was running in luck.

Most of the first post-operative day Grace Cowan spent under sedation. At 6:30 that evening, however, the private-duty nurse was on the phone.

"Dr. Carter," she said, "I'm sorry to bother you, but I'm having a bit of a problem with Miss Cowan. I spoke to Dr. Bronson, and he said to call you."

"What's the problem?" he said.

"The patient is complaining of pain, but she won't let me give her the hypo. She says she doesn't want any morphine."

"She didn't mention this to Dr. Robinson when he saw her this afternoon."

"I know. That's why I can't understand it."

"How is she otherwise?"

"Otherwise she's doing quite well. Her blood pressure is good. Her temperature is 102 and her pulse is fast, but I think you expect that."

"Is she taking her liquids?"

"Yes. Except for the morphine she's extremely co-operative."

"Then I'll tell you what you do. We'll give her something by mouth. Give her fifty milligrams of demerol. Give it every four hours if necessary, and if she asks what it's for, tell her it's to prevent the possibility of infection."

"You said fifty milligrams of demerol, every four hours if necessary?"

"That's right, and I'll be in to see her the first chance I get tomorrow."

"Thank you, Doctor."

It was now 9:34 in the morning when he looked at the chart. The temperature was 101 as expected and the blood pressure was good at 128 over 82, but the pulse was fast at 105, and the respirations shallow and rapid at 32 per minute.

She's having pain while she's awake, he thought, but if she won't take the morphine she's got to take the pain. Then he checked the fluid balance and saw that the intake at 2500 c.c.s and the output at 900 c.c.s were satisfactory, and he scanned the nurse's notes.

"Patient takes fluids well." . . . "Passing gas." . . . "Abdomen not distended." . . . "Patient complains of pain but refuses morphine as prescribed." . . . "Otherwise patient is extremely co-operative."

"Good morning," he said to the nurse, when he walked into the room. "How's everything?"

"I think we're doing pretty well," the nurse said, "except for some discomfort."

"Do you want to take a break for a few minutes?"

"All right, Doctor," the nurse said. "Thank you."

"You're looking pretty well," he said to Grace Cowan. "How do you feel?"

"Fair," she said.

There were two arrangements of mixed flowers in vases on the bedside table. Lying open in front of them was a Bible.

"How's the pain?" he said, taking her wrist and finding her pulse.

"Terrible."

"You know we can eliminate that."

"I know."

"What's this I hear about you refusing the medication I prescribed?"

"If it's the morphine you're talking about, I don't want any."

"It will not only take care of your pain but it will augment your recovery. Right now, because of the pain, you can't breathe as deeply as you should, and we want to get you breathing normally again as soon as we can."

"I'll remember to breathe deeply," she said.

"If it's addiction you're afraid of," he said, "you can ignore that possibility. There's no danger."

"I'm not afraid of that. It has nothing to do with that."

"Oh?" he said, stalling just to see what would happen.

"Warren," she said, "my brother-in-law, told me yesterday afternoon that he had a talk with you."

So that's it, he thought. So she's regarding this whole thing as a punishment visited upon her. So she's trying to eradicate her guilt with pain, or maybe I'm playing psychiatrist.

"Yes," he said, "we did have a talk. He was very concerned about you."

"You know that's not what I mean," she said. "Warren talks too much. I don't mean normally, but there was no need for him to bring that up at any time."

"He felt a need, and I'm a doctor."

"You know, my sister is really a very fine person. Warren and I have never wanted to hurt her."

"I'm sure of that."

"I guess you'd call it just one of those things," she said. "I guess what I'm really seeking now is absolution of my guilt."

"I understand."

"Have you ever read the Bible, Doctor?"

"I was brought up on it."

"I wasn't. It's new to me."

"I hope you're finding something in it."

"At least I'm trying," she said, and then: "How am I doing otherwise?"

"Very well, actually. You're doing so well that, if I had a hundred cases just like you, I'd be famous."

"It was cancer, wasn't it?"

"Yes, but I got it all out."

"Good."

I don't know whether that "good" is because she welcomes the disease as a guilt purgative, he thought, or whether it's for the cure.

"The growth was limited and confined," he said. "It hadn't spread, so we were able to get it all."

"I'm glad to hear that report."

"I'm glad to report it," he said. "Tomorrow morning we may be able to take that tube out. Later in the day we may let you up to walk to the bathroom, if you feel like it."

"That would be appreciated."

"Meanwhile," he said, "I want you to wiggle your toes once in a while, and occasionally bring your feet up and down."

"That's for my circulation?"

"Right, and I'm leaving that order for that medication if you change your mind about getting help for that pain."

"I won't change my mind. You might not think it, knowing what you do now, but I'm really quite strong-willed."

"I believe it."

In the hall the nurse was walking up and down near the door.

"Did you convince her to let me give her a hypo, Doctor?" she said.

"No," he said. "She doesn't want it, and she'll be all right."

"Honestly," the nurse said, "I don't understand some people, but I suppose it takes all kinds."

"That's right."

"Is it against her religion or something?"

"No. I don't know what it is, but we'll go along the way she wants it. Dr. Robinson will be in to see her this afternoon. He may leave an order with your relief to give her ten milligrams of sodium luminal if she's too uncomfortable."

"Honestly," the nurse said.

At the nurses' station he asked the talker to check on Mrs. Louise Brower again. Then he took Grace Cowan's chart out of the rack and wrote in his comments on the progress report.

How can that have gone on for twenty years, he was thinking, without her sister knowing? It seems impossible, but do you suppose she really doesn't know?

"Mrs. Brower has just checked in, Doctor," the talker said.

"Good," he said, looking at his watch. "Thank you."

If I skip Lynn Cummings and Anthony Trusco, he thought, I've just got time for Bernard Waterman. They'll still be doing the tests on Lynn Cummings, anyway, so Rob can see her late this afternoon. Anthony Trusco is curing himself, so Rob can tell him the good news, and I've got just enough time for Bernard Waterman before I do Mrs. Louise Brower and, finally, Mr. Scheller. Finally they'll let me get to my Mr. Scheller.

He put Grace Cowan's chart back and found Bernard Waterman's.

IX

"Oh?" he said, feigning surprise. "Am I in the right room?"

The nurse was standing by the intravenous stand at the side of the bed, adjusting the tube from the bottle of glucose and saline that was hanging inverted from one of the arms of the stand. She turned, surprised, when she heard him, and then she smiled at his small joke.

"That's right," she said. "This is the right room."

"Then this must be Dr. Bernard Waterman," he said.

"Hello," the boy said.

Bernard Waterman was fifteen years old. How many times Dr. Matthew Carter had worked over him on an operating table in the last six years only the records would show. He had twice performed major surgery, the last time two days before, to remove strictures in Bernard Waterman's esophagus, the passage by which food moves from the mouth to the stomach. Between those two operations he had periodically passed into the esophagus, through a tube called an esophagoscope, small steel ovals affixed to slender steel rods, hoping by that means to keep the passage open. In those past six years Bernard Waterman had gone under anesthesia at least thirty times.

"You know, Dr. Waterman," he said to the boy now, still trying to get a rise out of him, "I thought you'd be much older. I thought Dr. Bernard Waterman, the famous mathematician, would be about eighty years old, and have a long white beard."

"Do I still have to have all these tubes in?" the boy said, looking back at him through his black-rimmed glasses.

He was sitting up in bed. The intravenous tube ran to his right arm. The red rubber Levine tube that originated in his stomach and came out through his left nostril ran to the suction bottle beneath the bed. A third tube, draining the pleural cavity between his left lung and his chest wall, emerged from his left side and ran to another bottle on the floor.

"You mean you don't like these tubes? They're doing a lot of good work for you."

"When can you take them out?" the boy said.

"Well," he said, "I think we can take this one in your nose out tomorrow."

"When can you take the others out?"

"Oh, in a couple of days or so. You see, we like to keep you anchored to those bottles so you don't get up and run up and down the hall. We don't want you disturbing the other patients."

The boy just looked at him. His pale, thin, expressionless face did not change, and he said nothing.

"Except for the tubes," he said to the boy now, "are they treating you all right?"

"I guess so."

"You don't have any other complaints?"

"Nope."

"Then we've got to find something to do to make you mad. Do you know why?"

"Nope."

"When you get mad," he said, "we'll know you're feeling fine."

I wonder, he had often thought over the past half-dozen years, if Bernard Waterman ever gets mad. It is a strange desire to see another, especially a child, in anger, but I cannot make him laugh. I have tried, and I cannot even make him smile. I will never, of course, purposely try to anger him but at least we would know, after everything that he has had to take over these years, that there is still a spark in him if, just once, he would flare up in anger.

"So tell me something," he had said to Bernard Waterman the first day he had examined him. "What do you want to be when you grow up?"

"I don't know," the boy, who was nine years old then, had said.

"A baseball player? Would you like to be Ted Williams or Mickey Mantle, or that pitcher in Milwaukee—Warren Spahn?"

"Nope," the boy had said.

"He used to be interested in baseball," the father had said. "I explained the batting averages to him once, and he used to work out the average of every player after every game."

"That was when I was small," the boy said. "I don't do it any more."

"He's going to be a mathematician," the father said.

"Are you a mathematician, Mr. Waterman?"

"Me?" the father said, smiling. "No. I'm in the wholesale hardware business, but I think Bernie might be a mathematician."

"Maybe," the boy said, "but I haven't made up my mind yet."

He had been a poor eater from birth. Because he had instinctively learned to chew his food well in order to swallow it, there was no reason at first to suspect that there was any abnormality in his esophagus. As swallowing became more difficult, however, it was apparent that there was something anatomically wrong, and the X rays showed a stricture in the esophagus just above the point where it joins the stomach.

"What do you think it is, Doctor?" the father had said.

"I don't know. It's possible that it's tuberculosis of the lymph nodes. When the lymphatics become inflamed they contract and pull the nodes tight around the esophagus, like a napkin ring. Then a pocket forms above this stricture. When this pocket fills with food it overflows, in his sleep, into his lungs and that could account for the pneumonia and the chest colds he's had."

"What can you do about it?"

"We have to get that stricture out of there, so we'll remove that small section of the esophagus to clear the channel."

"You can do that?"

"Certainly. Although he hasn't been able to eat all the foods he needs and doesn't have any fat or much muscle on him he's otherwise healthy."

"You know he's our only child, Doctor."

"I know, and we'll cure him."

The operation took two and a half hours. When he removed the stricture, however, he was also forced to remove the valvelike guardian mechanism where the esophagus enters the stomach. It is this muscle which, following the passage of food, closes and prevents the regurgitation of that food back up into the esophagus. Its removal meant that Bernard Waterman would never again be able to lie flat while sleeping. For the rest of his life he would sleep in a semi-reclining position.

"But what caused his trouble, Doctor?" Bernard Waterman's father asked the day after the operation.

"I don't know," he said. "It was nothing that we could see or feel when we took it out. Now we're waiting to hear what the Pathology Department finds when they put it under a microscope. We'll have their report by tomorrow."

The pathology report was noncommittal. They could find no cause and merely described the abnormality as "inflammatory stricture." For two months, however, Bernard Waterman appeared to be cured. He was able to swallow solids and he started to take on a little weight. During the third month his difficulty began to reappear, and he became cautious and almost afraid to swallow. They reduced his diet from normal foods to baby foods, and brought him back to the hospital.

"What did you find this time?" his father asked.

"We found the stricture has re-formed."

"Doctor," his mother said, "you're not going to have to operate on him again?"

She was tall and thin and nervous, and it was obvious that when her son was in pain she was in pain, too.

"No," he said. "Not at this point. We're going to make another try at finding the cause of this. Meanwhile, I'm doing something else to help him. While I had him under the anesthesia today I re-enlarged the opening, so he should be able to swallow quite well again."

"You could do that?" the father said.

"Yes. I passed what we call bougies down through the stricture. They come in graduated sizes, and we start with the largest one that will go through and then increase the size by degrees to stretch the opening. This may work."

It worked, but with decreasing effectiveness, for six months. Following the treatment Bernard Waterman was able to swallow normally again, but Dr. Matthew Carter had the pathology slides and the remaining paraffin-preserved portion of the resected section of the esophagus sent from Mercy Hospital to Dr. Gustave Schroeder at University Hospital.

"If anybody can find the cause," he was telling his wife that night, "it's Gus."

"Gus Schroeder," she said, "is a boor."

"But he's a great pathologist."

Twenty-three years before, Gus Schroeder had left Germany to get away from Adolf Hitler, and then he had turned out to be a tyrant himself. He ruled the Pathology Department as if it were a duchy, and if he could have built a moat around it to exclude all surgeons he would have.

"You know he hates surgeons."

"He resents us," he said. "He envies the money and glamor associated with surgery."

"He should ask me about all the money and glamor," his wife said. "He's a boor, and I don't know how you can be so fond of him."

"Because a good pathologist is the only honest critic a surgeon has. Surgeons can't be completely honest with one another. I can't go down our staff and say: 'I rate you at ten points, you at nine and you at six, and I can't rate you because I haven't seen enough of your work.' You can't have any secrets from a good pathologist, though, because he does too many post mortems on the ones you lose. A surgeon can cover his mistake by closing the wound, but a Gus Schroeder reopens that incision and you're naked before him. A good pathologist is your conscience personified, and Gus Schroeder is great."

"Cy Winton hates him," his wife said, "and you like Cy."

"That's right," he said, "but that involves something else. They're in competition over hearts."

"Hearts?" she said. "Don't tell me old Gus Schroeder fancies himself a Don Juan."

"Of course not," he said, amused. "That's ridiculous. I'm talking about two men of science."

"Oh, please."

"I'm serious," he said. "Cy wants the hearts to dissect them. Gus wants to make beautiful, permanent plastic casts of them. He tells everybody around his lab: 'If Dr. Winton comes down to this end of the building he's not to put his hands on a heart. When those hearts stop beating they belong to me.'"

"Don't tell me any more about it," his wife said. "The whole thing disgusts me, and Gus Schroeder is a boor."

Two days later Gus Schroeder called him on the phone. There were no amenities.

"Matt," he said, "what's the matter with you?"

"I'm feeling all right."

"You shouldn't be."

"Why?"

"That esophagus you sent me, it's aberrant gastric mucosa."

That's right, he thought as soon as he heard it. Of course it is. It's the first one I've ever had and you won't get more than two or maybe three in a whole professional lifetime, but that's it.

"I might have guessed it," he said.

"Guess nothing," Gus Schroeder said. "You should have known. You know it can pop up anywhere in the alimentary canal."

"It's the first time for me," he said, "but I should have remembered a paper I heard Murchison give on it in New Orleans four or five years ago."

"You're too busy making money, all of you surgeons. You all want to get rich."

"Not me. I give mine to Uncle Sam."

"And he takes the money and builds national highways," Gus Schroeder said, "so more crazy people can kill themselves with their cars."

"I couldn't detect it by feel or sight," he said, "but I should have suspected it when I noticed that the wall was thick on one side."

"Now you're thinking," Gus Schroeder said. "How is the patient?"

"He's got a recurrence. I esophagoscoped him the other day and passed some bougies down through there and dilated it."

"It won't last," Gus Schroeder said. "You have to do him again."

"I know."

"And get it all this time," Gus Schroeder said. "I'll send you the report when we write it up. Tell them over there they should frame it and put it on the wall."

"I'll do that, Gus, and thanks."

"None of us is entitled to any thanks," Gus Schroeder said. "It's our job."

That night he told his wife. They were having a drink before dinner.

"Gus Schroeder found that kid's problem," he said. "He's got aberrant gastric mucosa. The mucous membrane that lines the stomach and manufactures hydrochloric acid, there's some of it up there in the esophagus which can't accept it."

"I'm glad he found it," his wife said, "but Gus Schroeder is still a boor."

The next day Carrie McKeen called Bernard Waterman's parents and asked them to come in to see Dr. Carter. Two days later Dr. Carter explained the problem to them.

"Your son's trouble," he said, "is caused by what is known as aberrant gastric mucosa. The mucous membrane that lines the stomach manufactures hydrochloric acid. Now, some of this membrane is present in your son's esophagus. The lining of the stomach is able to accept the high concentration of acid, but the esophagus isn't. As a result an inflammatory ulcer was bound to occur, and this heals in the form of a scar, or stricture. As it gradually closes, it forms a dam and blocks the passage of food."

"But you took that stricture out," the mother said. "That's what you told us."

"I did," he said, "but at that time we had no means of knowing the origin. It was impossible to tell by feel or by sight the cause of the stricture, and these things are so rare that a surgeon might go a whole lifetime without seeing one or he may see two or three at the most. In fact, it took a second laboratory analysis to discover it just three days ago."

"So you didn't get it all out?" the father said.

He's right, he thought. He's an intelligent man and he'll get an intelligent answer and we'll have to see what happens then.

"That's true," he said. "I resected what to all appearances and to the best of our knowledge was a sensible segment. There was no reason at that time to do anything more radical."

"I just don't understand this, Doctor," the mother said. "I don't understand it at all."

"Look at it this way," he said, but talking more for the father than the mother. "In the normal embryological development of the fetus in the womb all goes along in an orderly fashion. The ectoderm and mesoderm and endoderm come from three different sources at different times but they seek out each other and finally they all join up in proper fashion. The timing and the anatomical architecture are perfect.

"Sometimes, however, there's a slight mistiming. In that case, if it involves, let's say, the eye, astigmatism may result, so you wear glasses. The miracle, of course, is that with this same thing happening in the formation of all the organs and blood vessels and nerves and muscles and bones and tissues of the body so many people are perfect, or essentially perfect. In your son's case something wandered away from the parent group of cells of the gastro-intestinal tract. It was the wayward sheep that left the pack, and it ended up in the wrong location, in the esophagus."

"I see," the father said, nodding.

"But why?" the mother said. "Bernard is our only child. Why should this happen to him?"

"I don't know," he said. "No man can answer that."

"Please, Linda," the father said. "The doctor isn't God."

"I don't know," the mother said.

"So what do you recommend now?" the father said.

"Well," he said, "I've given him some relief by dilating the stricture, as I explained the other day. The probability is that it will only be temporary."

"But I don't want him to have another operation," the mother said, shaking her head. "I don't want that poor child to have to suffer any more."

"Please, Linda," the father said. "Why don't we just listen to what the doctor has to say?"

"But the poor child has suffered enough. He's never been able to do the things the other boys do. What kind of a life has he had? You just don't understand, Doctor."

"I do understand, and that's why I want to cure him."

"So listen to the doctor, Linda."

"The relief I've given him, as I said, will almost certainly be only temporary. We can effect a permanent cure only if we remove that section of the esophagus that contains the remaining gastric mucosa. That's the decision you'll have to make."

"I don't want him to have to have another operation," the mother said, shaking her head.

"You'll have to excuse my wife, Doctor," the father said. "She's upset now, and we'll have to have more time to think about it and make up our minds."

"That's completely understandable."

"What I want to know is, how long do you think he'll be able to swallow now? I mean, how long will he be all right as a result of this last treatment?"

"That's hard to say. That stricture may start to close again almost immediately, or it may close so slowly that it will remain open for weeks or even months. We don't know."

"Then when it closes, you'd do the same thing again that you did the other day?"

"That's correct. He'd have to come into the hospital and we'd have to put him under anesthesia and, using those bougies—those dilators— we'd enlarge the opening again. It's a simple procedure and not painful, but he'd lose a day or two of school each time."

"I'm not worried about his school," the mother said. "He's way ahead in school."

"He's just ten years old," the father said, "and he's teaching himself algebra."

"You may have a genius."

"He's just a little boy, Doctor," the mother said. "We don't want a genius. We just want a boy who can be like other boys his age and enjoy himself."

"It's good he has his brain and his books," his father said. "Otherwise what would he have?"

"I don't know," the mother said.

For almost ten years she was unable to bring herself to submit her son to another major operation. Over those years the periods of relief following the treatments shortened from months to weeks, and Bernard Waterman's diet was thinned from baby foods, mashed potatoes and Jello to beef juice, sherbets, fruit juices and liquid Jello. Dr. Matthew Carter saw more of Bernard Waterman than he had ever seen of any other patient, and yet he knew less about him.

"Did I hurt you today?" he would say.

"Nope," the boy would say.

"You know, I like you," he said to him one day. "What do you think of me?"

"I don't know," the boy said. "I guess you're all right."

When the boy was coming in for treatments once a month the mother finally consented. The night before the operation Dr. Matthew Carter, as he used to do regularly when he was younger but as he had not done for a long while, fell asleep planning his procedures.

I can take a section of the jejunum, he was thinking and meaning the middle portion of small intestine, and use it as a graft to replace the removed piece of esophagus. If I just take another piece of the esophagus and don't put in a graft of jejunum I'll have to pull the stomach up into the chest, so I'll use the jejunum. In the old days, he was thinking, they used to believe that the jejunum was empty at death and out of that came the word "jejune" to mean barren or dull or uninteresting or un- satisfying. It is not much of a word, jejune, because you cannot use it without making a show of it, like that girl at the Wintons' and she used it at least three times. The book she was reading was jejune and the play was jejune and so was everybody's apartment and I should have shocked her out of it by telling her to forget her bowels.

The operation took six hours, and it did not go as he had planned it the night before. After opening the chest and after removing the section of the esophagus containing the stricture, he decided that if he took a sufficiently long section of the jejunum he would put the blood supply to the intestines under too much tension. Instead, he chose to remove the spleen and mobilize the stomach so that he could connect it to the shortened esophagus, and he also opened permanently the muscular valve between the stomach and the duodenum to prevent retention of acids in the stomach.

Given this opportunity again, he was thinking, walking down the hall to see the mother and father, I'd still do exactly as I did today. That's the test, really, except that I'd cut the front lip of the esophagus longer because it joins the stomach at about a forty-five-degree angle. When I cut it straight across and it recoiled I lost about fifty minutes, and I had to put more tension on the sutures than I would if I had cut a semi-circular lip.

Rob knew it too, he was thinking. When it recoiled up under the arch of the aorta Rob knew exactly what I'd done but he was aware that I knew it only too well and he never said a word and he probably never will.

"Your son is doing fine," he said walking into the lounge and seeing them stand up to face him. "He's in the recovery room now."

"He's really all right?" the mother said.

"Absolutely. You'll be able to see him in a few hours."

"But it took so long," the mother said.

"That didn't bother him," he said, trying to reassure her. "You see, he had the anesthetist and her machine breathing for him. He was being fed intravenously, and he didn't have to move a muscle. He actually did less work than if he'd been just lying in bed."

"But did you get that stricture out, Doctor?" the father said.

"Yes, indeed. In order to get all that gastric mucosa that's been causing all the trouble I took a very generous piece of the esophagus."

"Then he's going to be all right from now on?" the mother said.

"I believe so. I certainly can't guarantee it, but it's my belief."

"Then you don't know for sure even yet?" the mother said.

"Who knows anything for sure, Linda," the father said. "Dr. Carter is telling us just what he believes."

"I know this," he said. "I know you should both feel very relieved. We've gotten to the core of your son's difficulty and I believe we've cured him. We'll put him on some solid foods in a few days and when you get him home he should be able to eat anything he wants."

"But when will we know for sure?" the mother said.

"If he's cured, as we believe, you're going to know it in three months."

"That long?" the mother said. "We have to wait that long?"

"It won't be just waiting. Your son is going to enjoy his food again and put on weight and gain strength. You three are going to enjoy some of the rewards now."

"Thank you, Doctor," the father said. "Thanks very much."

"Yes, thank you, Doctor," the mother said.

How I hope he's cured, he had thought, walking away. If he isn't, I've got two or three other procedures that I won't even burden them with because I'll believe we've cured him until I find out otherwise.

"So, Dr. Bernard Waterman," he said to the boy now, and it was two days later, "you're sure you have no other complaints, except about the tubes?"

"I'm hungry," the boy said.

"Fine," he said. "That's what I've been waiting to hear. You know, though, that you're getting a steak through that tube right from that bottle up there."

"I know, but it goes right through me."

"That's what it's supposed to do, but pretty soon we'll be giving you some real food. Then do you know what's going to happen?"

"Nope."

"You're going to go home, and you'll be able to eat anything you want. One day you're going to say to your mother: 'Mom, I'd like a real good steak.' I'm going to tell your mother that when you say that she's to call me, and that night I'll come over and buy you and your parents your first real good restaurant steak. Okay?"

"All right," the boy said, but his expression did not change.

"Any other complaints?"

"Nope."

"Excuse me, Doctor," the nurse said. "He'd like to hang his legs over the side of the bed. Is that all right?"

"Sure. That's fine."

"You see?" the nurse said. "I told you the doctor would let you."

"And in return for that, Dr. Waterman," he said, "can you explain combinations and permutations to me?"

"I don't know."

"Your father tells me you've been studying them and I want to learn about them this time from a real Doctor of Mathematics."

"I don't know whether I can explain them to you."

"All right. You can try to teach me that night I buy you that steak. Is that a bargain?"

"All right," the boy said.

"Dr. Robinson will be in to see you this afternoon," he said. "You like him, don't you?"

"I guess he's all right."

And I will buy him that steak, he was thinking, walking to the nurses' station. If his mother calls me, I will.

On Bernard Waterman's chart he filled in the progress report and wrote out the orders. When he looked at the clock he saw it was 9:47.

Mrs. Brower, he thought, Mrs. Louise Brower. The talker said she'd checked in so I'd better do her now down in Emergency, and Stan must be about finished in Three. If I'm going to get my Mr. Scheller in there as soon as I do Mrs. Brower he'd better be finished in Three.

"Excuse me," he said to the talker, "but is that Louise Brower on this floor?"

"Louise Brower?" the talker said. "Yes. She's in 435."

9:48 A.M.

X

Walk slowly, he was thinking, conscious of the urge to hurry but too long a professional to show it. Leonard Furman's old lesson: No matter how pressed you are for time, never exhibit it. Every patient has the right to think that you have nothing else on your mind but him. That was Furman's old lesson and I haven't even thought of it since I don't know when, and he must be dead now fifteen years.

"Oh, excuse me Dr. Carter," the nurse-anesthetist said.

She was coming out of the room, carrying her tray with the vials and the blood-pressure sleeve on it.

"My fault," he said. "I wasn't looking."

"This is your patient, isn't it? Mrs. Brower?"

"That's right. What's the trouble?"

"She won't let me prepare her," the anesthetist said, lowering her voice and motioning him aside. "I can't do anything with her."

"Why?"

"She says she doesn't want to be bronchoscoped. She says she's not having any discomfort now and she feels fine. She wants to go home."

That's just what I need, he thought. Right now, after what I've been through already this morning, I don't need this at all.

"Come back in with me," he said. "Let's see what I can do."

"I wish you luck," she said.

She stepped aside and followed him into the room. Mrs. Brower was sitting up in bed, middle-aged and plump and with a round, even face.

"Mrs. Brower?" he said. "I'm Dr. Carter."

"How do you do?" she said.

"I'm fine. How are you?"

"I'm fine, too."

"That isn't what your doctor told me on the phone this morning. That's not why you're here."

"Dr. Fineman?" she said. "I should never have called him."

"You were right to call him, and he was right to call me. Last evening you swallowed, or inhaled, a piece of meat that became lodged somewhere. Isn't that correct?"

"I thought so, but I must have been wrong. I don't feel anything there now, and I want to go home."

"Tell me what happened when the meat went down the wrong way."

"This whole thing is foolish, Doctor."

"Did you start to choke?"

"I'll say. It scared the life out of me. I couldn't breathe, and I got red in the face. At least my husband said I did. He kept hitting me, you know, pounding me on the back."

"How long was it before you could breathe all right again?"

"I don't know. It seemed like ten minutes, but it was probably two."

"When your coughing spasm was over, how did you feel?"

"Well, I felt a little bit better. I feel all right now."

"Why did you call Dr. Fineman?"

"Oh, you know. I didn't sleep much, and I was coughing. This morning I thought I could still feel something stuck down there. My husband insisted that I call him."

"I want you to tell me this, and I want you to tell me the truth. Do you feel any pain, and discomfort, down in the middle of your chest?"

"Not now. It's just like I told the nurse here. I don't feel anything now, and I'm sorry I even called Dr. Fineman."

If it were a sliver of bone and not a piece of meat and in the esophagus, he was thinking, it would be stuck where the aorta crosses and it would rub and penetrate as the aorta pulsates with each beat of the heart. If there's anything still down there it's in a lung where she wouldn't feel it.

"I want to explain something to you, Mrs. Brower," he said. "I want to tell you what we want to do, and why we want to do it."

"I don't want you to do anything. I'm quite sure there's nothing there any more."

"Now you're only guessing," he said, "because we really don't know. We're almost certain that there's nothing in your esophagus because you're feeling no irritation there now. If you did inhale a piece of meat, though, it's in your lung."

"But I don't feel a thing."

"There's nothing to feel with in the lung, so you can't tell. If it's in your lung, however, it's got to be removed. If we didn't take it out, it could lead to repeated bouts of pneumonia and lung abscess and eventually to destruction of that part of the lung. That's why we can't take the chance."

"Now you've got me scared, Doctor," she said, looking at him but then looking away and shaking her head. "It's just that I'm sorry that I mentioned it at all."

"There's nothing to be nervous about. It's a very simple, routine procedure, and it will only take me a few minutes. We just put you to sleep and I look down into your windpipe and lung with a scope—a tube. If there's anything down there I just reach down with some long forceps and bring it out. You don't know or feel a thing, and you can go home late this afternoon or early this evening."

"It sounds terrible to me, Doctor," she said. "I've never had an operation, and it just frightens me."

"I know it frightens you, but it shouldn't. If it will make you feel any better, I can tell you that I've done this—looked down into patients' lungs—thousands of times."

"You have?"

"Yes, and there's a boy—fifteen years old—just down the hall here, and I've put a scope down into him at least thirty times in the last six years. I've just operated on him to cure his problem, but he used to come in here once a month to be scoped."

"Really?"

"Yes, and it never hurt him. He wasn't frightened."

She's convinced, he knew, studying her. Bernard Waterman did it.

"But I just feel so foolish," she was saying. "If you don't find anything, I'll just feel so foolish."

"You'd be foolish if you didn't let us take a look," he said. "Miss Jasperson here is an anesthetist. She just wants to take your blood pressure and give you something to dry up your mucous membranes. That's all."

"All right, Doctor. I suppose you're right, but I'm just sorry to be such a bother."

"You're not a bother at all," he said, "and I'll see you downstairs in a few minutes."

"I still wish I had never told Dr. Fineman," she said.

When he got off the elevator at the O.R. floor Sarah Wheeler was walking down the hall toward him. She had her hands up behind her head, untying her mask.

"I thought you were taking your yacht to the Bahamas," he said. "What happened?"

"I realized it wouldn't be any fun without you," she said, "so I postponed the sailing until you could make it."

"Good," he said. "I'll be ready in about five hours."

"Not today you won't."

"Why?" he said. "How's Stan doing?"

"He's not. He's on his tenth pint of blood, and it's O-Negative. He cleaned us out, and we're getting two pints from University and the Red Cross is trying to round up a few of its emergency donors. It's a mess."

"What's he doing, anyway?"

"A duodenal ulcer that came in at 5 o'clock yesterday, and started to bleed again at about 4 this morning."

"He can handle that."

"It's not the duodenum that's giving him the trouble. It's the aorta, and he's really in a jam."

"He'll still handle it."

"Well, he's your boy," she said, "and I hope you're right."

"I'll do that bronchoscopy now down in Emergency," he said. "Then I'll check back with you."

"If you ask me," she said, "he's going to do it in the next half-hour, or he isn't, so I'll be able to get you in there in an hour or so."

"Thanks, Sal," he said.

And I'll bet I know exactly what Stan ran into, he was thinking, walking to the locker room. I'll bet he got one of those that come in vomiting blood and maybe even passing it, too, and you can't take an

X ray because they can't keep the barium down or, if they can, the tract is full of blood clots and you can't see the trouble. Sal says the problem isn't the duodenum but the aorta, so I'll bet it's where the third portion of the duodenum crosses the aorta and he's got an aneurism of the aorta that eroded into the duodenum. If you're doing general surgery you may see that about once every five years but I'll bet Stan didn't spot it early and the first thing he knew his field was full of blood and he's been scrambling ever since.

"Good morning, Dr. Carter," the intern said. He was sitting in the lounge chair, finishing a cigarette.

"Good morning," he said.

I can't think of his name, he was thinking. He's one of the new ones and he's never scrubbed with me but he's observed me a couple of times and I should remember his name.

"Excuse me, Doctor," the intern said, "but are you doing a pneumonectomy this morning?"

"Yes," he said, "when I can get in there. They've been rather busy."

"I'll say," the intern said. "We've had a real rough night."

"So I heard."

His name begins with *D*, he was thinking, hanging his jacket up in his locker. Not Darwin. That's not it. It's Darrow.

"You're Dr. Darrow, aren't you?"

"That's right, sir."

Darrow, he was saying to himself. Darrow. Remember Clarence Darrow. This boy is rather short and Clarence Darrow was taller and big-boned and he had long, straight hair that hung over one side of his forehead, if I remember his picture. Remember Darrow, but don't call this boy Clarence.

"I thought that, because I've got some time this morning, sir," Darrow was saying, "I'd observe you and Dr. Robinson and Jim Bronson."

"Good," he said. "This is undoubtedly a carcinoma of the right lung and it appears, on the X rays, to have invaded the mediastinum. You may see something interesting."

Especially, he was thinking, if it involves that vena cava of my Mr. Scheller. Then it's going to be more interesting than you think.

"It's all interesting to me," Darrow said.

"That's the way it should be," he said. "When I was your age everything interested and excited me, too."

When Pete Church was doing a chest, the word would spread and he'd be there somewhere. If he wasn't assisting he'd be there on the floor observing, or if he just had five minutes he'd be up in the gallery where you can't hear anything or see much but where he could at least try to feel a part of it.

He had stripped now to his shorts and his socks. He took off his wrist watch and slid it down inside his left sock. Then he reached into the locker and took the wallet out of the pocket of his jacket. He took out the bills and put the wallet back and slipped the bills down inside his right sock and flattened them around the ankle.

He did this now without thinking, but twice, years before, while he had been in there operating, his locker had been rifled. He lost a watch and between $150 and $200 in bills, and every now and then somebody would lose something. They figured it must be an orderly or one of the janitors because you can't pay them enough to get good help. As if you can buy honesty, he had thought, angry when it had happened, but it is an ironic ending to a beautiful operation to realize that while you were in there saving a life somebody was robbing you in the locker room.

"I think it was Osler," he said now to the intern named Darrow, "who once said that, if you practice medicine early and late, you can't hope to escape the malign influences of a routine life."

"I suppose that's right, sir," Darrow said, "but it's hard for me to imagine."

"It will happen to you," he said. "It happens to everybody, but the good ones fight it."

"It's not one of my problems right now," Darrow said.

"I'm sure it isn't."

He took out of his locker one of the wash-faded, starched, ironed-flat, short-sleeved, green scrub shirts and put it on over his head. He climbed into the scrub pants, pulled the draw string tight at the waist, and tied it at the right hip.

"There he is," he heard Maury Rand say, coming through the door. "I've been here since 8 o'clock, but he just starts to work at 10."

"Hello, Maury," he said.

"He keeps bankers' hours," Gene Parente said, coming in after Maury, "and he's got a banker's income."

"I'll say," Maury said, "but he won't be able to do that under socialized medicine. He'll have to be up before 7 every morning, and be on the job by 8."

"That's right," he said, sliding first one foot and then the other into the open-backed O.R. shoes, "and every afternoon we'll go home at 4. That's what they do, you know."

"That's what you do now, isn't it?" Maury said.

"Absolutely," he said. "As a matter of fact, quite often I get home for dinner by 8:30 or 9 o'clock."

"Oh, come on," Maury said. "You might impress Darrow here, but you can't impress us."

Darrow's eyes were following the back-and-forth of the badinage as if it were a badminton bird and he could actually see it.

"As a matter of fact," Gene Parente said, "under socialized medicine he'll be lucky if he gets any patients. They tell me that the G.P. holds onto the patient so long that, by the time he turns him over to a hot specialist like Matt, it's a terminal case."

"I'm not worried," he said, putting his white smock on over the scrub suit. "I could use a little leisure."

"The truth about socialized medicine," Maury said, "is that it's being forced by young doctors like Darrow here."

"Not me," Darrow said, shaking his head.

"Not at the moment," Maury said, "but in a few years. You'll want days off, vacations with pay, and an insured income from the start. All you young guys do, and that's where the pressure within the profession comes from."

"That isn't what I read," Gene Parente said. "From what I read it's us physicians and surgeons who are pricing ourselves out of the market. Isn't that right, Matt?"

"I don't know," he said, walking to the wooden box on the window sill and taking out a rolled surgical mask and a white cap. "Is that what they say?"

"He knows all right," Maury said. "One of his patients buys a Cadillac for six thousand dollars. Matt does that great pneumonectomy of his on him and the patient complains when Matt charges him fifteen hundred dollars for saving his life. Right?"

"I really don't know," he said, winking at Darrow who was watching him. "My secretary does all the billing, and I haven't the vaguest idea what she charges."

"I'll bet," Maury said.

"So we get accused," Gene was saying, "of pricing ourselves out of the market."

"Listen to this," Maury said. "I'm having one of the rooms at my office painted. I walked in yesterday morning and I hear one of the painters say to the other: 'You know, one of these guys killed my sister.'"

"I'm sorry, gentlemen," he said, tired of it, "but you wealthy doctors can sit around here all day and, when you get through talking about socialized medicine you can talk about golf and girls. I'm poor, and I have to go to work."

"I'd like to be so poor," Maury said.

"What are you doing?" Gene Parente said.

"A bronchoscopy."

"A bronchoscopy?" Maury said. "That's not work. I'll bet by now you can do one of those with your eyes closed."

"I can."

"That's a nice little thing to have going for you," Maury said. "How many of these do you do a month or a year, anyway?"

"You gynecologists should ask," he said to Maury. "How many of those D. and C.s do you do?"

"Why don't you go to work?" Maury said.

XI

"How many lives," he said once, "have been saved since Chevalier Jackson developed the bronchoscope no one can possibly calculate. All I know is that it may have saved my professional life."

In his senior year in medical school they were sitting at lunch in the cafeteria one day, and they were talking about sending out their applications for internships. Because it was a medical school with an inferiority complex, it had, throughout the half-century of its existence, inadvertently transmitted a sense of inadequacy to most of its students, and so most of its seniors applied for their internships to the smaller, less celebrated hospitals.

"How about you, Matt?" one of them said to him.

"Me?" he said. "I'm just applying to General."

"What?" the same one said. "And no place else?"

"Are you kidding?" another said. "You think they'll take you?"

"Sure," he said. "Why not?"

"I wish I had your guts."

"I'll take his marks," a third one said.

"You know," the first one said. "You might make it."

"I'll make it," he said.

Here I am, he thought later, playing the hero again. It's a chronic disease with me. I'm not even accepted yet, but it's like that time at the fraternity house when I said I thought I'd go to medical school and they all looked at me as if I'd already performed a completely successful frontal lobotomy.

Three weeks after he sent his letter of application and his transcript the answer came back. It was a form letter, its impersonality obvious in spite of the fact that it was addressed to, and was personally typed for, him. It thanked him for his application, regretted that its internships were already filled and it wished him success in his career. He read it through three times, looking for some encouragement and finding none.

"How are you making out with General?" one of them asked him a couple of days later.

"I don't know," he said, unable to shuck the hero image and admit it. "I haven't heard."

"They better let you know soon," the other said. "If they wait too long and then turn you down every other place will be filled."

"I know," he said, "but I'm not worrying about that yet."

Several nights later he recalled, by what process of mental association he never knew, that somewhere he had heard that Carleton Cheney Grant, the associate professor of surgery, had roomed in medical school with Franklin Pierce Church. Franklin Pierce Church was chief of surgery at General Hospital.

"I'll be glad to write Pete Church," Grant said the next day. "I don't know how much good it will do, but I can try."

About a week later Grant sent word he wanted to see him in his office. He had a letter from Church.

"I am impressed," Church wrote, "by your recommendation of Matthew Carter. Unfortunately, and as he already knows, our internships are filled and, like everyone else, we are short of funds and limited in living facilities. If he is as genuinely desirous of coming here as you say, however, we would be happy to have him as an extern, under one of our research fellowships. That means, of course, that he would be unable to live in, but if he can afford to live out he can take his meals here. If this is acceptable to him, have him write me and . . ."

"I'll take it," he said to Grant, "and thanks a lot."

"Can you handle it financially?" Grant said.

"Sure," he said. "I can get the money."

He borrowed it from his sister Ruth. She was married to a big Norwegian who operated his own plumbing business and they had a couple of thousand dollars in the bank. She agreed to lend him $25 a month, the money to be paid back when her son, then eleven, was ready for college.

He found a room a mile and a half from General Hospital. It was at the rear of the second floor of a brownstone house owned by a fat German widow named Koeppler, and it had formerly been a closet. He knew it had been a closet because there was just enough room in it for the iron cot, the straight-backed chair, and the washbasin in the corner, and the one window was small and high on the wall.

"The rent is fifteen dollars a month," Mrs. Koeppler said, "and no cooking in the room."

"Of course not," he said. "I get all my meals at the hospital."

After he had been there one month Pete Church called him into his office. Pete Church was a tall, pale-skinned, white-haired aristocrat with excellent facial architecture and a soft, even voice that never evidenced emotion.

"Dr. Carter," he said, "the executive committee of this institution informs me that, due to the straitened economic circumstances in which this establishment now finds itself, it will no longer be able to supply meals to the research fellows. This involves you."

"Yes, sir."

"In that I now find I can't live up to my contract with you, I thought I'd tell you this myself. I'm sorry about it, and I'll be glad to help you get any position that might interest you in another university or another hospital. I'll give you the highest recommendation, but if you can afford to pay your own way, I'd like to have you stay."

"I can swing it," he said.

"Good. I'm glad to hear that. Meanwhile, I'll keep you in mind for the first job that opens up and that you're qualified to handle."

"Thank you, sir," he said. "I'd appreciate that."

He wrote to his sister. After weighing the request for two weeks she wrote back that she would increase his loan to $35 a month. This left him, when he had paid his rent, $20 a month, or $5.00 a week, on which to eat and otherwise live.

He bought a second-hand one-burner electric grill, a coffee pot, a coffee cup, a plate, a knife, a spoon and fork. He smuggled them into his room that night, and from a wire coat hanger he fashioned a rack that would fit over the burner and hold two pieces of toast. This equipment he kept locked in the foot locker under his cot and each night, on his way home, he bought two eggs and, when he needed them, a loaf of bread or a pound of coffee.

"Every morning I'd put the water in the coffee pot and the eggs in the water," he was to recount years later. "Then I'd put the coffee in, and when the water started to boil I'd have soft-boiled eggs. For seven months I never saw a boiled egg that didn't have a coffee-colored shell."

At noon he would be working on pulmonary physiology in the dog lab. When the others would take off their smocks and wash for lunch he would refuse their invitations.

"I didn't have the guts," he was to say, "to tell them I couldn't afford lunch. I'd say: 'No thanks. I want to finish this, and I'm not hungry anyway.' I got the reputation of being a real beaver."

Once a week, at 5 o'clock in the afternoon, there would be a conference in Pete Church's consultation room, and they would serve coffee and crackers. By exerting admirable self-control he would limit himself to partaking only as much as the others, and for his one big meal, at 6:30, he would sit at a counter in a dirty, yellow-lighted, smoky, acrid-with-the-smell-of-frying-fat lunch wagon and have either Hungarian goulash or frankfurters and beans. They both cost thirty cents.

He subsisted like this for seven months. His stomach shrank, he lost fifteen pounds and, because his diet lacked the vitamins A to C to be found in green vegetables, pimples erupted over his body.

"Then I got an occasional job holding heads for bronchoscopies," he was to say. "Thoracic surgery was in its infancy then, and the nose-and-throat men did the bronchoscoping. I'd sit on a stool by the patient's head, and we had a stainless-steel mouth-bite, or clip. It fitted over the middle finger of your hand, and you'd bring your arm across under the patient's chin and bend your hand back and clip this over the lower mouth. You'd hold the head rigid and the mouth open that way."

The nose-and-throat man, for whom he worked most often, wore glasses. It was a stroke of luck, for as he assisted, sitting bent over and holding the head and lower jaw, he discovered he could trace the progress of the bronchoscope, with its small light at the bottom, down through the trachea and into the bronchi, by watching the reflection in the nose-and-throat man's glasses.

"He was getting fifty dollars for a bronchoscopy," he was to say, "and I got two dollars for holding the head. He'd do six in an afternoon, so I'd get twelve dollars, and that money looked so good to me I felt like I was stealing."

The first big meal he bought himself he lost before he got back to his room. He was ashamed to go back immediately to the same restaurant and order again, so he went to another. In those first two days he lost every meal he ate, until his stomach and his digestive system became accustomed again to a plenitude of food.

Two months later, when one of the interns contracted tuberculosis, he applied for the opening. He got the appointment, but the bronchoscope, as he was to say, may have saved his professional life.

XII

"Dr. Carter," the nurse said, "would you like to pick your forceps?"

She was standing in the door of the instrument room. She had seen him get off the elevator and walk down the hall toward her, opening the starched and ironed white cap and turning the bottom edge up about a half-inch so that it would fit flat on his head and not have a tufted ridge along the top nor come down to his ears.

"Sure," he said, putting on the cap and smoothing it and following her into the room. "How are you?"

"I'm fine, sir."

He looked at the dozen forceps lying in the slots of the wooden rack on the counter, each about sixteen inches long, slender and delicate, designed to be passed down through the bronchoscope and with the scissor-like handles at one end activating the small jaws at the other. If it should actually be a piece of soft hamburger meat, he was thinking, he would need the biopsy forceps with the flat spoons on the end, but if it turned out to be a sliver of bone or a piece of gristle he might get it more easily with a pair with tonglike jaws.

"I haven't the vaguest idea what Dr. Stanczyk is doing," he heard one of the two nurses in the back of the room saying, "but that orderly was down here again for another pint of O-Negative."

"I know," the other said. "The Red Cross dug up two donors."

"I'll need those flat, foreign-body forceps," he said, pointing, "and that one there with the smaller tongs."

"Yes, sir," the nurse said.

"Thanks," he said.

"Excuse me, Doctor," the nurse said, "but what *is* Dr. Stanczyk doing?"

"I don't know," he said. "I haven't looked in."

"I just wondered," she said.

When he walked out into the hall he saw Jim Bronson, big and blond and in his scrub suit, standing by the door of the emergency O.R. He was talking with the young intern named Darrow, and when they saw him coming they stopped talking and waited for him to say something.

"How's our eminent thoracic resident?" he said.

"Tired," Bronson said. "Do you know Paul Darrow here?"

"Sure," he said, nodding to Darrow. "We were just talking upstairs."

"That's right," Darrow said.

"Have you seen Benjamin Davies?" Bronson said.

"Yes."

"How is he now?"

"I put him back on the morphine."

"Did you see his wife and daughter?"

"Yes. I told them what to expect. I also told Mrs. Kirk's husband."

"You've had a great morning already, Doctor," Bronson said.

"You look like you had a great night."

"I did. I'm really bushed."

"What happened?"

"A lot of things. I don't want to bore you with most of it, but I almost called you about 2 A.M."

"Oh?"

"We got a guy, twenty-five years old, and his girl friend out of a car accident. They were coming home from a party right after midnight, and for some reason hit a fire hydrant. The girl wasn't bad—concussion, broken nose, and simple fracture in her right shoulder—but the boy friend was in shock, and when I examined him I could feel his fourth and fifth ribs moving here in front. You know how you can feel the broken ends click under your fingertips?"

"Yes."

"He probably hit the steering wheel."

"Undoubtedly."

"When he came in, his blood pressure was good—130 over 70. When I looked at the X rays to check the rib fractures I saw his heart shadow was enlarged."

Cardiac tamponade, he was thinking, listening, and I wonder if he spotted it right away.

"This scared me," Bronson was saying, "and when I took his blood pressure again it was now 110 over 90 in less than an hour."

It was cardiac tamponade all right, he was thinking and meaning that he was sure now that there had been bleeding within the pericardial sac that contains the heart. Because the blood was compressing it, the heart couldn't fill normally.

"Were the jugular veins more prominent?" he said, knowing that they would be distended due to the blood's inability to flow easily back into the heart.

"Definitely," Bronson said.

"So what was your diagnosis?"

"Cardiac tamponade."

"Good."

"So I didn't know whether to call you or not. I still don't know whether I did the right thing to tackle it myself."

"I can answer that. How's the patient?"

"He's fine," Bronson said, smiling. "In fact he pulled out of it great."

"Then you did the right thing. Congratulations."

"Thanks," Bronson said, enjoying it now. "Anyway, when I opened him and got in there the sac was so full of blood it was distended like a balloon. So . . ."

The left ventricle, he was thinking, listening to Bronson, thirty-one and a winner, forgetting his fatigue now and feeling like he might cure the world. One of those splintered ribs stabbed into the left ventricle.

". . . with the blood gushing it took me a little while to locate the source. When I finally found that it was a stab wound from a jagged rib that had penetrated the left ventricle I got my finger on it and closed it with two stitches and . . ."

And it is a great feeling, he was thinking, and the shame of it is that, as you get older, you experience it less and less.

". . . and after that," Bronson said, "we were just coasting home."

"So you see, Dr. Darrow," he said to the intern, who had been just standing there but following all this and nodding his head, "Dr. Bronson made an excellent decision for two reasons. I got my sleep, and he got an important win."

"I see," Darrow said.

"What Dr. Bronson and I know, however, is that the decision of whether or not to call the attending surgeon in the middle of the night sometimes isn't an easy one."

"I'll say," Bronson said. "If you call the attending out of bed or even away from a dinner party and it turns out to be something you could have handled yourself, you feel like a damn fool."

"In other words," he said, "it sometimes requires more courage to admit you're in doubt and to call the attending surgeon than to proceed on your own."

"I understand," Darrow said, nodding.

"But Dr. Carter doesn't seem to mind coming in," Bronson said, "no matter when you call him."

I'm glad I give that impression, he thought, but I hope he doesn't start buttering me and I wish they'd get Mrs. Brower down here and I wish I could get to Mr. Scheller. If it's actually in his vena cava and I do that graft I'll feel as good as Bronson.

"I assisted Dr. Carter a couple of months ago," Bronson was saying to Darrow, "on a case I was glad I wasn't handling alone at 3 o'clock in the morning."

"What one was that?" he said to Bronson.

"That pulmonary artery," Bronson said, and then to Darrow: "The tie had slipped off the pulmonary artery, with the heart already exposed and the blood concealing the opening. You know?"

Well at least he's picking a good one, he thought. I liked that recovery myself.

"So it was impossible to locate the source," Bronson was saying. "You couldn't see a thing, so Dr. Carter grabbed the heart with both hands and stopped it to arrest the bleeding. Dr. Robinson emptied the field with the tonsil sucker and put the clamp on the opening. Then Dr. Carter massaged the heart for about ten seconds to revive it, and the whole thing didn't take more than half a minute."

"I'd like to have seen that," Darrow said, nodding.

"It was great," Bronson said to Darrow. "You get a whole new concept, because although a patient is technically declared dead when the heart stops, life continues until the oxygen in the body is used up by the cells. You know?"

"I know."

"Here's my patient now," he said.

The orderly had pushed the bed off the elevator, and now he was pushing it toward them. The nurse-anesthetist named Jasperson was walking behind the orderly, and Mrs. Brower was lying flat on the bed, the sheet over her and only her head showing.

"How are you now?" he said to her.

"I was just saying," she said, looking up at him with that small-girl look they acquire with fear, "that I'll never eat another hamburger again. I never will."

"Of course you will," he said. "This is nothing. You won't feel a thing, and it will be all over in a few minutes."

"I never will," she was saying. Darrow was holding the door open and Bronson and the nurse-anesthetist named Jasperson were helping the orderly maneuver the bed into the room.

"Now we just want you to slide over onto this table," Jasperson said to her. "Sheet and all."

They had positioned the bed next to the operating table, and Bronson had lowered the table to the level of the mattress on the bed.

"I just feel so foolish, Doctor," Mrs. Brower was saying, on the table and her left arm out along the arm board. "I know you're not going to find anything down there and I'll feel so foolish."

"We'd all be fools if we didn't look. You'll be glad we did this."

"Now all you're going to feel," Jasperson said, "is a little pin-stick. It won't hurt, and that's all you'll feel."

"My heart is beating like mad," Mrs. Brower said. "It feels like it's going to burst."

"You're going to be all right," Jasperson said.

She had found the ante-cubital vein in front of the elbow on the arm board. When she inserted the needle Mrs. Brower winced just once.

"You see," Jasperson said, starting the Pentothal. "That wasn't bad. Now just keep your eyes open."

"She's giving you a cocktail," he said to Mrs. Brower. "What you're getting is a frozen daiquiri."

"Just keep your eyes open," Jasperson said, watching her.

"Do you feel sleepy?" he said.

"Yes," Mrs. Brower said, her eyelids fluttering and then closing. "I feel . . ."

He took the rolled white mask out of the pocket of his smock and took off his smock and tossed it on a stool. He shook out the mask and tied the bottom strings around his neck. He brought the mask up over his mouth and nose and knotted the top strings above his cap.

Bronson and Darrow and the nurse were adjusting the Emerson chest respirator, the semi-clear plastic shell with sponge-rubber flanges on its edges that fits over the front of the chest like a breastplate. From its top a hose, the size and composition of a vacuum-cleaner hose, runs to a suction pump, and it would breathe for Mrs. Brower.

Mrs. Brower would be unable to breathe on her own because of the curare Jasperson would introduce into her vein to paralyze her skeletal muscles and her diaphragm. It is a derivative of the natural drug with which the Amazon Indians poisoned the heads of their arrows, and so the automatic respirator would replace, with its even, alternating rhythm, her muscular function.

"How's she doing?" he said. He had put on the green operating gown, untied and hanging loose in back, and he was pulling on the thin brown latex gloves.

"Fine," Jasperson said.

"Shall I tie that for you, Doctor?" Darrow said, referring to the gown.

"Yes, please," he said, "although this will only take a couple of minutes."

How many bronchoscopies he had done in twenty years he would never know, but by now they must have numbered four thousand. Almost daily, and sometimes three or four times a day, he had looked into lungs, searching for disease, into the bronchi or the esophagus looking for chicken bones, pennies, nickels, dimes, peanuts, dental bridges, or the small gold crucifix that the baby pulled off the chain around her neck and swallowed.

"We're all set here, Doctor," Bronson said.

"Good."

He walked over to the stool at the head of the table and moved it up with his left foot and sat down. Mrs. Brower's head was level with the lower half of his chest.

And she's too far down the table, he thought. I'll wait until they get the table up before I show them, and then maybe they'll remember it. Bronson has seen me do enough of them so he should know it, if he weren't so tired.

"Will you pump the table up just a little, Doctor?" he said to Darrow.

"Yes, sir. Is that enough?"

"That's enough," he said, "but now we can see where this team didn't do its job."

"Sir?" Bronson said.

"The patient is too far down the table. You can see, that when I drop this head rest, her head won't fall back. What we're trying to do is essentially what the sword swallowers have done for years—line up the upper teeth, the throat, and the stomach. Let's slide her up about four inches."

"Just a minute, Doctor," Jasperson said, walking around behind him to check the intravenous needle in Mrs. Brower's outstretched arm.

She should remember how to position, he was thinking, while Bronson and Darrow moved Mrs. Brower up the table and toward him. She should never forget it since we had to move that fat woman about a month ago.

"That's fine," he said. "Are you ready to oxygenate her?"

"Yes, sir," Jasperson said.

"Watch out for her teeth," he said, winking at Bronson. "Her husband is a lawyer."

She fitted the black cone over Mrs. Brower's nose and mouth, and held it there with her left hand. With her right hand she started to squeeze the black pressure bag that would force the oxygen into Mrs. Brower's lungs.

"About a month ago," he said, "we had a 375-pound woman who swallowed the screw top off a salt shaker, and don't ask me how. Any-

way, they positioned her too low on the table and, once she was anes-
thetized, it almost took a block and tackle to move her. You remember
that one, Miss Jasperson?"

"I'll never forget her," she said, squeezing the pressure bag.

She'll never forget her, he thought. She'll never forget her, but she
still lets them position the patient too far down the table.

When the nurse handed him the tubular bronchoscope he held it up
to one eye and looked down through it. He could see no light at the
lower end, so he turned it over and adjusted the voltage regulator at the
top, and then saw that the bulb, the size of the head of a wooden
kitchen match, was burned out and blackened.

"This bulb is dead," he said, handing it back to the nurse.

"It was working a second ago."

"You may have had the current up too high. That's when they burn
out."

"It was working a second ago," the nurse said.

"You've got some other light carriers there. Let's get one in."

"Yes, sir."

"Now that everybody on this team seems to be missing his cues," he
said, "who knows what I'm doing wrong?"

"You?" Bronson said.

"That's right."

"I don't know."

"Dr. Darrow?"

"I don't know, sir."

"I'm not wearing my bronchoscopy shield," he said, meaning the cir-
cular, clear plastic disc that protects the face. "The fact that, for twenty
years, I have preferred to pick sputum out of my eye when the patient
coughs back at me, and just because I haven't contracted tuberculosis
doesn't make it right."

"She's ready, Doctor," Jasperson said, meaning that there was now
enough oxygen in Mrs. Brower's lungs to supply her blood during the
fifty seconds or so it would take him to get the bronchoscope into the
trachea, which is the windpipe.

"Thank you," he said. "If I had accustomed myself to the screen at
a young age, as I should have, I wouldn't find it a nuisance now when
it fogs up, and I'd use it."

He dropped the head rest and let the head down. The nurse handed
him the bronchoscope, and he turned it over and saw the lighted bulb.

He had the bronchoscope in his right hand, and with the fingers of
his left hand he pulled the upper teeth toward him while holding the

lower teeth away with his thumb. He placed the bottom end of the bronchoscope on the back of the tongue and, flattening the tongue on the floor of the mouth, he looked for the epiglottis, the hinged, erect cartilage at the root of the tongue that closes and protects the windpipe during swallowing. It looks like a shoe horn and hides the vocal cords, and now he lifted the edge of it with the end of the bronchoscope and slipped beneath it and, seeing the two vocal cords in the larynx, he went between them and was in the trachea.

As he leaned back on the stool, straightening his back, Jasperson connected the oxygen tubing to the small right-angle connector arm on the side of the bronchoscope. Then she turned on the chest respirator, and it began its breathing, in and out evenly, for Mrs. Brower.

"Good," he said.

Looking down through the top end of the bronchoscope now he saw that the trachea, pink-lined and with its cartilage rings, was clear. He moved the scope down to the bifurcation, the point where the trachea divides into the two large bronchi, one of each lung. He advanced the instrument carefully, moving it always not only by sight and feel but also by sound. As Mrs. Brower's breath brushed the end of the scope the sound was faint but like that made by blowing over the open neck of a bottle, and he had many times bronchoscoped just by feel and sound so that a student or intern could look through the upper end as he slowly maneuvered the bronchoscope downward.

"Right upper lobe negative," he said, using the long optical telescope with the right angle lens to look backward and upward at the three subdivisions of the upper lobe bronchus. Then he removed the telescope and, using just the bronchoscope tube, he could see the two divisions of the middle lobe and the five in the lower lobe.

"Nothing in the right lung," he said. He had withdrawn the bronchoscope back to the bottom of the trachea and was advancing into the left lung, to explore the three main subdivisions of its upper lobe.

"Left upper lobe negative," he said. "We may draw a blank on this lady."

He rotated the bronchoscope slightly as he altered the angle to enter the aperture of the lower lobe. As he did, he saw it lying there, in the circle of light.

"I have an announcement to make," he said, still looking down the scope. "We've just struck gold."

It's hamburger meat all right, he thought. It was about as big in circumference as a pencil eraser, but bleached and pale against the salmon-pink mucosa of the bronchial tube.

"It's in the lower lobe orifice," he said, straightening up. "Who wants to see a piece of misdirected hamburger meat?"

"I do," Bronson said, and he came around and sat down on the stool and put his right eye to the scope.

"Dr. Darrow?"

"Yes, sir," Darrow said. "I'd like to see it."

"You can really see it, too," Bronson said, getting up to let Darrow look.

"Let me have those soft biopsy forceps," he said to the nurse.

"Sir?"

"The flat, foreign-body forceps."

"Yes, sir."

"You see it?" he said to Darrow.

"Yes, sir. Very clearly."

The nurse handed him the long, slim-handled forceps with the almost flat spoons on the end and he sat down and slid them down into the bronchoscope. Then, looking down, he moved the ends carefully, maneuvering them until they extended beyond the bottom end of the scope and he had positioned them on either side of the piece of hamburger. Then he closed them on the meat, and withdrew the ends toward the mouth of the scope.

"I've got it," he said, still looking down the scope, "and now I'll employ a little trick you might remember. I've withdrawn the hamburger almost into the scope but not quite. If you try to pull it in, you run the risk of it breaking into smaller pieces and of losing it, so you bring the scope, the forceps and the piece of meat all out together—like this."

He brought the bronchoscope out then, the ends of the forceps still protruding from the bottom end. He handed it to the nurse and reached down and brought up the head rest and raised Mrs. Brower's head and snapped the rest into place. Then he stood up and straightened his back.

"In the old days," he said, pulling off his gloves and tossing them on the table against the wall, "box suppers were in vogue, and we were always doing old women without teeth who could only gum their chicken. Now it's cook-outs and hamburger."

He took off the gown and put it on the table, and then the mask. He looked at the wall clock, and it was 10:21.

"How's the patient?" he said.

"Fine, Doctor," Jasperson said.

"You look tired, Jim," he said to Bronson.

"I am."

"You're pale and your eyes are bloodshot and you can hardly keep them open and your voice is husky."

"I've had about two and a half hours sleep in the last thirty-four."

More than twenty years ago he had gone through it all himself, on for thirty-six hours and off twelve. At General they called it the House Officers' Quarters, and the phones were high on the wall so that you couldn't answer them from the bed and in your sleep. You'd have to get up, and when they'd wake you for an order, with not only the nurse but the night supervisor listening, they'd make you say it at least three times.

"Give him a quarter of morphine," you'd say.

"You said a quarter of morphine?" the nurse would say.

"A quarter of morphine."

"Then I'll write it down here," the nurse would say. "I'll write: 'Dr. Carter, a quarter of morphine.'"

"That's correct."

"You don't mean a sixth?"

"I mean a quarter."

"Thank you, Doctor."

Hours later, getting up, you wouldn't know what day it was or, sometimes in the winter when it was dark, whether it was 6 o'clock in the morning or 6 o'clock at night. You would open the window and look out to check the number of people on the street, and when you went over and checked in again the order would be on the chart. It would be on the order sheet with your name, and it would be correct, and sometimes you would not remember the call or the order at all. At least, he was to realize when fatigued in years to come, you learn then that your actual sleep-need is surprisingly minimal, and just that assurance can be a psychological stimulant when you need it.

"Why don't you knock off?" he said to Bronson now.

"I'd like to," Bronson said, "but you've got Mr. Scheller to do now."

"I think if you were to withdraw temporarily from this case," he said, smiling at Bronson, "the patient would still have a good chance of survival."

"I know," Bronson said, smiling now. "I didn't mean that. I'm down to assist, and I want to assist every time I can, and besides, I'm fond of Mr. Scheller."

"Look," he said. "Darrow here is off the medical service now and he was going to observe today anyway. I think he's scrubbed a few times, and would be happy to scrub in with me and the great Dr. Robert Robinson."

"That's right," Darrow said. "I'd like to assist."

"So hit the sack," he said to Bronson.

"Well," Bronson said, "I will if you say so."

"Good," he said. "How's our patient now?"

"Excellent," Jasperson said.

"Can you people get her back into bed if Dr. Darrow and I leave now?"

"I'll give them a hand," Bronson said.

"Thank you, everybody," he said, "and incidentally, save that piece of hamburger, I want it shown to this lady when she wakes up, but don't send it to Pathology. They might put it under the microscope and report a new disease."

If Mr. Scheller works out the way I believe he will, he was thinking, walking out with Darrow following him, Bronson should see it. It's too bad he's knocked out, because Bronson is going to be one of the good ones and he should see it.

10:24 A.M.

XIII

The elevator stopped at the second floor and the door opened. While two student nurses in their striped uniforms got on, and while the door was still open, he could hear a small child crying and, over it, the nasal, feminine voice on the page system.

"Dr. Rand. Dr. Maurice Rand. Dr. Levitt. Dr. Julius . . ."

When it stopped at the O.R. floor he got out, Darrow following him. Sarah Wheeler was standing halfway down the hall, talking with two maids. Her mask was hanging from her neck, and she was cleaning her glasses with it, and then she turned and walked toward him, putting her glasses on.

"Hello, Bahamas," he said.

"Hello, Bahamas yourself," she said.

"Don't charm me any more," he said. "Just tell me when I can get in there."

"In ten or fifteen minutes," she said. "Soon as we finish cleaning up."

"Then Stan is finished?"

"I'll say," she said.

"Oh?" he said. "What's the matter?"

"He lost his patient."

"Damn," he said, feeling it suddenly, never having even seen the patient and knowing nothing about him except that he was a human being, but knowing Stan.

"I know," she said.

"What happened?"

"Too much bleeding and then hypertension, I guess. A heart attack."

"Where's Stan now?"

"In the locker room, I think."

"When you call for them to start my patient down, will you let me know?"

"Sure. It'll be about fifteen minutes."

"I'll tell you what you do," he said to Darrow. "Why don't you go in and see if there's anything you can do to help them set up the room. I'll see you in there."

"Yes, sir."

"Have you seen Rob lately?"

"He's been up here a couple of times," she said. "I think he's down with your patient and his family."

"I'll see you, Sal."

"Sure."

When he had first opened his own practice, they had given him one case a month to do at the Veterans' Hospital. It was on the first Tuesday of every month, and they paid him $25. Because it was the only $25 he could count on every month, he had promised himself that no matter how busy he might become he would always do that case. Now they held out their most difficult or most interesting case for him each month, and on the first Tuesday he still made the hour's drive out over the Memorial Bridge and did the case and drove back again and they still paid him $25.

One first Tuesday he made the trip twice. He took out a right lung and left the comparatively simple, automatic, step-by-step closing to the staff surgeon named Halloran and the resident. He drove back over the bridge and when he got to Mercy there was a message to call Carrie McKeen.

"What's up?" he said.

"For John's sake, Matt," she said, "where have you been?"

"I stopped off in New Orleans for the Mardi Gras."

"Never mind that," she said. "Call Veterans'. They're in a panic over there."

"What's their problem?"

"Don't ask me. As near as I can make out, your patient has a hole in his pulmonary artery."

He called Veterans' and got the O.R. supervisor. She told him to hold on and she put the circulating, or floating, nurse on the phone.

"What's the trouble?" he said.

"There's a hole in the right pulmonary artery," the float said.

"What's Dr. Halloran doing?"

"He's standing there with his finger in it."

"Why doesn't he put a soft vascular clamp on it and tie it?"

"He says he hasn't got room. He says it's receded, and every time he takes his finger out it hemorrhages again."

"How's the patient doing?"

"Fine."

"Good," he said. "Tell Dr. Halloran to just stand there, and I'm starting back over right now. He knows as well as I do that as long as he keeps his finger in the dike the patient will do all right. I'll be over in forty-five minutes."

"Yes, Doctor," the float said.

It was February and it was sleeting and a trailer-truck had jackknifed, blocking two lanes of the bridge. Before he realized it, he was in the middle of the jam, cars and trucks ahead of him and on both sides and behind, the drivers swearing and blowing their horns and the police, red-faced from the cold and from anger, waving their arms and blowing their whistles and trying to clear the jam.

"Look," he said to one cop. "I'm a doctor and there's an emergency over at Veterans' Hospital. I can't get out of here, so I'm leaving my car while I make a phone call. I'll be back in two minutes, but if this starts to move push my car aside, will you?"

"Okay, Doc," the cop said, "but it ain't gonna move."

He found a phone in a cigar store with a billiard table in the back. Two men, their shirt sleeves rolled up and one of them with long sideburns, were shooting billiards, as if what was going on outside happened every day. While he waited, with the door of the phone booth open until the O.R. supervisor called the float to the phone again, he could hear the click of the billiard balls.

"How's the patient?" he said.

"The patient is all right," the float said. "Dr. Halloran is still standing there with his finger in it."

"How's Dr. Halloran feeling?"

"He's fine, too. He was hungry, so I got him a sandwich and a container of milk."

The absurdity of Halloran standing there with the float feeding him a sandwich and milk and Halloran holding his finger in the pulmonary artery struck him.

"What kind of a sandwich was it?" he said.

"It was a cream cheese sandwich," the float said, serious. "That's what he wanted."

"Good," he said, "that's prescribed in cases like this. Tell him I'm in a traffic jam on my side of the bridge. If it doesn't start to move soon I'll walk across the bridge and get the police to bring me in. I'll be there soon."

When he went out the sleet had lessened and was starting to turn to rain. He could see the boom of a crane on the bridge, and in ten minutes the traffic began to move into the funnel neck that was the cleared lane. In another thirty-five minutes he was at the hospital.

"How's he doing?" he said, looking in at the O.R. door.

"All right," Halloran said, standing there, his right hand hidden in the chest cavity and looking foolish and embarrassed.

"How are you feeling?"

"Stupid and tired," Halloran said.

"I'll be right in."

He got into a scrub suit and scrubbed again.

"What happened?" he said to Halloran.

"I was irrigating with the saline," Halloran said, "and I saw this black speck. I thought it was a fleck of carbon off the light, so I reached down with the forceps to pick it up. It was the frayed end of the silk tie, and it came off. When it did, the vessel retracted out of sight, so I reached down to locate it. When I put my finger down to stop the bleeding it went right into the artery, and here I am three hours later."

"Let me take a look," he said.

He knew he could get at the artery at its source, so he opened the pericardium, which is the covering over the heart, and went inside of it and clamped the artery there. Then Halloran found the artery and brought it into view and tied it off.

He had been driving to Veterans' for about four years when he realized he was always stopping, on the way back, at the same Esso station on the right-hand side of the road and just before the bridge. It was a one-man business with just two pumps, and over the door of the one-room gray clapboard building adjoining the garage with the grease-pit in it, was a board painted white with black lettering that read: J. S. Stanczyk.

"Fill it up, Doctor?" J. S. Stanczyk said to him one day.

"Yes," he said, "but don't put so much water in with it this time."

"Water?" J. S. Stanczyk said, then looking at his face and getting it. "Oh, yes. Well, you see, Doctor, that's the way I have to make my profit until the customer gets wise."

"I figured that," he said.

That was the way he got to know J. S. Stanczyk. J. S. Stanczyk and his wife lived in a white Cape Cod cottage on the hill behind the gas station. There was a field-stone path that led up to it and a rose arbor over the walk near the front door, and from the cottage they could look down over the green slope of Wendell's Evergreen Nursery to their right and they could see the river and the bridge.

"You know what you ought to do?" he said to J. S. Stanczyk one day.

While J. S. Stanczyk had been filling the tank he had walked into the station and, because he was hungry but had no time to eat, he had taken a Coke out of the machine. He was finishing the Coke when J. S. Stanczyk came in, wiping his hands on a rag and looking at the black under his nails.

"What?" he said.

"Expand your establishment. Put in a lunch counter."

"No, thanks," J. S. Stanczyk said.

"Why not? Then a busy man who has no time to stop for lunch could grab a sandwich while you're servicing his car."

"You hungry, Doctor?"

"I am today, but I haven't got any time to eat."

"You gonna do another operation now without eatin'?"

"I do that all the time."

"If I'd known that," J. S. Stanczyk said, "I woulda had my wife put a couple of extra sandwiches in my lunch box."

"That's very nice of you," he said, "but this Coke will fix me up fine."

The first Tuesday of the next month, when he stopped at the station again, J. S. Stanczyk was putting oil into a car standing at one side of the pumps. It was raining hard, the water running off the brim of his old fedora hat when he bent over the engine and the rain beating at his yellow slicker.

"If you've got a minute, Doctor," he said, when he had come over and had motioned for him to put the window down, "would you mind stepping into the place?"

He followed J. S. Stanczyk into the station. J. S. Stanczyk took his black lunch box down from beside the cash register and opened it and took out two sandwiches, wrapped in waxed paper, and handed them to him.

"Here," he said. "Have some lunch with your Coke."

"Wait a minute. I don't want to be eating your lunch."

"It's not mine. My wife put in two extra for you."

"That's very nice of her, and it's nice of you, too."

"Enjoy it while I'm fillin' your car."

There was a ham sandwich and the second was Swiss cheese. As he was starting on the Swiss cheese J. S. Stanczyk came in, shaking the water off his fedora and taking off his slicker and shaking it before he hung it up.

"How are the sandwiches?" he said.

"They're great, but your wife shouldn't have bothered."

"No bother."

"What do I owe you?"

"It took four dollars and thirty cents' worth, Doctor."

"And how much are the sandwiches?"

"No charge for the sandwiches. It's our pleasure."

"Oh, come on, now. Let's be reasonable. I want to pay for these. I don't want any favors."

"Look, Doctor," J. S. Stanczyk said, "every time you help some sick person you're doin' them a favor. The least we can do is a little favor like this for you."

"But I get paid for that," he said. "I charge those patients, you know."

"I know," J. S. Stanczyk said, "but when you save somebody's life they can't begin to pay you enough. That's the way we feel about your business, and we'd like to do this for you."

"I'm not accustomed to hearing people talk like this about doctors," he said.

"Ain't I right, though?"

"I don't know," he said, "but thanks again."

"Our pleasure," J. S. Stanczyk said.

He knew, driving away, that on the next first Tuesday there would be sandwiches again. There were sandwiches every first Tuesday, and so he began, every third visit or so, to bring a box of candy for Mrs. Stanczyk. He also began, on the last week of every month, to watch his gas gauge, trying to deplete the gas in the tank so that, when he got to J. S. Stanczyk's, it would take close to twenty gallons. Several times, leaving Veterans' Hospital, he was afraid he would run out of gas before he got there, and he wanted to end the whole relationship and forget the J. S. Stanczyks.

But after she's made those sandwiches I can't leave them there, he thought. This thing is ridiculous.

"Gee, Doctor," J. S. Stanczyk said to him one of those times, "you better watch your gas gauge, or maybe it's busted."

"Why?" he said. "Did it take much?"

"It must have been almost empty. It took a whole twenty gallons."

"I'd better watch it," he said, eating his second sandwich and enjoying his victory.

"You don't wanna run out, goin' to some hospital," J. S. Stanczyk said. "I notice you been runnin' pretty close every time lately."

"Have I?" he said.

After that he decided to compromise, and he would pull into the station needing fifteen or sixteen or maybe only ten or twelve gallons. One day, and he would remember it was in the spring, he drove up to the pumps but, when he got out of the car, he could see J. S. Stanczyk nowhere. Instead a woman came out of the station.

"May I help you?" she said.

"Is Mr. Stanczyk here?"

"No," she said. "I'm sorry, but he'll be back in about an hour."

"Are you Mrs. Stanczyk?"

"I am," she said, smiling.

She was of medium height and in her early fifties. She had small features and delicate nostrils and she was wearing a clean light blue cotton dress and had a pair of men's white work gloves in her hands.

"I'm Dr. Carter," he said.

"Oh," she said, shaking hands. "I'm pleased to meet you."

"I'm glad to meet you, and to thank you personally for feeding me all these months."

"I'm happy to do it, Doctor, and thank you for the candy. That isn't necessary."

"Neither are the sandwiches," he said. "Here. Let me help you."

"Oh, no," she said. "I'm good at this."

She had put on the gloves and, as he watched, feeling embarrassed, she started to pump the gas into the car.

"Your lunch is waiting for you in Jack's lunch box by the cash register," she said. "Why don't you go in?"

"Mr. Stanczyk isn't ill, is he?" he said, when she came in.

"No," she said. "He had to go to the bank on some business. We can't afford any regular help, so I fill in for him once in a while."

She must have been quite pretty when he married her, he was thinking, and there is an air of refinement about her, even when she is pumping gas.

"You don't have any children?" he said.

"Oh, yes," she said. "We have a son nineteen, but he's in college."

"Your husband never mentioned him to me."

"Jack doesn't like to brag," she said, "but we're very proud of our boy. In fact, he's going to be a doctor."

"I'm glad to hear that," he said. "We need good doctors."

"I think he'll be a good one."

"How are his marks?"

"He gets A's and B's."

"I'd like to meet him."

"I'd like you to meet him," she said. "You know, my husband will be embarrassed when I tell him I mentioned Frank to you, but you understand we're not asking any favors."

"I know that," he said.

He met Frank Stanczyk a month later. The boy was home from college for the summer, and the next week he was starting to work as a laborer on a road-construction project. He was an inch under six feet, with good shoulders and a slim waist and flat hips, and he had brown hair, cut short, and dark brown eyes. When he said something to you he looked right at you, as if he were studying the effect of his words.

They talked about his courses and about medical schools, and he did not see the boy again that summer. He saw him only two or three times during the next two years, but on the first Tuesday during the Christmas –New Year vacation of Frank Stanczyk's second year in medical school he found him tending the gas station for his father.

"How's school?" he said to him, sitting in the station and having the sandwiches and Coke.

"It's pretty rugged," Frank Stanczyk said.

"Why do you want to be a doctor?"

"It's hard to say," Frank Stanczyk said. "As long as I can remember, my folks have been talking about my becoming a doctor."

"That's no reason."

"I realize that," Frank Stanczyk said, "but I think it's also true that if I didn't feel strongly myself that I wanted to be a doctor I would have revolted against my parents' wishes. I did that on a number of minor issues during the process of growing up."

"So why do you want to be a doctor?"

"Well, it may sound corny, but I'd like to feel that in my work I'm providing a necessary service. I can't see myself contented just working at a job, like my dad does, or going into an office or selling some product nobody needs. You know what I mean?"

"I know what you mean," he said, "but your dad provides a service. I need gas and oil to keep this car running, and so does everybody else."

"Don't get me wrong," Frank Stanczyk said. "I respect my dad."

"I know you do."

"He's worked hard and deprived himself and my mother of things to give me an education, but keeping cars running isn't what I want to do. There are too many automobiles on the road, too much moving around in our society anyway. This isn't essential. My dad fills up some crazy kid's gas tank, and the kid cracks up and kills himself and maybe takes two or three other people with him, too. Who needs that?"

"Let me tell you something," he said. "A couple of months ago, in my examining room, I had one of this country's great naval heroes. In the waiting room, waiting to get into the examining room, was a man, described by the newspapers anyway, as this section's—and maybe one of this country's—biggest racketeers. According to the newspapers he runs off-track betting, numbers, and maybe narcotics."

"Is that right?"

"That's right, and it so happened that I was able to help both of them. Now these were two men, both severely ill, and it wasn't up to me to judge between them. I can't take any more credit for what the admiral does with the rest of his life—that life I have preserved—than I can be blamed for what the hoodlum does with his."

"I see your point, Doctor," Frank Stanczyk said, looking at him and nodding. "That's very interesting."

"I'm no different than your dad. When somebody drives up here for gas it isn't up to him to decide what the driver is going to do with that car. That crazy kid has a legal right to drive—a license—and the hoodlum has a legal right to remain out of jail or he wouldn't be in my office as a free man."

"But that's an exception. Most of the people a doctor treats are decent people."

"And they drive cars."

"You're right," Frank Stanczyk said, smiling. "What I mean about being a doctor, though, is that you extend life. When you strip our society of its non-essentials and then get down to the lesser essentials, you come, finally, to the one basic essential—the need to go on living. The way I feel, if I just preserve for one person one more day of life I'd be doing more, really, than I could do in any other profession or business."

"I see."

"But don't get me wrong, Doctor. I'm not looking for a halo. This just happens to be the way I am, and what I want to do to satisfy myself. Anyway, I suppose that just preserving for one person one more day of life doesn't seem like much to you, but I'm just beginning and when I get older I'll probably lose sight of that."

"I hope you never do," he said.

He's a fine kid, he was thinking, driving away. If I had a son of my own I'd want him to be like this, but if I had a son like this I'd probably spoil him, and J. S. Stanczyk and that good wife of his haven't spoiled him one bit.

He saw, in Frank Stanczyk's senior year in medical school, that Frank Stanczyk had applied for an internship at Mercy. There were 106 applicants for the six openings in surgery, and as the attending thoracic surgeon he saw their applications and their records and he sat on the examining board with Ross Young, the chief of surgery, and the three others.

They interviewed them over a period of three weeks, sitting behind the big table in the main conference room with their name plaques in front of them, and the applicants coming in and sitting down in the chair facing them. They alternated, one examiner asking the questions of one applicant, and when he saw Frank Stanczyk walk in, the third applicant on the very first day, he felt it in his stomach and he was glad that it was not his turn to question him and that it was Ross Young's.

Ross Young said that they had all seen Frank Stanczyk's record, and that they wanted to know why he had chosen to apply to Mercy Hospital for an internship. Frank Stanczyk said that he hoped, during his training, to acquire as much varied experience as he could, and that Mercy Hospital had the most active ambulance service and was the most active hospital in the area.

Thank the Lord, Matthew Carter was thinking, listening, that he's not saying it's because of the excellence of the staff. I should have known that he wouldn't try to flatter his way in, as too many of them try to do.

"But I suppose," Frank Stanczyk was saying, and showing no sign of nervousness, "that every applicant tells you that."

"Not exactly," Ross Young said, "but tell me this. What are your interests outside of medicine?"

"Like everyone else in medical school," Frank Stanczyk said, "I haven't had too much time for hobbies, but I play a little tennis and I

enjoy classical music and I collect hi-fi records, when I can afford to
buy one."

"You know, I suppose, that Billroth had an interest in music," Ross
Young said. He was referring to the great nineteenth-century German
pathologist and surgeon after whom a whole series of abdominal operations of his own invention are named, and Matthew Carter knew that
Ross Young was testing Frank Stancyzk's professed interest in classical
music now. He was testing it to see if it were genuine or merely borrowed to give the appearance of the well-rounded young man.

"Yes, sir," Frank Stancyzk said. "In fact, he and Brahms were good
friends."

"That's right," Ross Young said. "Didn't Brahms play much of his
chamber music at Billroth's home before introducing it publicly?"

"Yes, and Billroth played the piano quite well himself," Frank
Stanczyk said. "He must have been quite a man."

"I guess he was," Ross Young said.

He asked Frank Stanczyk if he had any other interests. Frank
Stanczyk said that, while in high school, he had been fascinated by the
mechanics of the internal-combustion engine, but that he had outgrown
his interest in cars except as a means of transportation. He said that he
hoped to take up woodworking, when he had the time and the money
for the equipment.

"As a medical school senior," Ross Young said, "you know that it will
be a long time before you're able to earn the money, and when you do,
you probably won't have the time."

"I realize that," Frank Stanczyk said, smiling.

"Then may I ask you," Ross Young said, "why you want to be a
doctor?"

Frank Stanczyk was saying now what he had said two years before,
sitting that afternoon in the clapboard building by the gas pumps, but
he was saying it better. As Matthew Carter listened, he heard Frank
Stanczyk explaining that he didn't believe in confusing self-service with
public service. He was saying that, because of the nature of his own
personality, for which he could take no credit, and because, perhaps, of
his own emotional needs, he could conceive of being happy in life only
if he could be doing something for a common good. Like everyone else,
he was saying, he was merely seeking his own fulfillment, and in his
case it happened to be in medicine.

"I simply feel," he was saying, looking right at Ross Young, "that if
I could just extend one human life just one day I would be doing more
than I could be doing in any other field. I realize that any doctor does

much more than that—that, as a doctor, I'd better do more than that—but I'm not quite a doctor yet and when I am I'll probably forget all about such a limited concept as that."

"I hope you never do," Ross Young said, and Matthew Carter heard his own words coming back to him from the garage on the other side of the Memorial Bridge.

Ross Young thanked Frank Stanczyk then for coming in to see them, and Frank Stanczyk got up and thanked them and left. As they watched him turn and walk out Matthew Carter realized he had never told any of them that he had ever heard of Frank Stanczyk before, and while he had been in the room their eyes had never met.

"I'd like to make a prediction, gentlemen," Ross Young said. "We've still got one hundred and three to go, but I predict we'll find that this young man is the best of the crop, and if it so happens that you gentlemen agree with me, I'll predict he'll make the best house officer we've got."

Then he pushed the button on the desk in front of him to signal his secretary. In a moment the door opened and the next applicant came in.

It evolved as Ross Young had predicted that it would, and as Matthew Carter had known that it would. Frank Stanczyk was the best of the interns and he became the best of the surgical residents. He had the mental capacity and the emotional stability, the physical resiliency and the manual dexterity. He had the curiosity and the appetite for it, and he was as demanding, in the easy, natural but persistent way of his questioning, of the members of the surgical staff as they were demanding of him.

It was obvious, although no one else knew the beginnings of it, that he idolized Matthew Carter and that Matthew Carter saw in Frank Stanczyk an extension of himself. Two years after Frank Stanczyk had completed his chief residency and had started out in general surgery he was still known as "Matt Carter's boy."

XIV

When he walked into the locker room he saw that Frank Stanczyk was alone, sitting back in the lounge chair, his head back and his eyes closed. His hair was still damp and matted from his sweating under the cap and he needed a shave. He was still in his scrub suit, and had sweated under the arms and there was also an island of it, gray on the light green, on the front of the short-sleeved shirt.

"Oh, hello, Matt," he said. "How are you?"

"I'm all right. How are you?"

"Lousy."

"Why don't you get out of that suit and take a shower?"

"I'm too bushed right now. It's warm in here anyway."

"At least get out of that shirt," he said and he turned and walked into the lavatory and shower room. He took a clean bath towel off the shelf and walked back.

"Take the shirt off," he said. "C'mon."

Frank Stanczyk got up and pulled the shirt over his head and turned and threw it at the hamper. It hit the edge and hung there and he took the towel and toweled himself off, his chest and back and under the arms. Then he draped the towel around his neck and sat down again.

"Pull that foot rest out and put your feet up. You'll have varicose veins before you're forty."

"That's the least of my worries," Frank Stanczyk said.

"I know."

"You heard?"

"Yes."

"Who told you?" Frank Stanczyk said, looking right at him.

"Sally Wheeler. Stop worrying about your reputation."

"I'm not worried about that."

"I know you're not. Sally told me because I follow you into that room."

"I'm sorry to hold you up."

"Don't be ridiculous."

"For over six hours I fought that thing, Matt," Frank Stanczyk said. "I actually thought of calling you but I knew you had that 8 o'clock case. I tried everything I know. Three times I thought I had it won. You know?"

"Of course I know. Don't you think I get those, too? You do everything you can, and when that's not enough you take your shower and try your best to put it out of your mind."

You try your best to put it out of your mind, he was thinking, but you never quite do.

"I did everything. I did everything including making the mistake that got me into the mess in the first place."

"Look," he said. "You know there isn't a man alive who hasn't made his mistakes. That's trite but it's still true, and I could tell you a few of my own."

"But it looked so easy, Matt," Frank Stanczyk said. "It looked so damn easy."

That's the kind that trap you, he was thinking, listening. The enemy leads you into that false sense of security and you walk in there and he hits you from the side and if you haven't prepared your escapes, the first thing you know he's all around you and behind you and then there's no way out.

It had occurred to him once, years before, that it is like the time that new infantry outfit came up into the Huertgen during the war. The first day they were in there they sent two companies out to take those two small towns that were sitting right out there in the open and that looked so easy. He could never remember the names of those towns, but the Germans had the woods on both sides and the high ground beyond. They were just sitting there, waiting, as they had been waiting for weeks, and when the two companies moved in they closed on them and cut them off and it was plain slaughter.

He didn't see the first of the wounded they managed to get out and move back through battalion and regiment and division until late that afternoon. He was operating then in the kitchen of a church social hall and he worked all night and all the next morning and until about 1:00 the next afternoon. Some years later he met a colonel from the outfit that had been relieved, and when he mentioned the towns the colonel, although it must have been six or even eight years later, was still irate.

"Damn foolishness," the colonel said. "They were absolute damn fools. When they relieved us we filled them in on everything. We gave them all our intelligence and we said: 'Don't take those towns. We've been looking at them for three weeks, but we know what they are. They look sweet, but they're sour. The easy way to those towns is not the short way, but through the woods.'

"I guess the damn fools were just starting to feel their oats and they wanted to make a show," the colonel said. "I guess they wanted to make a show on the map at Corps and Army, and they damn well did."

It is like that with surgery, he had thought after talking with the colonel. It is never a matter of making a show, but it takes time, this going, you might say, from tree to tree, even though with modern anesthesia you've got the time and nobody has to take a leg off in twenty-eight seconds as Liston could do more than a hundred years ago. Of course, any man who doesn't take the short way whenever he can is either incompetent or a coward, but if he's brave enough he'd better also be knowledgeable enough to know what's on both sides of him and cautious enough to keep his escape routes open until he finds out what's ahead.

"It just looked so damn easy," Frank Stanczyk was saying, "that when I first got in there I thought it was going to be a snap."

"You're not the first one to make that mistake, either," he said. "What was the problem?"

"He came in about 5 o'clock yesterday afternoon," Frank Stanczyk said, "vomiting blood and passing bright red, and pretty shocky. He was fifty-four and he had a history of a duodenal ulcer about ten years ago but it hadn't bothered him in years and there was hardly a trace of tarry stool.

"Anyway, he couldn't keep the barium down so we couldn't X ray him. We gave him the first two pints of blood and his pressure responded and it looked pretty good for the time being. About 3 A.M. he started vomiting again, unchanged bright red, and his pressure dropped and they called me. I opened him and found this duodenal scar, but there was no swelling around it. There was blood in his entire G.I. tract, though, and you know what it was?"

"Aneurism of the abdominal aorta?" he said, meaning a blood-filled tumor of the main artery that carries the blood from the left ventricle of the heart.

"That's right. It took me some time to realize what it was because I'd never seen one quite like this. The aneurism, in expanding, had become fused with the duodenum and, finally, had perforated into it. There was no blood in the abdomen, but it was leaking into the duodenum itself, as if it were an ulcer."

"So what did you do?"

"Well, I felt around it, and I got cocky, I guess. The aneurism wasn't much bigger than a large grape, and I've done big ones with so little blood loss that I figured the simplest thing to do was to put a tangential clamp at the base of the aneurism, take the duodenum off, close the duodenum, and close the aorta."

"It would have been a nice trick if you could have brought it off," he said, but he was thinking: He should have gone upstream. He should have dissected around the aorta above in order to cross clamp it and leave himself an escape. He should have gone through the woods, as he knows well enough now.

"And then all hell broke loose," Frank Stanczyk was saying. "I isolated the aneurism and put the clamp on, but there wasn't any room to sew. So I repositioned the clamp, and it tore."

"And you were looking down the open end of a rifle barrel."

"That's right. I had to scramble like hell to dissect and get a finger around the aorta. You can imagine what was happening to his pressure. The blood bank here was low on O-Negative and they had to borrow a couple of pints. They got the blood to me all right, but—hell, Matt, do you know how I feel?"

"Of course I know," he said. "I want to . . ."

He heard the door from the hall open and hit the rubber stop. He turned and saw Arnold Jaffrey walk in with Maury Rand, still in his scrub suit, behind him.

"And don't think I don't mean it," Jaffrey was saying to Maury Rand. "I've got every ruddy right to be incensed, and I'm going down and see Baumgartner right now and point out to him that if he thinks he's running an efficient institution here he'd do well to look around."

He picked a great time to bust in here, he was thinking, and he's sore because they had to postpone his gall-bladder, or whatever he's doing. Instead of threatening Baumgartner I wish he'd threaten to take down his shingle and do it.

He had known Arnold Jaffrey for twelve years and of late had watched the decline of what was once considered his highly successful and enviable society practice. Arnold Jaffrey was only fifty years old but a remnant of the depression, of the days when the primary requirement for admission to too many medical schools was your ability to pay for it. Too many smart kids couldn't afford it and too many rich kids could, although Arnold Jaffrey may have been rather bright. He probably couldn't drive a nail into a board, because he had never had to, and he had had a year at Oxford, which had been a help. When he contracted osteomyelitis and affected a cane, for which he had no real need, it gave him the license to affect the accent and complement his British tailoring and his prematurely gray hair, for all of which he had great need.

"Arnold Jaffrey shouldn't be a surgeon," Marion had said one evening, driving home from a dinner party that had included Arnold Jaffrey and his quiet, pleasant, but not very bright wife. "He should be a cruise director."

"Why do you say that?" he had said, amused and knowing very well why.

"He'd make a great cruise director," she said. "He could lead everything from the conga line to the sunrise service."

"It's strange you should feel that way," he said. "He always seems to like you."

"How thrilling," she said. "He's one of those phonies who makes a play for every woman he thinks attractive, and if one of them ever took him up on it he'd probably die of fright."

"Considering that possibility, why don't you take him up on it?"

"Oh, please," she said. "Who could stand all that fawning around and that accent?"

"He seems to get along very well with his wife."

"He'd better," she said. "I understand she has all the money now."

"His patients adore him."

"The way they're declining in numbers I doubt that."

"Actually they do," he said. "He's especially good with the dying, and he's the soul of comfort to the family."

"Even though he was a contributing factor in the demise of the deceased?"

"No. I don't mean that at all. Nobody is referring the tough ones to him any more, and if they did he wouldn't attempt them. He's a coward and that's fine. He can do his appendectomies and handle his gall-bladders and spleens and hernias and the results are all right."

"I'm glad to hear that," Marion had said.

"Oh, hello, Matt," Arnold Jaffrey was saying now, noticing them for the first time. "Stanczyk. Didn't see you there."

"Good morning," he said.

"Hello," Frank Stanczyk said.

"Isn't this preposterous, Matt?" Jaffrey said.

"I'm sorry, but I've been talking to Stan here. What's your difficulty?"

"Difficulty? You've been delayed, too, haven't you?"

"That's right."

"And that's what I mean. How long are we going to put up with the utter confusion one has to face here merely trying to practice his profession in this so-called house of mercy? I don't mind telling you, as I've been telling a few other people this morning and as I'm going right down and tell Baumgartner, that I'm incensed."

"I can see that."

"And with one good reason. Do you know what they've done to me?"

"No."

"I've had my patient scheduled for 8 o'clock this morning for three days. That incredible Miss Wheeler, Miss Sarah Wheeler, knows full well, or she should know after all these years, that I always do my cases at 8 o'clock. . . ."

Your two cases a week, he was thinking, so you'll be in plenty of time for a nice leisurely lunch at the club.

". . . and this morning she phones me at 7 o'clock to inform me that due to some confusion, the details of which don't interest me in the slightest at that hour, my room won't be available until 11."

"They did have a rough night around here."

"And isn't that what any hospital should be prepared to accept? One would think this was Gettysburg after the third day."

"What's your case?" he said, seeing Maury Rand, standing behind Jaffrey, raise his eyebrows and shrug his shoulders.

"An inguinal hernia," Jaffrey said, "and that reminds me of something else. Do you realize that this patient has been on the waiting list for three weeks just to get into this place?"

And he probably had his ruptured groin for five years before he even came in to see you, he was thinking. If all of us didn't have to live with you around here I'd like to straighten you out or see somebody do it.

"As a matter of fact," Jaffrey was saying, "my investigation reveals that the confusion that apparently existed here last night, and I can well believe it, had little or nothing to do with my being delayed. It turns out that my room would have been available at 9 o'clock, but I was displaced by Dr. Berkman, whom I don't even know, incidentally, on the pretext that he was doing a child."

Berkman would be the one to straighten you out, he was thinking. Berkman put himself through college working summers in a steel mill and was the intercollegiate middleweight wrestling champion and he'd straighten you out. Unfortunately he might do it with a forward chancery and bar, and that would be something to behold.

"Berkman is doing a child right now," Maury Rand was saying.

"Regardless," Jaffrey said, turning on Maury Rand. "I'm as fond of children as anyone on this staff and I've successfully done my share of them, too. This business of not wanting to keep them fasting in the morning is carried to a ridiculous extreme. Anyone knows you can keep them hydrated with an intravenous which is what you're going to do on the table, anyway."

Great, he was thinking. Just great. The kid wakes up hungry and sees the other kids eating and doesn't know what it's all about and starts to cry, and you want to start an intravenous.

"Do you gentlemen know what I'm going to do now?" Jaffrey was saying. "Miss Sarah Wheeler informed me that it was her belief that she could give me a room at 12:30. Can you imagine that? Having postponed me for three hours, she finds me here on time . . ."

You're always on time, he was thinking. Promptness is your greatest virtue.

". . . and then she has the insufferable gall to tell me I'm to be delayed for another hour and a half. Who does she think I am?"

She thinks you're the Great Jaffrey, he was thinking. That's what she calls you.

"So I told her a thing or two. I told her that if she can't run an O.R., this institution had better find somebody who can. I told her to take my case off for today, and I'm on for 8 o'clock tomorrow morning. I'll do it then."

And if it's a simple inguinal hernia, he was thinking, it would take a good man a half-hour but it will take you an hour and a half. As refined as you may appear, you've never learned to refine your work, and you'll reminisce about all the big cases in your glorious past to impress the nurses. The patient won't suffer but the nurses will, and, it has got so that lately the house staff has been drawing lots to see who has to scrub with you.

"And if I weren't being decent and concerned with the public image of this institution," Jaffrey was saying, "do you know what I'd do? I'd go right up and apprise my patient of what this is all about."

That's enough of this, he was thinking. I'd get out of here, except for Stan. This must really brace up Stan.

"Excuse me, Arnold," he said. "I don't mean to interrupt."

"That's quite all right," Jaffrey said. "You see my point."

"I do, but I've got a little business to transact with Stan."

"Oh, that reminds me," Jaffrey said, looking at Frank Stanczyk. "I note that you're one of the fortunate ones around here."

"Fortunate?" Frank Stanczyk said, looking at him.

"You're blessed with a towel. The last two occasions when I've had some need of a clean towel there hasn't been one. It seems to me that if we had an extra orderly around here we might stand a chance of having our minimal and modest needs answered. Excuse me, gentlemen."

He turned and they watched him stalk out, his cane over one arm. Maury Rand was standing in the doorway to the shower room, holding the door open.

"After that," he said, "I have some minimal and modest needs of my own that I'm going to answer right here and now."

"Enjoy yourself."

"After that cathartic it'll be easy," Maury Rand said. "Excuse me, too."

"Did you ever hear anything like that?" Frank Stanczyk said.

"Yes. I've heard him before."

"He wants another orderly. Every time he operates he has one of them in here shining his shoes."

"Forget him," he said. "There's nothing we can do about his kind, but attrition takes care of them. You're young and you know you're good, and I'm concerned right now about you."

"Honestly, Matt," Frank Stanczyk said, "right now I feel like chucking everything."

"Don't be ridiculous."

"I'm not being ridiculous. It's the way I feel."

"All right, but I don't have to go over the lesson you learned today. You've already learned that."

"I'll say."

"You did what you believed was right at the time. Also, you've heard it said, and you know it's true, that the coward who underoperates does the same disservice as the man who gets too brave."

"I should have saved this one, Matt."

"All right, but I want you to remember something else. I recall very well why you got into medicine and then surgery in the first place. You said it, and I heard you say it twice, that you believed that if you could extend one human life one day you'd be doing more than you could do in any other endeavor."

"I was a kid, just talking, Matt. Besides, I didn't extend that one today."

"You weren't just a kid talking, and what I want you to remember now is not just the tough one you lost today, but the many tough ones you've already won. We're all inclined to forget those. I can't tell you how many there are already in your career, or in mine, either, but you wouldn't want to support all yours for the rest of their lives, would you?"

"Hardly."

"That's what I mean."

"Matt?" Bob Robinson said, standing in the doorway.

"All right, Rob."

"Hello, Stan," Bob Robinson said. "I'm sorry to hear about that."

"Thanks, Rob," Frank Stanczyk said.

"They'll be ready in about five minutes, Matt. Have you got time to go up and see Mrs. Scheller?"

"Why? Anything wrong with her?"

"No. She's just nervous about her husband. She's got her son with her, and they'd like to talk with the great surgeon himself."

"Where are they?"

"They're waiting for you in the lounge on the sixth floor."

"Okay."

"I'll see you inside," Bob Robinson said. "Take it easy, Stan."

"I will."

"I'll tell you what," he said to Frank Stanczyk. "Why don't you come up to the place for dinner some night next week?"

"I'd like that."

"I'll check with Marion, and let you know."

"Thanks a lot, Matt, and thanks a lot for everything. I appreciate it."

"Then snap out of it. Start bouncing back."

"I'll try."

He'll bounce back, he was thinking, walking to the elevator. We all bounce back, but the trouble is that we never bounce back all the way. We lose a little of our resiliency with each one, and it is like that poet said, something about no man being an island and every man being a piece of the continent and every man's death diminishing us. It goes something like that.

XV

"You have to learn to handle your deaths with grace," he said once. "You have to learn not to take them out on your associates, your wife, and certainly not on your next patient."

He had learned to handle his deaths with grace. He had learned to carry them around the hospital and around the office but he had never learned how to leave them there or how to carry them, with that same grace, into the presence of his wife.

"What happened?" she asked once.

"Who told you?" he said.

"You always do," she said, "by the way you walk through that door."

It is strange, he had thought often, how we can be with death hundreds of times and yet we can never quite accept death. We understand, as the layman doesn't, that whole series of immutable changes by which the progression of living becomes the process of dying. We accept this inevitable metamorphosis as a basic law and it controls our medications and the mechanics of our surgery, but we never quite accept death.

He must have been four or five years old when he became vaguely aware for the first time of the ending of life. His mother had planted flowering bushes against the back of the house and one morning he noticed the butterflies settling in the warmth of the early sun on the small yellow blossoms. The butterflies were brown with round spots on their wings and must have been buckeyes, and when they settled they brought their wings up and together and he discovered that, if he stood almost still and moved his hand slowly, he could pick them up by their wings as by a handle.

He found a cardboard shoe box and began picking them off the blossoms and putting them into the covered box. Their brown coloring powder came off on his fingers and stained them brown and his fingers felt more smooth than they had ever felt to his own touch. This tactile sensation pleased him and his greed grew until he became almost fanatical, and there must have been dozens of the brown butterflies in the box when he tired of the game and left the covered box under the bushes.

He did not think of the box again until sometime the next day. When he opened it the brown butterflies with their purplish eye spots, some with folded wings, some with open wings, some with broken wings, were inert. They had died, of suffocation and dehydration, but he did not know this or conceive of this as death. It was merely something that happened to brown butterflies when you put them in a box. Many years later, because he could still see a small, rompered boy picking brown butterflies off yellow blossoms and putting them in a cardboard shoe box and then finding them dead, because these scenes still played across his mind with all the clarity of a technicolor motion picture, he realized that he had actually then, for the first time, been aware of, and affected by, death.

As he became older his father let him watch when he killed the chickens for Sunday dinner and when the Mexican ranch hands slaughtered a steer. His father would take the small gray-and-white, protesting Plymouth Rock fryers and pull their wings down to their legs and, holding the wings and legs in his left hand and his hatchet in his right, the chickens convulsing as he held them, he would behead them on the upturned cottonwood log. The Mexicans would truss the steer by its legs, the steer lying on its side on the barn floor, its eyes bulging with fright. With the 8-to-1 pulleys attached to one of the crossbeams of the barn they would pull it up by its hind legs until its head hung at the level of their knees and then they would cut the carotid arteries in the neck and catch the blood in the buckets. All this he observed with a feeling of pity and sadness but with a curiosity he couldn't explain but that made him watch.

When he was seven years old he was allowed to walk into town twice

a week with his brother, who was then twelve. They would pull their
wooden hand wagon to the general store and load it with the groceries
and pull it back home again. They would each buy a penny length of
licorice rope and the trick, on the way back, was to make the licorice last
until they reached home.

"When you go to town this morning," his mother said to them on
this day, "I don't want you to go near the Jenkins' house."

"Why?" his brother said.

"There's smallpox in that house," his mother said.

"What's smallpox?" he said.

"It's a terrible sickness," his mother said, "and there's already death
in that house. Mr. Jenkins is dead and Mrs. Jenkins is sick and dying,
so you stay away from it."

"How far away from it?" his brother said.

"I don't want you to go into the yard for any reason," his mother said.
"You just stay on the road. You don't have to run past it and make a
scene, but I don't want you standing there and staring at the house,
either. Do you understand?"

As they walked down the road, the dirt- and gravel-grating sound of
the iron rims of the wooden wheels of the wagon following them, they
could see the house ahead, standing white in the morning sun and about
fifty feet off to the right of the road. It did not look any different to him
from the way it had looked before, but as they neared it and then passed
it, walking faster and looking at it out of the corners of their eyes, it
seemed more alone and still and silent than any house he had ever seen.
It seemed to be standing, its shades drawn and its white paint peeling
and powdering but still glaring in the sun, in the middle of a thin, in-
visible something that separated it from the road and the fields and everything else around it; and that something, he thought, must be death
and what it looks like, even though you can't really see it.

When he was nine years old he began to pull the wagon into town
alone one afternoon a week to collect beer bottles. He would work the
alleys behind the houses, searching through the trash barrels. The people in the town buried the leavings of their food in their back yards or
in the fields beyond the town, but the barrels held tin cans and broken
glass, old shoes and old corsets, sometimes eyeless dolls' heads and
dented, worn-out coffee pots, and after a while he learned in which barrels to look for the beer bottles.

He had an old burlap sack in the bottom of the wagon, and when he
had a dozen bottles in it he would take it to the saloon and carry the
sack of bottles down into the cellar. When he came upstairs the bar-

tender would go down and count the bottles and give him ten cents for the dozen. While the bartender was downstairs he would take a cold roast beef sandwich from the free lunch at the end of the bar and put it inside his shirt, and pulling the wagon on the way home he would eat the sandwich and feel of the pennies or nickels or of the dime in his pocket and think of the flashlight or the Daisy air rifle he would some-day buy in the general store.

"Whenever you're in town and you hear gun shots," his father had told him and his brother, "you're to run right home. I don't care what you're doing or where you are, you run home. Out here gun shots mean hunting, but in town they mean killing, so you run home."

On this afternoon he had just started to work the alleys, and his wagon was still empty, when he heard the shots, three of them, clear and sharp like claps. He ran, the wagon bouncing behind him, until he could run no more, and then he walked the rest of the way home. About two hours later his cousin came out from town and found him.

"You ever see a dead man?" his cousin said.

"Nope," he said.

"You wanna see one?" his cousin said.

"Who's dead?" he said.

"The sheriff," his cousin said. "Somebody shot him."

The sheriff was his first real hero. For a while his first hero had been the Mexican who moved from ranch to ranch, breaking the new horses, but after a time he had come to realize that the Mexican was not really a hero. He was just big and heavy and he held the horn of the saddle and didn't really ride and he just broke the horses with his weight, and wasn't really a hero like the sheriff.

Why the sheriff was a hero he never knew. He never heard of anything brave that the sheriff had done, but somehow he had derived from things he had heard his father and the other men say that they all looked up to the sheriff. The sheriff was big, but not heavy, and his skin was sun-tanned and he had light blue eyes and one day, when he was in town with his wagon, the sheriff had nodded to him and said hello.

"But don't you want to see him?" his cousin was saying. "He's lyin' right there in my dad's."

His cousin's dad, his own Uncle Frank, was the town furniture dealer and undertaker. He was a short, stout, red-faced man who chewed to-bacco, and the corners of his mouth were always brown.

"I don't know," he said to his cousin.

"You scared?"

"Nope."

"Then why don't you wanna see him?" his cousin said.

He walked with his cousin back into town. They went in through the front of his Uncle Frank's store, past the overstuffed furniture in the window and the dining-room furniture and then the kitchen tables and chairs stacked near the back.

"There he is," his cousin said.

The sheriff was lying, but it did not look like the sheriff at first, on his back on the undertaker's slab. He was naked, and he seemed so white, because only his hands and wrists, his neck and face were tanned, and there was a small hole, singed black, in his left chest.

"A gunman shot him," his cousin said, "but he killed the gunman, too. You wanna see the gunman?"

"Nope," he said, and he was afraid that he was going to be sick.

"Why not?"

" 'Cause I have to go home."

"Don't you wanna stay and play?"

"Nope," he said. "I have to go home."

On the way home he felt that he would be sick and then he felt that he would cry. He could see the sheriff alive, sun-tanned and tall and walking, and then he could see him dead, pale, and not so tall, and lying there not like a real person at all. For several days he kept seeing the sheriff first the one way and then the other way until it became difficult for him to remember the sheriff alive and he saw him only lying there; and he decided that death was when you didn't look like a real person any more.

"You will remember," his Gross Anatomy professor was saying thirteen years later, "that the cadavers to which you will be introduced within the next few minutes were once human beings. I remind you of this not to unnerve you, but to caution you that they are to be treated with the respect to which a human being is entitled."

It was the second day of medical school. On the first day they had registered in the morning, and signed for and picked up their instruments, their microscopes and their books. In the afternoon they had sat in the amphitheater and had listened for an hour while they were told that if they were not ready to do their best every day this was their time to leave medicine for another field. On the way out they had all complained, and that night he had had an asthmatic attack for the only time in his life.

"As a matter of fact," the Gross Anatomy professor named Thiel was saying the next morning, "one of these cadavers was a highly respected member of the profession you are about to enter, and a graduate of this institution. He willed his body to his school, so that you might learn as he did. Only I know which of the bodies was his, and none of you will ever know, for they are all to be regarded with the same respect. Who are we to judge the dead?"

Then Thiel, gray-haired, wearing his white smock and those thick-lensed glasses, led them down the hall. In their own smocks they had lined up and paired off alphabetically, two for each cadaver, and their footsteps echoed in the hall and here and there along the double column someone murmured something to his partner.

"Let's try to get a thin one," Stu Chase said to him. "They say it's easier to get to the anatomy if you don't have to go through a lot of fat."

"I know," he said, although he had never thought of it before.

Thiel opened the door and they walked in. It was a large, cement-floored, gray-walled room, and down the length of it ran four rows of narrow, hip-high tables, each one covered with a black oilcloth bulked up from beneath by the body.

He and Stu Chase started down the middle aisle, and he was aware of his nervousness and of the heavy but sharp scent of formaldehyde. Halfway down the aisle the two in front of them stopped and he and Stu Chase walked around them and Stu stopped two tables beyond and looked at him and they pulled the black oilcloth and then the damp, yellowish-gray cheesecloth down.

"Does he look all right?" Stu said. "I mean, is he thin enough?"

"I guess so," he said.

"Where does a guy get sick around here?" Stu said.

"I don't know," he said. "I was wondering the same thing."

It looks like a mummy, he was thinking, looking at the nut-brown, taut-over-the-chest-and-cheekbones skin. He needs a shave, and there's no reason to be nervous about a dead man. I saw the sheriff when I was just a kid and there's no reason to be nervous if you're going to be a doctor, and this is where you have to start being a doctor right now.

"You think it's that doctor?" Stu was saying. "I mean the one who willed his body?"

I hope not, he was thinking. I hope he wasn't a doctor and I'm glad I don't know who he was or what he did.

"I don't know," he said. "I don't think so."

"I don't think so, either," Stu said. "He doesn't look like it."

"He looks like a mummy."

"Yeah," Stu said, "but what are we supposed to do now?"

"May I have your attention?" Thiel was saying, standing back by the door and raising his voice. "You will have the rest of the morning to

acclimate yourselves as you desire. Tomorrow morning you will bring
your manuals and you will start dissecting, but before that you will wash
your cadavers. You'll find the soap, towels, and everything you need in
the room here to my left. You may do that today, or at the start of class
tomorrow morning. That is up to you, and unless there are any questions
I have nothing more to say today."

Out of the whole class only one pair washed their cadaver that day.
The rest of them covered them again and wandered out to gather in
groups outside on the steps in the September sunlight and make small
jokes that seemed much funnier than they were and concerned how
they had felt in the lab and whom their cadavers resembled and what
the deceased probably had done for a living.

The next day it pleased him that he felt remarkably composed as he
and Stu Chase washed and dried the body. Before the period was over,
however, it surprised him and he felt a sense of small shock and of guilt
that so soon, and so easily, they could sit there, Stu on a stool on one
side and he on a stool on the other, their Cunningham's *Dissecting Manuals* open on the varnished oak racks in front of them, and that they had
already cut into this body and that Stu was dissecting the right arm and
he the left.

At the end of each session they would cover the dissected areas with
cheesecloth soaked in formaldehyde, and the formaldehyde burned in
their nostrils and brought tears into their eyes. No matter how often he
washed, the smell of it seemed to be under his nails and all the food he
ate tasted of it, and he found that, for more than a year after the
course was completed, he could never eat fried pork chops because of
their color.

Because the laboratory periods were never long enough most of them
also dissected at night and on Sundays and holidays. They would often
bring sandwiches and pint bottles of milk to the lab and sit on the wide
window sills and eat, and there were several who, once or twice, made a
show of unwrapping their sandwiches on the chests of their cadavers and
of sitting right beside them while they ate and made casual talk.

There were no displays of sadistic exhibitionism, but they heard of
the time that Thiel found the left lobe of a human liver on the steps
outside and of the night when he walked in and saw the student skipping
rope with a small intestine in the aisle next to his cadaver. Thiel told him
to take his dissecting kit with him when he left, because he was expelled,
but the only incident in their year was relatively mild and Thiel never
heard of it or, if he did, he never mentioned it. Somebody inserted a

theater-ticket stub through the superior vena cava into the right atrium of the heart of the cadaver of the only two girls in the class.

If there were a ghoul in the lab, it was Tony. Tony was the custodian and he was in his mid-forties, small, sallow-skinned, and balding. He wore a black rubber apron over his worn rust-brown trousers and blue short-sleeved shirts, and he moved around almost noiselessly in his dirt-gray, stained sneakers, cutting off arms and legs with his hack saw, carrying them out under his arm and every now and then coming back with a spare part from the basement.

Only Thiel and Tony had the three keys for the three doors that led to the long narrow room in the basement where the cadavers were pre-served. There was the door from the hall, the middle door and then the final steel door, and the cadavers, chains under their arms, were sus-pended upright in the tank in the concrete floor, the tops of their heads about three inches below the surface of the embalming fluid.

For a long while he thought that Tony was a mute. Tony never spoke to any of the students, but one day he heard Tony say something to Thiel and when he discovered that Tony could talk he wondered what Tony talked about when he got home at night.

Only twice, after the first day, did he feel any uneasiness or revulsion. In the fifth week they started dissecting around the eye, and that open brown eye, looking back at him, bothered him. Months later, when they were down to the leg, he detected a foul odor, and when he lifted the leg he saw a cluster of what seemed to be moving eggs, almost the size of flies and the color of cigarette ash. When he showed them to Stu Chase, Stu made a wry face and turned away.

"Maggots," Thiel said. "Tell Tony to cut it off."

By the time he and Stu had reached the legs it would no longer have occurred to him to stand back and look at what was left and say: "That's a man." They had dissected to isolate each organ, to trace each muscle from its origin to its insertion into the bone, to follow each nerve that motivated that muscle and each blood vessel that nourished it. What remained might have been the model of an early airplane or an in-vention of Leonardo da Vinci, all lines and levers, and he himself, more easily than he might once have thought possible, had made the step that would leave him forever stranded, one foot in the world of the medical scientist but the other still anchored in the world of what he had been and would be still, although he would see death approach and understand its causes and see the living die hundreds of times in his professional life.

"The degree to which you are affected by a death," he was to say, "depends upon several things, but in large part upon the degree of your emotional involvement with the patient. I don't think I'm being dramatic when I say that you die a little with each, that something, however small it may be, goes out of you. I know that the older you get, the more you try to shield yourself from this. I know that you ask yourself how much emotional investment, how much empathy, how much more of myself can I continue to give along the way and still have anything left?"

The beginnings of his giving were in the second half of his second year in medical school. At the lectures in Physical Diagnosis the patients with their heart murmurs, their breast tumors, their skin diseases would walk or be wheeled into the amphitheater, as mute and submissive as chastised children. Just sitting there and looking at them, he felt more a part of them than he did of the professor who, it occurred to him, discussed them and their ailments with the aloof objectivity of an engineer analyzing a drainage problem or some other kind of land-reclamation project.

Then they went around to the wards, five or six in a group with an instructor. The instructor would listen to a heart and then he would step aside and they would take turns listening, and again he felt pity for the patient and guilt in his own health. Finally this pity was mixed with fear of the patient when he was sent into a ward alone to make his own examinations and his own diagnoses.

"Excuse me," he said to the patient, the first time. "I'm Dr. Carter, a student doctor, and I wonder if I can examine you?"

"Are you a specialist?" the old man, who was a heart case, asked.

"No," he said. "I'm a student doctor assigned to report on your case."

"Then, please, you're going to be taking care of me from now on?" the old man said, not having heard his answer. "You're going to make me well, Doctor?"

"You're going to be all right, I'm sure," he said, trying to keep his guilt from showing. "There are great doctors here who will help you."

"Then you're going to take care of me now, Doctor?" the old man said. "Please."

There were the ones who, embittered by the first realization that nature had not provided them with ever-healthy bodies, resented him. Having already been examined by their own doctor, by an intern, and by an assistant resident, and checked by the resident, unaware and unconcerned that he, to prove himself, had to make the most detailed report of all, they resisted him.

"So you feel this patient's difficulty during pregnancy is due to hypertension?" the professor said.

"Yes, sir."

He had just presented his first case. They had wheeled the woman out onto the floor of the amphitheater, the nurse present to protect the patient's modesty, the professor standing to one side, his arms folded across his chest. She was one of those who resented and had resisted him, and now, before the whole class, he had gone through the past history into the present illness, the tests, the studies, the diagnosis, and the therapeutic plan, with the management outlined, A, B, C, D. Then the professor had thanked the patient and the nurse had wheeled her out.

"The tests for albumen in the urine, did you do those yourself?"

"Yes, sir."

"Have you examined the patient when she was completely at ease in the quiet of the evening?"

"Yes, sir."

"Do you feel her blood pressure might be influenced by her mood?"

"Yes, sir."

"Has she had any trouble with her nurses?"

"I don't know, sir."

"Oh?" the professor said. "You don't know? What about her relations with her husband?"

"I don't know, sir."

"Well, we know she's about to have a baby, so we do know she's had some relations and we presume that they were with her husband."

"Yes, sir," he said, and he heard a couple of them in the class laughing behind him.

"But you don't know if, perhaps, her husband might have a disturbing emotional influence on her?"

"No, sir."

"You didn't check in on her after a visit by her husband?"

"No, sir."

"All right, Carter," the professor said. "That was still a good presentation. Thank you."

He waited for Stu Chase to come down out of the seats and they walked out together.

"You did all right, Matt," Stu said.

"Sure," he said. "I always leave them laughing when I say good-bye."

"Wait till some of those guys have to stand down there and present a case."

"Do you think he knows something about her and her husband?"

"You mean that it isn't his baby?"

"I don't know. How should I know?"

"I think he was just making a point," Stu said.

"He made it all right," he said.

The point had been, of course, that when the emotions may be involved you cannot know too much, but in his internship and then his residency he was to find that the more he knew the more his own emotions were involved. He was encouraged to know not only the patient but the patient's family, to act as a buffer between the family and the surgeon, to appear to answer their questions when he was never allowed to tell them anything, and so he became an accomplished liar, or performer, as he was to call it in later years.

"But Doctor," Mrs. Kroner said to him, sitting beside her husband's bed, "from Dr. Williams we still know nothing, and they must have now the report."

"No," he said, lying. "It takes quite a while to make those tests, and Dr. Williams will let you know as soon as he learns the results."

Dr. Williams had known for three days. Three days ago he had opened Herman Kroner, a sixty-two-year-old carpenter, and found an inoperable cancer of the esophagus. Within fifteen minutes the Pathology lab had called back to say it was an adeno-carcinoma.

"When it's a squamous-cell carcinoma," Dr. Williams had said to the resident and to him, "it'll take X-ray treatment, but when it's adeno-carcinoma it originates in the stomach and by the time it has spread this far it's resistant to everything."

"But what's going to happen now?" he had asked Williams.

"He'll probably go with pneumonia within three weeks," Williams said. "You know that we produce about a quart of saliva a day. When nothing can get through the esophagus the saliva overflows into the windpipe and when they sleep at night they can't cough it up. As a result pneumonia gets them."

"But isn't there anything that can be done?" he said.

"Yes," he said, "you can keep the patient as comfortable as possible. The wife is too upset right now about the operation to be told. She's got two grown daughters and a sister of hers and I can see they'll be on my neck all the time. I'm going to tell them to appoint a spokesman and I'll deal with that one and nobody else. In a day or two I'll tell her what we've found, and she can tell the others or the patient as she sees fit. What I've told you, of course, is professional between us."

"Yes, sir," he said, but he had walked away wondering if Williams wasn't giving up too easily, wondering if Williams could be wrong, if maybe there was someone somewhere who could do something that Williams couldn't. Doesn't he know, he wondered, that this is a nice old guy and these are nice people and that nobody wants to die?

As it turned out, Mrs. Kroner was the one whom Williams told. He did not tell her that Mr. Kroner would be dead within weeks, but he did tell her what they had found and that there was no known cure. He said that they would do everything they could for Mr. Kroner and, having explained all that, and because there was then nothing that he could do that the house staff couldn't, he had seen less and less of the patient and of Mrs. Kroner and he had had no time for the two daughters and for Mrs. Kroner's sister, who had traveled halfway across the country by bus to be there in this time of trouble.

All of this had come as a shock to Dr. Matthew Carter, six months out of medical school and on his first terminal case. In his mind was still that picture of the old family physician keeping the bedside vigil, and even as he found Dr. Williams was now primarily occupied with those cases he could cure or give relief, he found himself drawn more and more to Mr. Kroner and to his family.

When he could answer their questions he did, and when he could not he professed ignorance and then tried to find something to say to ease their anxiety. It was three weeks before Christmas, and when Mrs. Kroner, short, plump, and pink-complexioned, found that often he missed a meal and would grab a snack when he could she brought him a box of home-made Christmas cookies. She called them *kuchen* and there were three or four kinds, some flat and thin and brittle and in the shape of Christmas trees and stars, some round and soft and with grated nuts in them and others smaller and round with a hollow shell of what must have been egg white and sugar on top.

"You like them, yes?" she said the next day. "Sometime, then, you come to our house and I cook you a meal. Yes?"

"Yes," he said, knowing that it would never be. "I'd like that."

Before and after visiting hours, when he had the time, he would stop by and sit and talk with Mr. Kroner. At first he did this because he felt sorry for Mr. Kroner and wanted to ease Mr. Kroner's loneliness, but by the second week he knew that he did it, too, to ease his own loneliness because he was many miles from home. In this way he came to know all about Mr. Kroner and about his life and his dreams and about what hopes he still had.

Mr. Kroner, he learned, had been born in a small town in Germany, the only son of a cabinet maker, and from his father he had learned his trade. He had married Mrs. Kroner in that town, and in 1899 they had come to this country because in this country, surely, there would be more need for a good cabinet maker.

"But in this country," Mr. Kroner said, "no one cares for good cabinets. Everything is factory, factory. In this country I find all of the furniture is made in Grand Rapids, and this is not cabinets. This is boxes with a shiny front. This I cannot make myself to make, so I become a carpenter instead and there I can at least do good carpentry, and cabinets I make for my own house and for my friends."

As he talked with Mr. Kroner he found he was telling him about his own beginnings and his own career. This was a simple man to whom he could talk about his own simple dreams as he could to no one else in these harried, hectic halls of professionalism where everyone seemed to be carrying so many burdens of his own that there was no room for those of another.

"You will be a good doctor," Mr. Kroner said to him, "because you care for people. You will be a better doctor than Dr. Williams because I do not think he cares for people."

"Oh, yes he does," he said. "Dr. Williams is a great surgeon, but he's very busy."

"I know," Mr. Kroner said, "but you will be better, and I tell you what I do. If I get out from this place I make you a cabinet. I make a cabinet for when you have your own office, and I make it from mahogany with the inlay on the front around the edges of the doors and around the top edge. No doctor will have a more beautiful cabinet than I make for you. I be proud to do it, and of this cabinet you can be proud, too."

"Yes," he said, again knowing. "I'll be very proud of it."

"Then first you must get me out from this place. Right?"

"Right," he said.

Thus it was that, as he watched Mr. Kroner die, he carried this burden of his own creation. Three weeks ago neither he nor Mr. Kroner had even heard of the other, but thus it was that it was he who was alone with Mr. Kroner, holding Mr. Kroner's pulse when, at 2:30 in the morning two days before Christmas, that pulse stopped beating.

"Well," Dr. Williams said when he called him and told him at 8 o'clock, "the family was prepared for it."

"That's right, sir," he said.

"You've gotten along very well with that family, haven't you?" Williams said.

"Yes, sir."

"Then it will probably be better if the wife hears it from you," Williams said. "Ask her for a post-mortem, too. It's always better to get those permissions before the family has too much time to talk it all over, and I'd like an autopsy."

"Yes, sir."

"And while I've got you on the phone," Williams said, "how's that thoracoplasty I did yesterday, that Mrs. Woodman?"

"She's not one of mine, Doctor," he said. "I think Bill O'Donnell has her."

"That's right," Williams said. "Thanks anyway, Carter."

"You're welcome, sir," he said.

So it was that he knew that none of it in medical school, none of that with the cadaver and Physical Diagnosis and Surgical Anatomy and the rest of it then and since, had changed him. So it was that he wondered if he were really fit to be a doctor, and he asked himself how he could possibly continue to lose some of himself like this, time and time again, year after year, and he remembered something Pete Church had said after he had just lost a case and they were walking together out of the room.

"Have you ever wished you were a horticulturist?" Pete Church had asked him, suddenly.

"A horticulturist? No, sir."

"I have," Pete Church had said, "because when a flower dies, nobody cries."

About a month later a letter came from his father. His father had written it late at night, after his mother had gone to bed.

"Something strange is happening to your mother," his father wrote. "No matter how warm the house is she's complaining all the time about being cold. She also has trouble thinking of words, and yesterday she slapped a woman. You don't know the woman, Mrs. Kelly, but your mother has been friendly with her for years and you know your mother was never like that. She has me worried."

When he read the letter he knew, or felt he knew, what it was. He had just finished some studies on the brain, and he inquired about brain specialists in the Southwest and that night he called his father and gave him the name of the man. Five nights later his father called.

"He wants to operate," his father said.

"How's Mother?" he said.

"She's having trouble even speaking."

"Then he's got to operate," he said.

"I don't know," his father said. "Your brother is against it and I'm not sure."

"Of course he's got to operate," he said. "Who are you and Mark to doubt the decision of a man who has devoted his whole life to this work? Your wife and our mother is entitled to the knowledge of our time."

So he convinced his father and three days later they operated and found a malignant brain tumor. On the fourth post-operative day, without ever speaking again, his mother died, and when they called him that afternoon and told him he asked for a post-mortem, because he knew he would ask this of many others, and then he went to his room and locked the door and he sat for a half-hour and thought of his mother as he remembered her.

He remembered her singing around the house and how she was always spouting those philosophies and how he and Mark used to grab her and dance her around the floor until she was red in the face and out of breath from dancing and from laughing. He remembered how, once, when Mark had started to smoke a pipe and she had complained that the house always smelled of it, they had wrestled her to the floor and he had held her nose and Mark had put the pipe in her mouth and made her puff on it.

"Can't you treat me with some dignity?" she had said when they had let her up and they were unsure whether she was going to cry or laugh. "Can't you remember that I'm your mother?"

After dinner in the summer either he or Mark would do the dishes with their father, and the other would walk with her out to the knoll behind the barns. She wanted to see the sun set, and they would watch it go down at the end of the valley and she would always say the same thing.

"Tomorrow will be beautiful," she would say. "It's going to be a beautiful tomorrow."

Now he knew that for her there would be no more tomorrows and he knew again that nothing had changed him or would ever change him. He wondered again if he were really meant to be a doctor and then he got up and unlocked the door and walked out.

Forty-five minutes later, because they were short-handed in Emergency, he was riding the ambulance through the dusk to Main Station. The driver swung the ambulance right up beside the train and when they got out they saw two conductors or trainmen down near the end of the platform, a small crowd around them, waving to them to come down to the second car from the end. In his white uniform and carrying his black bag he ran down the dimly lighted platform, the driver and the attendant running after him with the stretcher, and he climbed up and into the car.

"A heart attack, I think, Doc," one of the trainmen was saying. "I think it's a heart attack."

Halfway down the aisle two sailors were bending over a man lying face down on the floor. One of the sailors was administering artificial respiration and the two sailors and the man were blocking the aisle so that the women in the seats on either side were unable to get out. The women were sitting, he remembered when he reconstructed it later, with their feet up under them, trying to withdraw as if there were a mouse or a rat in the car.

"Turn him over," he said to the sailors.

"It was like somebody shot him," one of the sailors said, while the other, who had been kneeling over the man got up and then the two of them, lifting the man, turned him over. "He was just walking down the aisle when he dropped like he was shot."

"Do something for him, Doctor!" one of the women was saying. "Do something!"

He looked at the big man lying on his back now on the floor and filling the aisle, his tie pulled down and his collar opened. He saw that the big man's jowled face was purple and his eyes were glassy and he opened the big man's shirt and pulled up his undershirt. With one hand he was trying to feel the pulse, but could feel none, and with the other he was putting on his stethoscope and then he was trying to hear the heart.

"Do something, Doctor!" the woman was saying. "Can't you do something?"

"Will you please keep still?" he said. "I can't hear a thing in this noise."

He could hear no beat. Listening, listening, he realized that his own heart was pounding from running down the platform and from his excitement and now what he was hearing was his own blood pressure pounding in his ears. He took off his stethoscope then and reached into his bag and found an ampoule of adrenalin and a long needle and then he inserted the needle into the chest and injected the adrenalin right into the heart.

"Come on!" he said, calling to the driver and the attendant standing down the aisle. "Let's get this man out of here."

"Is he alive, Doc?" one of the sailors said.

"I'm not sure," he said. "Thanks a lot for your help."

"Oh, my God!" one of the women said.

"That's all right, Doc," the sailor said. "He just dropped like he was shot."

It was a tight squeeze in the aisle but the attendant and the driver got the big man onto the stretcher and started him down the aisle. They had to jockey the stretcher at the end of the car to make the turn and get it down the steps onto the station platform.

"A heart attack, Doc?" one of the trainmen said.

"It looks that way," he said.

"He alive?"

"I doubt it, but I'm not sure yet."

"That's the second one I had this year," the trainman said.

In the parked ambulance he took out his stethoscope again and he put it once more to the big man's chest. All he could hear was the steam hissing from between the cars of the train still standing on the track so he closed the ambulance door. When he still could hear no beat he took the stethoscope off and the attendant, without saying anything, put the black oxygen mask over the big man's mouth and nose.

"This guy's dead, Doc," the attendant said after a while.

"Just let me check something," he said.

He took the small mirror from his bag and held it close to the big man's mouth. When he looked at it there was no steam on it, and he found his ophthalmoscope in his bag and, shining the light first in one eye and then the other, squinting through the tiny lens, he tried to find an artery beating behind the pupils, but he found none.

"Well, where you wanna go, Doc?" the driver said. He had climbed behind the wheel and had shut the door on his side.

"Where do I want to go?" he said.

"Yeah," the driver said. "You wanna take this guy to the hospital or the morgue?"

"There's no sense in taking him to the hospital, is there?" he said, still stalling. "He's dead, isn't he?"

"Whatever you say, Doc," the driver said. "We'll drop you off at the hospital on the way."

The house staff at General had two traditions. If you delivered a baby in the ambulance you bought a case of beer for the weekly house-staff party, and if you brought a Dead On Arrival back to the hospital instead of to the morgue, you also had to buy one, and you knew that, long after the beer was gone, they would never let you forget it.

When they dropped him at the hospital and he sat down in Emergency to fill out his report, he began to sweat out the waiting. He was just finishing the report when one of the nurses called him and said the morgue was on the phone.

Oh, no, he said to himself, he's not alive. He can't be alive. How can he be alive? He's got to be dead.

"Yes?" he said, on the phone.

"Dr. Carter?" the man's voice said.

"Yes?"

"On this D.O.A.," the voice said, "you forgot to fill in the hour of death."

"Oh," he said, relieved now. "I'm sorry. Put down 5:45 P.M., and thanks a lot."

But what kind of a doctor can I be, he was thinking when he had hung up, when I'm hoping a man is dead just so I won't be wrong? Can it be that I wanted him dead just to preserve what reputation I might have around this place?

In the space of two hours on one afternoon, through the deaths of his own mother and of a complete stranger, he had learned that his own attitude toward death was, and would be, controlled not only by the degree of his emotional involvement but by the extent of his professional involvement and his pride as well.

10:37 A.M.

XVI

I should have asked Rob what this Mrs. Scheller looks like, he was thinking, waiting for the elevator. It was only last week that she came in with her husband, a nice little woman, but I'm not so good on the faces any more. All I remember about her is that she was about six inches shorter than her husband and had dark brown hair and was wearing a dark blue dress. She said they'll be married thirty years next month and she was just about as nervous as her husband but she didn't have the disease and he did, so it was one of those times when I got more of the truth out of her than I did out of him. He wanted to belittle the pain in the shoulder and the coughing but she wouldn't let him and I should have asked Rob to describe her again in case there are two or three other women there when I walk into that lounge.

"Where to, Doctor?" the elevator operator said.

"Oh," he said. "Just up to the sixth."

"You're really circulatin' this morning, Doctor."

"That's right," he said. "That's the way I keep in shape."

"I could use a little exercise myself," the elevator operator said.

When he walked into the lounge Mrs. Scheller and a rather tall young man about thirty years old were sitting on the sofa. They were the only ones in the room, and Mrs. Scheller had on the same dark blue dress, or one like it, and the young man was saying something to her and she was nodding.

"Good morning," he said, walking over to them.

"Oh," Mrs. Scheller said, looking up. She stood up and her black handbag slid off her lap onto the floor. As she started to bend over, the young man bent down and picked it up and handed it to her.

"I'm so nervous today, Doctor," she said, shaking hands, "I don't know what I'm doing."

"I understand," he said, "but there's really no reason to be."

"I want you to meet my son," Mrs. Scheller said. "This is my son Harold."

"Hello, Doctor," the young man said, shaking hands.

"I'm glad to meet you," he said.

It had been late that afternoon the week before. He had just finished with his last patient for the day and he was sitting at his desk, starting to look at his mail.

"You busy, Matt?" Bob Robinson said.

"No," he said. "What's up?"

"Take a look at these," Rob said.

Rob walked over to the light panels on the wall behind the desk and snapped the two X rays up under the clips. Then he lighted the two panels and stepped back and they looked at them together.

"What do you think?" Rob said.

"I think they're pretty poor pictures," he said, annoyed by the lack of definition but still able to make out the shadow, light and rather irregular and the size of a small lemon, just above the root of the right lung.

"I know," Rob said, "but for some reason it was the best they could do."

"What's the history?" he said, still looking at the films and at that shadow.

"He's fifty-four years old," Rob said, looking at the sheets of paper in his hands, "and a house painter. About six months ago he was coughing and he spit up some blood. When the bleeding stopped he figured it was a cigarette cough and he forgot it. About two months ago he started to spit blood again. A chest film showed nothing abnormal, but about a week later—and his wife tells me this although he doesn't want to admit it—he felt some pain and there was more blood in his sputum. This has continued, although the pain has gone."

"I'll bet."

"Anyway," Rob said, "that's what he says now. He says he feels fine, but his wife says his appetite is poor. He's lost almost ten pounds, and she says he's also short of breath."

"He's here now?"

"Yes. I started him because you were tied up, but Carrie says you're clear now so I thought you should look him over and talk with him. He's pretty nervous."

"They all are."

"This guy's really scared. His wife's upset, too, and I judge they came here expecting to see you."

"How far have you gotten with him?"

"I've got all his history. Everything seems all right except for the chief complaint. His pulse is strong and a little fast, probably because of the nervousness, but his temperature is normal and his blood pressure is okay."

Mr. Scheller, stripped to his shorts, was sitting on the examining table. He was about five feet eleven, pale and lean, his graying, straight, light brown hair receding at the temples and thinning on top.

"Mr. Scheller," Bob Robinson said, "this is Dr. Carter."

"Oh," Mr. Scheller said, getting off the table and putting out his hand. "Hello, Doctor."

"Hello," he said, taking Mr. Scheller's hand. "How are you?"

"Oh, I don't know," Mr. Scheller said. "I don't feel too bad."

"Good," he said. "Then I wouldn't worry too much. Too many of us worry about nothing."

He's nervous all right, he was thinking. His hand wasn't damp and cold like most of them but he can't look at me.

"Excuse me," Bob Robinson said. "I'll go out and talk with Mrs. Scheller for a few minutes."

"Fine," he said, and then to Mr. Scheller: "Just stand here relaxed. I just want to turn you around a little and look you over."

He was starting the search now, the systemic review. It would not end until six days later, when he opened Mr. Scheller on the operating table, but he was looking now for every clue to that shadow in the X rays, for any indication of its spread and for any sign that might identify Mr. Scheller as an operative risk.

"You've got a pretty good build," he said, trying to relax Mr. Scheller. "You've kept yourself in pretty good shape."

"Well, I work hard," Mr. Scheller said.

Rob said he's a house painter, he was thinking, and that's why his flexors and extensors in his right forearm are more developed than in the left. That goes for his biceps and triceps and for the whole shoulder girdle on the right side, too.

"What business are you in?" he said.

He was feeling the trapezius, the shrugging muscle in the shoulder. He was searching for any metastasis, or spread, of a cancer to the spinal accessory nerve. The spinal accessory, or eleventh cranial, nerve is affixed to, and motivates, the trapezius muscle, and when the nerve is affected the muscle atrophies. Now the trapezius, on the right side as well as the left, felt solid but still supple under his fingers.

"I'm a painter," Mr. Scheller was saying.

He is perspiring at that, he was thinking, but more on that left side than the right. He's actually sweating plenty under the left arm but not much under the right and I'll bet the sympathetic nerve chain on the right is invaded by cancer. That's why his right palm was dry when we shook hands before, and if that's it, if the cancer is not only in the lung but has spread up there far enough to knock out his sympathetic nerve chain there isn't anything I can do to help this poor man.

"So you're a painter?" he said, feeling now for verification in the lymph nodes over the sympathetic chain low on the right side of Mr. Scheller's neck. "How long have you been in the business?"

When he was a younger surgeon, and before the neurosurgeons took over the management of high blood pressure, he occasionally operated for it. When portions of the sympathetic nervous system are removed the blood vessels open and reduce the pressure and it so happened that a couple of his patients were salesmen who were delighted with the unexpected bonus. They had been embarrassed, and had felt handicapped, by their cold-clammy handshakes when they met customers and now, although they overperspired on the left side, their right hands were dry.

"In the painting business?" Mr. Scheller said now. "Too many years. Since I'm eighteen."

On the basis of this experience he had once won a bottle of brandy from another young surgeon named Pete Vilella at the state tuberculosis sanitarium. The patient's X rays had shown a shadow high in the apex of the right lung and, because the sputum studies had been negative for tuberculosis and there was no significant pain, Vilella had diagnosed it as an old, healed TB scar, while he had held out for cancer.

"You know what you're doing, don't you?" Vilella had said, while they were scrubbing in for the operation. "You're operating for an old, healed TB scar."

"I'll make you a bet," he had said.

"Okay," Vilella had said. "A bottle of Martell."

"That's a bet," he had said.

He had not told Vilella that, two days before, he had sat the patient down in a warm room and had played an infra-red lamp on his face. After fifteen minutes, when the patient was sweating only on the left side of his face and not on the right, he had known for sure that it was cancer that had invaded the right sympathetic nerve chain. He didn't tell Vilella, in fact, until after they had opened the patient and found the cancer, and Vilella had delivered the Martell and they were having a drink together. Considering how he had been trapped, Vilella had taken it quite well.

"How did you get to be a painter?" he said to Mr. Scheller now. He had instinctively, as he felt for the nodes, let his gaze over Mr. Scheller's shoulder drift to infinity so that he would not be distracted by visual impulses and could better concentrate with his fingers, and yet he was unable, probing, to feel them, cancerous and hard and like peanuts under the skin.

"My father was a painter," Mr. Scheller said. "I learned it from him."

"Good," he said. "Will you just turn and look toward that light over there?"

The pupil in the right eye is smaller than the left, he was thinking now, so it's got to be the sympathetic chain. It's strange that I couldn't feel those nodes.

"Then I guess you really know the painting business," he said.

"I know the business all right," Mr. Scheller said.

"I just want to take a closer look at you here now," he said.

He was examining the skin on the neck just above the right collar bone now, and he saw it. It was an old, small, hairline scar, not more than a half-inch in length and hidden right in a natural skin fold.

"You've got a little scar in your neck," he said, thinking: So that's it; so a stabbing knocked out that chain and the nodes are clean. "Where did you get that?"

"Oh, that?" Mr. Scheller said. "I got that when I was a kid."

"How?"

"Oh, you know. Fooling around. I was fooling around with a pen knife with another kid and I fell on it. A doctor sewed it up in his office."

He's luckier than he knows, he was thinking. He hasn't any idea how lucky he is.

"But surely you must have noticed that you don't perspire on the right side, under the arm and in the hand, like you do on the left."

"That's right," Mr. Scheller said, "but I don't even think of it. I mean, that must have been forty years ago, and I don't ever think of it any more."

"Good. We get accustomed to little things like that."

He was moving his left hand, flat, over Mr. Scheller's left chest, tapping the middle phalanx between the first two joints of his middle finger with the tip of the middle finger of his right hand. When, in medical school, he had first learned to percuss, to distinguish the different shadings of sound, he used to lie in bed at night and tap out the borders of his own heart.

"I never even think of it," Mr. Scheller said.

When he worked under Pete Church they used to percuss a patient before they looked at the X rays. Then they would compare their separate findings and their diagnoses before they checked them against the pictures for verification.

"Just take a deep breath," he said, "and then let the air out and hold it a second before breathing in again."

He was sounding out the lower border of Mr. Scheller's left lung with the lung deflated. He could hear the resonant sound as he tapped over the lung, and then the flatter, duller sound where the lung stopped opposite the ninth rib.

"Good," he said. "Now take a deep breath again, but this time don't let it out. Just hold it a few seconds."

He was testing the respiratory capacity of Mr. Scheller's left lung, the lung on which Mr. Scheller would have to survive if he had to remove the right. As he sounded now, moving his left hand down and tapping, he could hear the resonance down to the eleventh rib, and so he knew the expansion of two intercostal spaces was adequate.

"Good," he said. "Now you can breathe normally again. All right? Now take a deep breath again, and hold it just once more."

He had moved to the right side. He was sounding out the level of the diaphragm below Mr. Scheller's right lung.

"You can breathe out again now," he said, thinking: It's involving his phrenic nerve, though. The right diaphragm is normally a little higher than the left but this one is two inter-spaces too high and doesn't move like the left and it's his phrenic nerve.

He put on his stethoscope and he started to move the bell of it over Mr. Scheller's left back and then left chest. The heart rhythm was good and the left lung was clear, but he wanted to re-establish in his ears and his mind the sounds of normality as, away back in medical school, they had stethoscoped themselves and one another on and off for days, learning the normal sounds before they went into the wards.

"All right," he said. "Now put your right arm up over your head, like you're painting a ceiling."

"I've painted many a ceiling," Mr. Scheller said, putting his arm up.

"That's why you've got good muscles in the arm and up here in the shoulder."

He listened, the bell of the stethoscope at the axilla, or armpit, and then he told Mr. Scheller to put his arm down. At the back he placed the bell over the right shoulder blade, to listen to the right upper lobe of the lung, then down between the shoulder blades. He listened over the auscultatory triangle, formed where the muscles, the trapezius and the latissimus dorsi, meet in back of the apex of the lower lobe. Then he moved around to the front and placed the bell over the pectoral muscle, at the level of the second rib and again opposite the upper lobe.

He's got it all right, he was thinking. There's no doubt about it and those X rays, fuzzy as they are, aren't lying and it's in the upper lobe. He's got it and we'll be taking that lobe and probably the whole lung if it hasn't gone too far already.

"Do you like to paint ceilings?" he said. "I've often thought that would be the toughest part of the job."

He had heard it clearly. A healthy lung gives out the sound of leaves rustling in a tree. The bronchial breath sounds in Mr. Scheller's right lung were like those of a door squeaking or of a broken reed on a saxophone.

"Oh, I don't know," Mr. Scheller said. "Ceilings have to be done, so you get used to it."

"But you'd rather paint walls?" he said, trying again to relax him.

"It doesn't much matter," Mr. Scheller said. "I've got a painter works for me who'd rather do ceilings."

"He sounds like a good man to have around," he said. "Will you step up on that little platform there and sit down on the table again?"

"I don't know," Mr. Scheller said, getting up on the table. "I'd like to be able to do just ceilings, if I had to, for a few more years."

"Why not?" he said. "You're not an old man. You'll do a lot of ceilings yet."

"I don't know," Mr. Scheller said.

"As a matter of fact," he said, "I was thinking, while I was listening to your chest, that in a year or two we've got to have some more painting done around here. I was thinking that you might be interested in doing the job."

It was a variation of an old device that he had used many times. When they are frightened, afraid that they are incurably ill and may not have long to live, you try to project them into the next day, the next week, or the next year.

"Believe me," Mr. Scheller said, "I'll be glad to do it, if I'm still around."

"Are you planning on moving away?"

"No," Mr. Scheller said. "It's not that."

"Look," he said, looking right at Mr. Scheller. "Are you scared?"

"Well, I'm a little nervous."

"Why? What do you think your trouble is?"

"I don't know."

"Then why are you so worried?"

"Well, I've never been in a hospital in my life. I've never had anything wrong with my chest. I never had pneumonia. I never even had a cough before."

"I want to tell you something," he said, still looking right at him. "If there's any worrying to be done you should let me do it. You know I'm an expert at my business."

"I know that."

"So you don't think for a minute that I'd have anything to do with you if I didn't think I could help you. Do you?"

"I guess not," Mr. Scheller said, looking at the floor.

"Of course not. You have to remember that I'm pretty well thought of, and I have a reputation to consider. Just to protect my reputation I have to get you well."

"I understand."

It is something you have to do with so many of them, he had often thought. Although most of them never even mention it, they come in with a pretty good idea of their trouble and they're scared. All that publicity on cancer gets some of them in earlier than they would come in otherwise, but it also scares them and you have to get them away from themselves. You have to get them believing in you, so that they don't quit on you when you need them.

"How's your appetite?" he said, although he knew Bob Robinson had been through this. He was examining Mr. Scheller's scalp, finding that the hair, although thinning, was not dry and stiff as is often true in cases of vitamin deficiency.

"I eat pretty good," Mr. Scheller said.

Rob said his wife reported a decrease in appetite, he was thinking. His skin color isn't too good, but part of that is due to his nervousness.

"How's your digestion? Your bowels?"

"All right."

"Do you have much gas?"

"Nope."

"How about heartburn?"

"Nope."

"Do you get up at night?"

"Sometimes. Not always."

"Do you feel a burning sensation when you urinate?"

"Nope."

"What color is the urine, yellow or white?"

"Yellow usually. Isn't that all right?"

"That's good. Do you have any headaches?"

"Nope."

"You don't wear glasses?"

"Just when I read or watch television."

"You haven't had to have your glasses changed lately?"

"About a year ago I did."

"And you still see all right with them?"

"That's right."

"How's your hearing?"

"It's all right."

"Your wife doesn't complain that you're turning up the television set too loud?"

"No. She likes it louder than I do."

"I just want to look in your ears," he said.

He turned Mr. Scheller's head with his left hand and, with his right, he lighted the otoscope and shone the light from the black plastic right-angle nozzle into first one ear and then the other. Peering through the small magnifying lens he saw that there was no perforation on the drum and no drainage and that the waxing was no more than normal. The drum was flat and not convex as it would be if there were pressure in the middle ear.

"Good," he said. "Now I want to look down your throat. Will you stick out your tongue?"

He watched the tongue, normally moist, come out evenly. When it comes out to one side or the other it is a sign that the hypoglossal, or twelfth cranial, nerve is affected, and he held it down now with the wooden depressor.

He says he's never been in a hospital, he was thinking, shining the flashlight into the mouth and then down into the throat. He's still got his tonsils but there's no inflammation except for some irritation of the pharynx and that's probably from too much smoking. His teeth are good, just one gold inlay and a few silver fillings, and this is one of those cases where, ironically, good oral hygiene may have delayed the detection of his disease.

Pain is usually such a late sign of cancer, he had often thought, that a foul mouth, infected with bacteria, may actually have a salutary value. The spirochetes, aspirated into the lung, may cause an infection, such as pneumonitis. The patient coughs and produces sputum and goes to his doctor. The X rays show the pneumonia patch, but if he also happens to have cancer it reveals that, too, and he can thank his foul mouth for an early detection.

"All right," he said, withdrawing the wooden depressor and snapping off the flashlight. "How's your sense of smell?"

He was starting, with the olfactory, or first cranial, nerve, to check out the rest of them, looking for any possible invasion of them by the spread of cancer. In medical school they had used one of the few socially acceptable mnemonics to memorize them—"On Old Olympus' Towering Tops, A Finn and German Viewed Some Hops"—but he had long ago forgotten it. He had also forgotten the one, concerned with Oscar's love life, that they had used for the eight branches of the external carotid artery, and another, involving one of Tillie's undergarments, that was the key to the eight carpal, or wrist, bones.

"My sense of smell?" Mr. Scheller said. "I guess it's all right."

I'll bet he can't smell turpentine, he was thinking, any more than I can smell ether after all these years, but I'll bet he says he can.

"You can smell turpentine, can you?"

"Not that so much," Mr. Scheller said. "I've been working with it so much all my life that I don't notice it much any more. Besides, we don't use it like we used to."

That was honest enough, he thought. Maybe he's relaxing a little.

"How about when you come into the house and your wife's cooking dinner? Can you detect that?"

"Sure. Especially if we've got something like pot roast."

Good, he thought. He's not faking that and his olfactory nerve is all right.

"Your wife cooks it with a little vinegar?"

"That's right. How do you know that, Doctor?"

"I enjoy German cooking myself. Now I just want to take a look at your front teeth. Just show them to me, as if you were smiling for a photographer."

He was no longer interested in Mr. Scheller's teeth but he was still looking for any possible metastasis, or spread, of the cancer to the brain. One of the evidences of it is a drooping eyelid and another is in the way a patient smiles or frowns, but Mr. Scheller had done neither. Now, as his face pulled back symmetrically as he bared his front teeth, it was apparent that the facial, or seventh cranial, nerve was intact.

"You've got good teeth," he said.

"They never give me much trouble," Mr. Scheller said.

"Now just follow my hand, will you?"

He was standing about two feet from Mr. Scheller, and he moved his hand slowly back and forth. Seeing that Mr. Scheller's eyes tracked evenly, he knew that, in all probability, the oculomotor, the trochlear, and the abducent, or third, fourth, and sixth cranial, nerves were unimpaired.

"Fine," he said. "Now I just want to take a closer look at your eyes. Just hold your head back slightly, so you can look right at me."

With the ophthalmoscope, and squinting through the lens hole, he looked into the retina of each eye. He saw that there was no edema, or swelling, at the head of the optic, or second cranial, nerve, and he could see that the dimple at the end had not filled and that the small arteries and veins, pulsating normally, were not obscured.

"Good," he said. "Your eyes look all right."

"They don't give me any trouble," Mr. Scheller said.

"Tell me this," he said, wanting to check out the vagus, or tenth cranial, nerve. "Do you experience any thickness in your voice, any hoarseness?"

"No," Mr. Scheller said. "I don't think so."

"How about when you stay up too late and maybe drink too much and smoke too much?"

"I know what you mean," Mr. Scheller said. "Occasionally I'll be a little husky the next day, but I don't do that very often."

Well, he's honest about that, he thought, but hoarseness, come to think of it, probably wouldn't have any bearing on his case anyway. On the right side, where his tumor is, the branch of the vagus nerve to the vocal cord barely reaches the chest and isn't near the tumor site on his X ray.

"How about your face and your scalp?" he said, thinking of the trigeminal, or fifth cranial, nerve. "Do you ever get any sensations of pain in the face or up here in your scalp?"

"Nope. Never that I've noticed."

"Have you noticed any swelling in your neck? I mean, have your shirt collars been getting tight?"

"Nope," Mr. Scheller said. "There's no swelling there that I know of."

As a matter of fact, he thought, his shirt collars are probably a little loose on him. Rob said he's lost about ten pounds, but he is not mentioning that.

"How about your hands?" he said, taking Mr. Scheller's right hand and examining the joints. "Have you had any bursitis or arthritis or any pains there?"

"No. My hands are all right."

"How about your legs? Any stiffness in the joints?"

"None. I work on my feet, so my legs are in pretty good shape."

"Do your feet get cold, say at night when you're in bed?"

"Nope."

Now for the pain symptom, he was thinking. If I'm right about the phrenic nerve being involved, and if I can get him to confess he'll admit it's up there high in the right shoulder. One of the roots of origin of the phrenic nerve is the fifth cervical nerve in the neck and it has a sensory branch in the shoulder, and I'd like to get the truth out of him on this.

"Now tell me about any pain you've been having," he said. "Tell me where it is, and describe it to me."

"Well, I haven't really had any pain, to speak of," Mr. Scheller said. "I don't feel anything now and I've felt pretty good for the last couple of days."

"But what was it that got you to go to your doctor who had your X rays taken and sent to me?"

"Well, early last summer I got a kind of a cold in my chest. That was the beginning of it."

"Do you usually get colds in the summer?"

"No. That was the first one I ever had in the summer."

"Were you sneezing with it?"

"No. Maybe it was just a cigarette cough."

"How much do you smoke?"

"Oh, I don't know. Maybe a pack and a half a day."

"How long have you been smoking?"

"Oh, more than thirty years, I guess. Since I was about nineteen. Maybe thirty-five years."

"Have you ever thought of cutting down on the cigarettes?"

"Once in a while. Sometimes I try to cut down for a while, but I've been smoking so many years it's hard."

"When you had that difficulty last summer did you spit up any phlegm?"

"Some."

"Was it white or greenish-yellow and kind of thick?"

"Kind of thick, and like you say."

"Did you detect any blood in it?"

"A little, but then I didn't see any more so I figured it was maybe just from the cigarettes."

"And then, a couple of months ago, you began to get some blood again?"

"That's right. I figured maybe I tore something in there, coughing, but my wife wanted me to go to our doctor, so I went and he had some X rays taken."

"And then, about a week later, you began to have some pain and more blood, and last week you went back?"

"That's right. Like my wife and I told Dr. Robinson."

So now he admits to pain, he was thinking. It's a shame to trap them like this, but their fear turns them into children and you have to do it.

"Do you notice any shortness of breath?" he said, diverting him but preparing to lead him around to it again.

"A little, maybe, but I'm not as young as I used to be."

"You probably notice it when you're climbing stairs, especially if you're carrying some of your equipment."

"That's right. I get a little winded."

"Oh, I forgot to ask you," he said. "Is the pain worse during the day or in bed at night?"

"At night," Mr. Scheller said.

He had known that, if he could get him to admit it, he would say that. During the day the field of consciousness in the brain is assaulted by sight, taste, smell, and touch, but in the quiet darkness of the sleep hours the pain sensation is without competition and dominates.

"When you feel it at night," he said, "is it down here?"

He was diverting him again. He had placed his hand low, on the ribs on the left side.

"No," Mr. Scheller said. "I don't feel anything there."

"How about higher up? How about here?"

"Nope."

"How about over here?" he said, placing his hand low on the right side.

"Nope."

"Up here a little higher?"

"Nope."

"You do a lot of work with your right arm," he said, putting his hand up on the right shoulder. "What you probably feel is a pain up here."

"That's right," Mr. Scheller said. "That's where I feel it."

"Is it a sharp, pulsating pain," he said, knowing that it would not be, "or is it one of those slow, steady aches we get once in a while as we get older?"

"That's it," he heard Mr. Scheller, walking into the trap, say. "It's a kind of steady ache. I put heat on it and rubbed some stuff in, but it doesn't help much."

"All right," he said. "I haven't got any more questions, so you can get dressed now."

"What do you think, Doctor?" Mr. Scheller said. "I mean, what are you going to do?"

I'll wait until he's dressed and we're with his wife, he was thinking.

"Well, we know we're going to help you," he said. "You remember I have to cure that cough and that pain just to protect my own reputation. Right?"

"I guess so," Mr. Scheller said, starting to dress.

"Tell me something," he said. "If you paint an office like this, where we've got patients in here every afternoon, can you work weekends?"

"Oh yes," Mr. Scheller said. "That's when we have to work in business places and offices like this."

He kept Mr. Scheller talking about the painting while Mr. Scheller dressed and he mentioned again that he wouldn't want it done for a year or two. Then they went out and he met Mrs. Scheller in Bob Robinson's office and they sat down.

"Are you really worried about this husband of yours?" he said to Mrs. Scheller, trying to ease their nervousness first.

"I am, Doctor," she said, looking at her husband, "and he is, too."

"But that's just jumping at conclusions," he said. "Why should you be so worried?"

"I don't know," she said, still looking at her husband. "Next month we'll be married thirty years."

"Well, congratulations," he said. "You're going to have a fine anniversary."

"I don't know, Doctor," Mrs. Scheller said. "What do you think his trouble is?"

"What did your family doctor tell you when he sent you here?"

"Not very much. He just said he wanted you to look at the X rays and make your own examination."

Here we go, he thought. I've got to tell them and this is the moment.

"Well," he said, turning to Mr. Scheller, "you've got something in your right lung, and we've got to take a look at it and get it out of there."

"Oh, no," Mr. Scheller said, shaking his head. "I don't want any operation."

"Are you sure, Doctor?" Mrs. Scheller said, looking at him.

"Yes," he said, "but there's no reason to be so upset."

"I was afraid of this when I came here," Mr. Scheller said.

"Please just listen to the doctor," his wife said.

"I feel pretty good," Mr. Scheller said. "I've never been in any hospital and I don't want to go in any now."

"He tells you he feels pretty good, Doctor," his wife said, "but he's awake every night with the pain now. He doesn't tell you that."

"Yes, he said he has some pain."

"More than he says," she said. "He doesn't think I know it, but I hear him get up and walk around the house and cough."

"You make it sound worse than it is," Mr. Scheller said.

"I don't," she said, and the tears were starting to come into her eyes. "Believe me, Doctor, I don't."

"I know you don't," he said, "and I want you both to listen to me. There's something in that lung that absolutely has to come out, but there's no cause for all this worry. I do operations like this every day in the week. I've done thousands of them."

"I know," Mrs. Scheller said, looking over at Bob Robinson, sitting behind his desk. "Dr. Robinson told me."

"Then why are you both so upset?"

"Well, I'm not used to being sick," Mr. Scheller said.

"We all have to get used to it as we get older," he said.

"But when would he have to go into the hospital?" Mrs. Scheller said.

"Today's Thursday, so he should go in next Monday. Miss McKeen can call and find out if they can take him then."

"Next Monday?" Mr. Scheller said. "So soon?"

"Waiting isn't going to help you," he said. "The sooner you go in the sooner we'll have you out and you'll be back to work."

"You're finishing a job this week," his wife said. "You could go in Monday."

"How long will I have to be in there?"

"Oh, a couple of weeks. Then, when you get home, you'll have to take it easy for a couple of weeks more."

"I'll lose an awful lot of time."

"Harry can look after things," his wife said. "For heaven's sake, he's old enough now."

"They have a son," Bob Robinson said. "He's in business with Mr. Scheller."

"Oh?" he said. "Then you haven't got any worries there and you've both got to stop being so worried about this, too. We'll stop at Miss McKeen's desk on the way out, and she'll check with the hospital right now. All right?"

"I guess it's the right thing to do," Mrs. Scheller said, looking at her husband.

"It's the only thing to do."

He waited while they shook hands with Bob Robinson and then he walked them out to Carrie McKeen's desk. He shook hands with them there, and when he walked back into his office Bob Robinson was sitting there looking at the X rays still on the lighted panel.

"Well, what do you think now?" Rob said.

"He's got a cancer all right."

"I presumed so."

"When I put the stethoscope on him I could hear the wind whistling right by that lesion."

"You know what this is like?" Rob said.

"Like?"

"I've been thinking lately," Rob said. "You know, when you have to tell them they've got cancer it's like you've got a loaded forty-five right in your hand."

"I know what you mean," he said, "but we don't have to tell this one for a while."

"Sure," Rob said, "but whether they admit it or not, they've got a pretty strong suspicion of what's wrong when they come in here. Once they eventually learn it was a cancer, you realize that from the moment you told them they had to submit to an operation their lives would never quite be the same again. Even when we cure them it still hangs over them. It's like a forty-five."

"That's true."

"Anyway," Rob said, "what kind of shape is he in otherwise?"

"Fortunately, not bad. As I guess you got in his history, he has no unusual headaches, his vision hasn't changed, and he has no significant pains in his joints. His kidneys and digestive habits are standard and there's no evidence of any metastasis to any of the areas of the brain from which the cranial nerves originate."

"It hasn't spread much then?"

"Well, it's probably spread into the mediastinum," he said, meaning the space between the lungs and containing the heart and the major blood vessels. "There's no swelling of his neck veins, but it's involving his phrenic nerve, because his right diaphragm is a couple of spaces too high, and I got him to confess to the pain high in the right shoulder."

"How come it doesn't show on these pictures?"

"They're poor, and if he didn't breath in hard enough it might not be obvious."

"Do you think we've got another Brazilian lawyer here?" Rob said then. He had got up and had walked over to the X rays and he was pointing to the shadow at the inner edge of the upper lobe of the right lung, just above the root. "Do you think he's another Roberto Leon?"

"We can't tell from those," he said. "He may be."

"I've been thinking of that little Brazilian lawyer for a year now," Rob said.

"I have, too," he said, "but it's more than a year. It's about eighteen months."

"It's a funny thing," Rob said. "I wouldn't want to wish it on a dog, but I'd like to see us do another one some time."

"We've got four live dogs in the lab to prove we can do it," he said.

"Mr. Scheller may be the one at that," Rob said.

"We'll know on Wednesday," he said.

Mr. Scheller may indeed be the one, he had thought, driving home that night. His symptoms indicate it's even more advanced than that Roberto Leon's and, as Rob says, we've been waiting for another one to invade the superior vena cava and Mr. Scheller can be the one. If he is we can do it. I know we can do it and, as Rob says again, I'd like to bring it off some time and this could be the one.

"I'm glad to meet you, too," Mr. Scheller's son was saying now, standing beside his mother in the lounge. "We just wanted to wish you luck, Doctor."

"I thank you," he said, "but I don't want you and your mother to worry now. Your father's going to be all right."

"I certainly hope so," Mrs. Scheller said, shaking her head and trying to hold back the tears.

"Now look," he said. "As I've told you, I've done thousands of chest operations and I'm going to take the best of care of Mr. Scheller."

"I know you will, Doctor," the son said.

"I'm sorry that we've been delayed," he said, "and you two don't have to stay here. You can go home and come back in about four hours. If you're not here when we've finished either Dr. Robinson or I will call you to give you the report, and perhaps you can see Mr. Scheller this evening."

"I certainly hope so," Mrs. Scheller said, still shaking her head and blinking back the tears.

"Now please," he said. "You must believe in me."

"I do, Doctor," she said, nodding and shaking his hand. "I'll try not to worry so much."

"And you too," he said, shaking hands with the son. "You take care of your mother. I'll take good care of your father."

"I know you will," the son said, "and good luck again."

"Fine," he said.

I hope I don't have to count on my luck, he was thinking, walking away, but I know what they mean when they always wish you luck. You count on your skill and it's only when you come up short on skill that you need your luck. If we've got another Roberto Leon here I know I've got the skill now and I won't need that luck we could have used then but didn't get. That was one day when we certainly didn't pull any luck.

XVII

"What time is it?" he had said that evening, walking down the hall from the operating room.

"7:45," Bob Robinson said.

He had worked it out, then, the simple mathematics of it. At 1:00 they had opened Roberto Leon and at 7:30 they had lost him.

"I'm bushed," Bob Robinson said. "You know that was six and a half hours?"

"I know," he said. "I'm tired, too."

They both knew, without saying it or without it even becoming a conscious thought, that it was not the hours alone but the empty frustration of failure that was the catalyst of their fatigue. Often, after an emergency, he had walked out of the operating room at 3 or 4 o'clock in the morning so exhilarated that he knew he would be unable to sleep and wishing that his regular operating schedule for the day could begin then and not five or six hours later.

"I'll phone it in," Bob Robinson said. "I just want to get out of this suit."

"No," he said. "I'll phone this one in myself."

"Whatever you say," Rob said.

"I'll see you back at the office."

"Don't you want to eat?"

"Maybe later," he said.

He went into the booth next to the nurses' station and closed the door. He sat down and picked up the phone and heard the dial tone. When he dialed 7 the tone altered to a higher pitch and when he dialed 1 the tone ceased and he knew that the recorder in the booth in the office downstairs was turning and that he had five seconds in which to begin talking.

"Patient's name," he said. "Leon. L-e-o-n. First name, Roberto. Date, May 11, 1960."

Exactly one week before, Roberto Leon had walked into the office for the first and, as it was to turn out, the only time. He had flown up from São Paulo alone, bringing with him, in their large brown envelope, his X rays. He was forty-six years old, five feet five inches, swarthy, dark-haired and dark-eyed, and he spoke excellent English, with only that typical rising inflection at the end of his sentences. The shadow in his right lung had been picked up three weeks before in a routine examination by his doctor in Brazil, and his only symptoms were an unproductive cough and some pain in his right shoulder.

"You think it is cancer, Doctor?" he had said at the end of the examination.

"I can't be sure at this point."

"As I told you, I am a heavy smoker."

"If you're convinced of the correlation between smoking and lung cancer, why don't you give up cigarettes?"

"That's what you call the calculated risk," Roberto Leon said. "I work hard at my profession and I enjoy smoking. I am not concerned with just life alone but with living. Smoking a lot and drinking perhaps a little more than I should are among the pleasures of living for me. Can you understand that?"

"I understand perfectly."

"I think too many people deprive themselves of living just to live," Roberto Leon said. "Then you will have to operate?"

"Yes. I have to get in there to see what this is."

"Then you have to operate. When can you do this?"

"I can do it as soon as we can get you a room at the hospital. Can you go in within the week?"

"Yes. I have several days' business with an associate here for whom I do work in South America, but after that I am ready."

"You told me that you're married. Did your wife come up from South America with you?"

"No, because she does not care for airplane travel, but she understood that I might have to have an operation."

"And a major operation?"

"Oh, yes. You were highly recommended to me in São Paulo, and I am aware of your reputation and I have confidence in you."

"That's good to know."

"Oh, yes. They have explained to me, because I asked, that if it is cancer you may have to take out my lung."

"That's correct, but we don't know that yet."

"If you have to take out the lung," Roberto Leon said, "you have to take out the lung. I have confidence."

"Good," he said. "I have confidence, too."

Not many of them make it as easy for you as that, he had thought after Roberto Leon had left, and I like this little guy. He's the manic type and decisions come easy for him and if he were not a good lawyer and had the skill in his hands and the liking for it he would have made a good surgeon. All the best ones among us are that same type.

When he opened Roberto Leon he found that the cancer had spread from the lung to the pericardium, the covering over the heart, and to the superior vena cava, the large vein that drains the blood from the upper half of the body to the right atrium, or chamber, of the heart. It covered the lateral and anterior, or side and front, walls of the superior vena cava over a longitudinal area of about two and a half centimeters, or almost an inch, and so he knew that he could not simply remove the infected section and sew the two severed ends back together because the tension would be so great that the sutures would tear out.

It was a problem he saw about once every two years and it had been baffling him as it had the rest of the profession which had been talking about it for twenty years. To leave the cancer there would mean death for Roberto Leon within six weeks or two months. Those surgeons who had tried plastic grafts or bypasses had found that, because the body tends to reject a foreign graft and because the blood flows so slowly in the vena cava, as in any vein, the blood had clotted and the patients had died within three days.

"What do you think?" he said to Bob Robinson.

"I think he's got just one chance, Matt."

"You're right," he said, "so we have to give it to him."

They had been working on an experimental procedure on and off for several months. One evening after they had closed another patient, forced again to leave the cancer-invaded superior vena cava, it had come to him suddenly and he never knew why or from where, that, although foreign grafts had failed, a graft made from the patient's own right pulmonary artery might be completely compatible.

"After all," he said to Bob Robinson the next day, "when we take the right lung we're also taking the right pulmonary artery."

"You know something, Matt?" Rob said. "You might just have it."

"It's worth a few hours in the dog lab, isn't it?"

"I'll say," Rob said.

The next Saturday morning they tried it for the first time in the old red brick wing that had been the original hospital building, with the animal smell hovering there and with the intermittent chorus of barking coming through the two doors between them and the kennels. In a human being the superior vena cava and the right pulmonary artery are, in diameter, about the size of a man's thumb. In the animal that they used, the two vessels were about as big around as a lead pencil, and when they had removed the right lung and its artery he fitted the section of the artery to be grafted over a three-inch length of polyethylene tubing at the ends of which he had flared a collar or flange with the heat from a match flame. His plan was to clamp off the superior vena cava to stop the flow of blood, remove a section, insert the tubing, and snare it at both flared ends. Then he would release the clamps, which would permit the resumption of the flow of blood through the tubing and prevent damage to the brain. He would suture the ends of the artery to the ends of the vena cava, but just before he put in the final sutures, he would clamp the vena cava again, remove the tubing, finish the graft, and release the clamps.

It failed. It failed because, when he severed the vena cava, the ends retracted and the vessel collapsed and, before he could bring the ends close enough to place the tubing, snare it, and remove the clamps, the damage had been done to the brain. While the carotid artery had continued to pump blood into the brain the clamps had prevented it from draining out.

"But there's got to be a way, Matt," Bob Robinson said. "It's just a matter of procedure."

"I know," he said. "We've got five minutes, at the most, while that clamp is on. I should have left a floor in the vena cava."

What he meant was that, instead of cutting through the vena cava, he should have made two cuts, one at either end of the section to be removed, but that each cut should have been only about two thirds of the way around the vessel. The wall that remained would prevent the retraction and provide a floor on which he could slide the tubing into place.

"That'll work," Bob Robinson said. "We've done that with the aorta."

"I know," he said. "Tell me why I didn't try it here."

The following week they tried it and it worked. About a month later they were successful with another dog, and so they had two living animals to prove they could do it when he decided, because he had no other choice, to attempt it on Roberto Leon.

What happened then he would never forget. He had placed the tubing with its sleeve of artery around it and he had snared it at both ends. He had removed the section of vena cava containing the cancer and, with the tube in place and the blood draining again, he was sewing the bottom of the arterial section to the lower portion of the vena cava when he saw the blood and heard Bob Robinson.

"Christ, Matt!" Rob said. "The tube's popped out!"

"Clamp him," he said.

The tube had slipped its snare at the upper end. With the vena cava clamped again he knew how much time he had, but trying to bring down the retracted and collapsed end of the vena cava and trying to get it back over the end of the tube was like attempting to fit the taut neck of a toy balloon over something larger than itself.

"His pressure's dropped, Doctor," the anesthetist was saying. "It's down to 60 now and his pulse is extremely weak."

"All right," he said. "I'm having trouble but I'll get it."

"I'm sorry, Doctor," she was saying, "but his face is puffy and his eyes are bloodshot. His color is terrible. He's as blue as ink."

"I'll have this in a moment," he said, keeping his voice even and trying to assure her and the rest of them. "I'm getting it now."

He got it, but not in time. He got the tube back in and completed the graft, but the blood pressure never responded. When it became imperceptible they tried, for an hour, intermittent manual massage of the heart and then ten grams of calcium through the intravenous tube and then an injection of one c.c. of 1:10,000 dilution of adrenalin right into the heart.

"I'm sorry," he said, finally, suddenly feeling his own emptiness and then aware that the whole room had gone flat around him. "He's gone. What's the time?"

"It's 7:30," Bob Robinson said. "I'm sorry, too, Matt."

That was all they said. It took them about fifteen minutes to close the chest and sew back the skin. Out of habit, because it is the right way to close a chest, and out of respect for the body, they used the same interrupted-silk technique they would have used if they had been successful and Roberto Leon still lived. Then they were walking down the hall and he again asked the time and then went into the booth to start dictating the report.

Twelve paragraphs and as many minutes later, his sweat drying on him now and conscious of the chill, he was at the end. When he paused then, silent for more than those five seconds at which the timing mechanism of the recorder is set, he heard the shrill whistle in the receiver.

"At 7:30 P.M.," he said, and the high-pitched whine stopped, "six and one-half hours after the beginning of the operation, the patient was pronounced dead. The chest was closed in layers with interrupted-silk technique. Dictated by Matthew Carter, M.D."

So that's that, he was thinking, walking to the locker room, and when I get back to the office I've got to call that associate of little Mr. Leon. I've got to call and tell him and find out if he'll call the wife in Brazil or whether I should. I don't even know whether the woman speaks English and my poor bastardized Spanish won't stand up to that. They speak Portuguese down there anyway, although, if she's like her husband, she probably speaks Spanish and maybe even English, too. If she doesn't speak English he'll have to do it.

Rob put that snare in, he was thinking, but I don't think it was the snare. After the tube slipped and I had to take that snare off, it seemed tight enough, and if it wasn't the snare it had to be the flare on the tube itself. We did those three dogs the same way but, for some reason, the flare on that tubing just wasn't big enough, and that has to be it.

His own office was dark but there was a light in Bob Robinson's. Bob Robinson was sitting at his desk, looking through his mail, and sipping at a drink. He had mixed another, and it was standing on the corner of the desk with the ice and the twist of lemon in it.

"You know, Matt," he said, "what makes it such a damn shame is that we can do that thing."

"I know we can," he said, "but we didn't."

"I've been sitting here thinking about that snare," Rob said.

"It wasn't the snare."

"I'd have sworn I had it tight enough."

"You did. It wasn't the snare."

"I took two turns around it before I tied it down."

"It wasn't the snare," he said. "I could tell it was tight enough when I took it off. It had to be the flare on the tubing."

"But why?" Rob said. "It looked all right to me."

"It looked all right to me, too, but obviously it wasn't flared enough and my technique wasn't smooth enough, either. If I'd been smoother putting those sutures in below it never would have popped out above, even with the flare it had on it."

"I don't know," Rob said. "I'm not sure."

"You know it as well as I do."

"But let's face it, Matt," Rob said. "If we hadn't tried it he'd have been done for anyway."

Oh, come on, Rob, he thought. You're saying that I didn't kill him; that I just didn't cure him, but what difference does that make right now to little Mr. Roberto Leon, who had all that confidence in me, and to his wife down there in Brazil?

"You know what I've thought occasionally?" he said.

"What?"

"The profession to be in is civil engineering."

"Civil engineering? Why?"

"An engineer is never allowed to forget his mistakes. I envy him this, really."

"I don't get you."

"An engineer designs a lousy bridge or building and if it stands at all, it stands as a monument to his idiocy all the rest of his life and beyond."

"I'll never buy that," Rob said. "Our profession doesn't need a public audience or a public jury."

"The profession doesn't," he said, "but at a time like this I think the individual does."

"Stop berating yourself," Rob said. "If you hadn't tried that bridge, Mr. Roberto Leon would have died on that shore waiting for a boat that was never coming. You know that."

"You said that before," he said. "What are you doing Saturday?"

"Saturday?" Rob said. "Nothing. Why?"

"I want to do another dog. In fact, I want to do at least two more dogs."

"I'm all for that."

"Are you sure you're not doing anything Saturday?"

"Come to think of it," Rob said, "I am."

"What are you doing?"

"I'm assisting while you do a superior vena caval graft from a right pulmonary artery on a dog. Do you want another drink?"

"Not right now," he said. "I've got to call that lawyer."

"Who?"

"That associate of Mr. Leon."

"Do you want me to call him?"

"Of course not," he said. "Don't be so solicitous."

"Who needs a public jury?" Rob said. "Certainly not you."

So the wife must know by now, he was thinking, lying in bed four hours later. That lawyer took it all right. That lawyer, when I finally located him, was very decent about it but who knows how the wife is taking it? All that wife knows is that her husband came all the way up here alone to the great Matthew Carter and now she hears this and who knows what she thinks or how she's taking it?

Anyway, he was thinking, I've told the lawyer. I've done that and on Tuesday afternoon I'll stand up at weekly conference and I'll do that, too. That resident, that young Bauman, will present the case and then he'll pause and look at me and I'll stand up. I'll stand up in front of Ross Young and Maury Rand and Gene Parente and Stan and Sid Berkman and the Great Jaffrey and the rest of them. The Great Jaffrey is great all right. The Great Jaffrey is great at editing operations. He never says he could have done it. He just implies it, but there'll be no implications by me. There'll be none of those inferences that, after all, any operation is a team effort and that maybe the patient got light under the anesthesia and moved or that there were unexpected complications. I'll stand up there and tell them what I tried to do and why I tried it. It's true enough that he had no chance if I didn't make the try, but I'll tell them what we've done in the dog lab and what happened and when I get done it will still all come down to the same thing and I'll say that this patient died of a technical error. When I say it young Bauman will write it, T.E., write it in that big, long, cloth-bound book, and it will be there after my name.

"Matt?" his wife said, from the other bed.

"Yes?"

"Why don't you try to get some sleep?"

"I will."

"For God's sake, Matt," she said, "after all these years you know what kind of a surgeon you are."

"I know," he said. "Get some sleep yourself."

"I will," she said, "if you'll stop turning every two minutes."

"All right," he said. "Good night."

"I hope you're not asking yourself why you ever wanted to be a surgeon. You haven't done that in years."

"I'm not doing it now," he said. "Good night."

And I'm not doing it now, he was thinking. I wanted to be a hero. They were all my heroes. It was that old hero fixation that I've had all my life and I can remember when it was obstetrics. It was obstetrics because it's the beginning of life, the beginning of everything, and you think then that you'd like to be a part of it always. If there's a birth during lunch hour you're running off to watch it and you sit there at the lectures about the right oblique and the left oblique and the buttocks presentation and the internal podalic version and you can't wait to get your first one just to deliver one of your own and when you get it you're so scared that you're afraid your hands will shake and the poor woman will know it and ask you if you're really a doctor or just a medical student and then you'll have to tell her the truth.

They never ask, though, he was thinking. They never ask and I went out on that first one with that field nurse who seemed to me to be about sixty years old but she probably wasn't more than forty. We went out in her new Ford and she'd been taking medical students through it for a dozen years and she said: "Are you scared?" I was honest because I was too scared to lie and she was driving and she said: "Relax. It'll be easy. It's this woman's sixth, and remember what they say about taxicab drivers. The mortality rate is lowest in the hands of a cab driver because he doesn't know what to do and so he does nothing. Ninety-five times out of a hundred, nature takes care of it and you won't have any trouble."

That's what she said and it was out at the east end of town in one of those factory houses and it was about 7:30 in the evening in the spring of that third year and the woman was still about two hours away. The husband was down at a bar getting courage and the grandmother had taken the other kids and we sat there, that nurse and I, on the porch listening to the groans and counting the length of time between the pains. When it came, it popped its head first and there was that rotation so that the shoulders would come as they should. You get one shoulder by depressing the head and when you see part of the arm you put your forefinger under the armpit and deliver the arm. Then you raise the head, if I remember it now, until it shows you the other arm and after you get the shoulders it's easy. The hips are smaller than the shoulders and it takes only a little pressure on the abdomen to get the hips and after I'd clamped the cord and tied it off I held it that way with the ankles between the thumb and forefinger and middle finger and whacked it and when it cried I turned it up and handed it to the nurse and she took it and said: "Congratulations." Then, leaning forward with that baby, and it was a boy, between us, she kissed me and that woman lying there saw it and said: "Cut it out, you two. That's the way I got into this trouble."

For ten days I saw that woman and those were the first house calls. She never knew, none of them ever knew, the real truth, so I was a big doctor instead. I was a big doctor and a big hero all right with my how's your appetite? Your bowels? How many pads are you wearing now? Fine, and how's the baby feeding? Well, that's the main thing, that you and the baby are both fine, and I'm sure that when work picks up at the factory again your husband will cut down on the drinking and everything will work out again just fine.

So the baby was fine, he was thinking, and I can remember resolving then that I would follow that kid all his life and I don't think I've thought of it in twenty-five years and he must be twenty-six, no, twenty-seven years old now if he's still alive and I haven't even the faintest idea of his name. I don't know any of their names, any of the names of the dozen I had in the six months and the next thing was gynecology and what a hero I was going to be there, reconstructing the damage from childbirth, repairing, you might say, the woman you delivered. There was the curiosity involved there, too, the desire to see in great detail all the anatomy, the mysterious anatomy of which you've been conscious ever since you pulled on your first pair of long pants, or pulled them off, you might say, and then there was the wonder about what the effect of all this would be. The fact was that it had no effect whatsoever, that even after you've seen it all a hundred times you haven't changed a bit and any thoughts of the corrugations of the vagina or the size of the labia still never enter your mind.

Your mind, the human mind, he was thinking, and what an arena for personal heroics that was going to be. Every psychiatrist is a hero to his patients and it's great in class with everybody reading the seven volumes of Havelock Ellis when they won't read the other things and everybody looking for paranoidal tendencies in everybody else. It's completely fascinating and you can't get enough of it until they take you out to the psychiatric pavilion and without warning they walk you into the lunch room and there they are, some of them rubbing the food into their hair and some of them throwing it at one another and the keepers finally herding them out like animals.

And upstairs. And upstairs in that bathtub, in that bathtub with the canvas jacket on him with the ropes on it and the four orderlies trying to hold him was that big red-haired O'Connell. I can't remember his first name but I remember him and I remember that little blond cheer leader he was babbling about and how when he used to wrestle for us he'd just pick the other man up and throw him onto the mat. That's how big and powerful he was and he won the conference title and he may have won the nationals, too, for all I know, and nobody knew I knew him. I can see him now, right now trying to get out of that tub, red-faced and the jugulars showing in his neck and the orderlies holding him and big O'Connell babbling about that girl. I can hear the lecturer explaining when we got outside, explaining that the patient had fallen in love but that, actually, it had been nothing more than a mental romance. He had never even spoken to the girl, because he was extremely religious and they were of different beliefs and so, he was saying, what we had just witnessed was the result of his sexual desire versus his rigid religious training and what that lecturer said after that I don't remember.

I remember, though, that nobody had to write me a letter to tell me it wasn't for me. Nobody ever had to write me a letter, really, to tell me that for me it was Pete Church and Alex Johnson and even Leo Kastner, and after Pete Church took me those years went like months and I remember standing in his office that afternoon when he made that phone call. He picked up that phone and told his secretary to get Alex Johnson and when he got him he said in that quiet way of his: "Alex, I've had a young world-beater here with me now for five years. I've taught him all I know, but apparently that's not enough and now he wants to work under you."

So Pete Church gave me $25 out of his own pocket and I drove for two days and two nights to get there for that interview, driving that old black Chevy coupe and sleeping in it at the side of the road and washing and shaving in the men's rooms at the gas stations and there were twelve of us applying. Twelve of us wanted three jobs and Alex Johnson was sitting at his desk with the twelve cards in front of him and he looked up and said: "Good morning. As long as Pete Church recommends you, you can't be all bad." Then he got up and straightened a picture on the wall. He was always doing that while he was talking, straightening a picture or moving a chair or rearranging the papers on his desk into neat piles and walking with that exaggerated backward arch in his spine from the Pott's disease, the tuberculous caries of the vertebrae, from the TB he picked up as a young assistant and that hit him first in both lungs and then the spine and finally the kidneys.

When you think of it he was imprisoned in a plaster cast and lying on his back for two years and they rigged up mirrors and that typewriter from the ceiling and he wrote, like that, the first book of thoracic surgery. He reviewed, first, all the world's literature on TB and then he wrote that first book and it's still the classic text book of thoracic surgery after almost forty years.

"So you think you'd like the job?" he said on the third day. I said I certainly would and he said: "I can't pay you the first year and you'll need about $125 a month. Have you got any money?" I said: "No, but I can borrow it." "Good," he said, and then about a week later the wire came from him and I can still remember the wording. I can still see it on that yellow telegram paper and I can still remember it said:

BENEVOLENT DONOR HAS ESTABLISHED ENDOWED INSTRUCTORSHIP STOP IF YOU HAVEN'T BORROWED MONEY IT WON'T BE NECESSARY SIGNED ALEXANDER JOHNSON.

There were the three of us there with him then and one of the things he was proudest of was that he never kept any secrets from us and he always left that door open between his office and ours. When he wanted one of us he'd just call through the open door and I'll never forget when he came back from the three months in Arizona and I'd been running his service like crazy and he called me in and started walking around the room and straightening things and I couldn't tell what he was getting at when he started to talk.

"As you know," he was saying, walking and straightening, "I came here in 1922 as an assistant professor of surgery. As you also know the Board of Regents then saw fit to promote me to a professorship and each year since then they've seen fit to reappoint me. Also, over the years, we've developed the service to the point where it's well known throughout the world. Now on January first of this year I went to Arizona and I went feeling secure that everything would be under control and that I wouldn't be greatly missed. On April first I returned and I did so to discover that I had not only not been missed but also to discover that we've now got two services here. We've got the Johnson service and the Carter service, and I've called you in here now to ask you if perhaps I might be allowed to work on your service."

I just didn't know what to say. I remember I just looked at him and he said: "You've done a fine job. As a matter of fact I've come to the conclusion that in all my years you and Byron Frank are the two best I've ever trained and I thought it was time I told you."

He knew he'd had the best of it by then, too. When the tuberculosis finally hit his kidneys and one of them quit, his bladder would hold only an ounce of urine, so to finish an operation he had to have that rubber bag, that water bottle, strapped to his leg and when I went back and scrubbed with him for that last time he emptied it into the slop sink before we scrubbed.

The night before, though, at that dinner party, he was standing by the fireplace while they were all having drinks before going in to eat and he saw me come into the room. I remember him calling across the room and I didn't know how bad it was then but streptomycin was still new then and he was taking four grams a day instead of one and it had knocked out his eighth nerve and he staggered.

"Say, Matt," he said, calling across the room. "Come over here and tell me about all the money you're making." So I went over and he was leaning on the mantel over the fireplace. Then he put his arm around my shoulder and, talking to me, he walked me over to somebody else he wanted to talk to and I realized then that that was the way he got around the room. It was the way he got to the O.R., too, because when he was operating there at the end there were always a couple of nurses who waited around outside the locker room door for him to come out. When he came out they'd say: "How are you today, Doctor?" and they'd put their arms around him and, kidding with him, one on each side, that was the way they'd walk him to the O.R. Then in the O.R. they'd strap him to the side of the table and that was the great thing. He could barely walk, but strapped to that table he was as steady as he'd ever been and he was as great as he'd ever been, too.

And I remember, too, before he got that bad and I'd been away maybe five years and I couldn't wait to show him my segmental resection, my segmental resection that I'd refined and refined some more until I thought, and I still do, that I could do it better than anyone else in the world. He watched me do three and then he said: "It's no good." It was like a slap in the face and I looked at him and I said: "What do you mean, it's no good?" "Oh," he said, "it's beautiful. It's absolutely lovely, but rating it as a contribution to the whole field of thoracic surgery it's a luxury. In China they couldn't be bothered with it."

He was right. I was getting a swelled head over it and so he placed it in perspective although he knew as well as I did that it's a lovely surgical shot to have in your repertoire. It wouldn't be any good in China and it's strange that I should be thinking of this now, twice within a week, because before the insurance companies get done they'll turn it into a luxury in this country, too. He'd be amazed, Alex Johnson would be amazed, that those statisticians will end up dictating what we do. He'd be amazed that those statisticians have it all figured out that if you take a lobe of a lung it's worth so much, but that if you do a segmental resection, if you take only a segment, it's only worth half as much. So what they're penalizing you for is the precision you've perfected and before they get done posting their price tags precision surgery and perfected post-operative procedures that get the patient out of the hospital in eight days instead of two weeks will be a luxury that only the independently wealthy surgeons will be able to afford to perform.

It's true, and it's strange that it was just this week that Carrie showed me the letter and the senior statistician, or whatever he is, wrote: "In reviewing the surgical procedure performed by you, we feel that the fee for the service performed should not exceed $750." So I said to Carrie: "What did we bill him?" And she said: "We sent a bill for $1500. For John's sake, Matt, the man makes $30,000 a year and for what you did for him I've figured out that we charged him five per cent of his annual income. I'll bet you he pays three times as much for a new car." And I said: "I don't care about that. What I care about is that statisticians who are unequipped to perform, edit, or assess surgical procedures are now putting a price not only on talent but also on operative difficulties."

So Carrie said: "Don't tell me." She said: "Don't ask me to write a letter. You write it." So I sat down and I wrote it and I said: "Should the surgeon be penalized because through his skill the operative procedure took two hours instead of four? Is the surgeon to believe that his fee will be reduced because his proficiency and close post-operative supervision allows the patient to be discharged from the hospital in eight days rather than the usual two weeks? Should the surgeon be encouraged to take larger segments of lung to get a larger fee when an anatomical segmental or sub-segmental resection requires more surgical skill and post-operative attention but preserves the patient's function and allows him to return to normal pre-operative activities? Is it possible that you believe that all surgeons are of an equal skill and ability that can be regulated by a standardized fee schedule? Are you saying that I, as the leading proponent of this operative procedure and with more experience than perhaps any other surgeon in the world in this particular procedure should receive the same fee as the graduating resident?" I wrote that, and then I wrote: "In answer to your request for an adjustment, my adjusted fee is $1500. Sincerely yours."

That's what I wrote and now they can take it from there. They can take it from there, but Alex Johnson would be amazed, amazed that my segmental resection may yet be as big a luxury here as it would be in China but my letter would have pleased him. Can you imagine them putting a standard fee on a skill like Alex Johnson's? That letter would have pleased him, but the man to write the letter was Leo Kastner, except that Leo never would have been interested in a nicety like my segmental resection. Refinements never meant anything to Leo because with Leo it was all simplification, not refinement, but when somebody crossed him or even challenged him he could blast them and he would have been the one to write that letter and I would have loved to read it.

He was a genius, Leo was, or close to a genius and it would have been some letter because he would have blasted them like he did that cop that first day when we were going to lunch and there were no parking spaces and he double-parked that Cadillac he was driving and the cop came along in the patrol car. All the cops knew him and he knew all the cops and the cop said: "I'm sorry, Leo, but you'll have to move that." And Leo turned on him and said: "I'm not going to move it and if you get out of that car I'll break your goddam jaw." So the cop just pulled his head back in and drove off and we went into the restaurant and had a drink and he was telling me that three nights a week he played violin with a string trio and I reached over and took his left hand to feel the calluses on his fingers and he turned on me and he said: "You doubted it? Well, from now on remember that whenever I tell you I can do something I can do it and don't you dare doubt it."

I doubted it because he looked like a gorilla. He really did and it was a shock when you first met him because I'd been hearing those stories of how he did three majors in two hours and twelve operations in a day and I'd been saying it was impossible and I went there full of antagonism. I was late getting there and it must have been about 9 o'clock and I said to the O.R. supervisor: "Is he operating?" And she said: "Oh, a whole bunch." And I said: "What room is he in?" And she said: "Oh, he hasn't come in yet. He always starts at 10."

So I waited for him in the locker room and when he came in and we started to strip down I couldn't believe it. He had those long arms to mid-thighs and he sloped from his ears to his elbows, with a big neck and those powerful, sloping, but narrow shoulders and while I was looking him over he saw my nose and he said to me: "Do you box?" I said: "I did in college." So he said: "I wrestle. I was wrestling this morning."

He was getting out of his shorts when he said it, and when he turned to hang them in his locker I saw that hematoma on his left thigh. He was black and blue from his belt line to his knee and I said: "Did you get that wrestling or were you hit by a truck?" And he said: "No. My horse kicked me. I've got the greatest animal in the world but he's the meanest sob you ever saw and every day it's a contest between us. He kicks me and I belt him, but he's a great animal."

Then we got into our scrub suits and he reached into his locker and took out this white stocking cap with a wool ball on top that his wife knitted for him. He never operated without it but he never wore a mask and when we went into the O.R. there were seven or eight and sometimes a dozen observing him and he always had them banked up on those rolling metal stands. He kept them at a distance where they could observe but where they couldn't learn his tricks and the only reason he let me come up close was that I was from out of town and I was no competition to him.

So he did those three in the two hours before lunch. He did a cancer of the rectum and a hysterectomy and a gall bladder and then before we went to lunch he made rounds. I remember we walked in to see that one old man and it was five days after he'd removed the gall bladder and the old man was still running a high fever. So Leo said to the nurse: "What's causing this patient's temperature?" She said: "I don't know, Doctor." Then he turned to his assistant and said: "What's causing the temperature?" The assistant said: "I don't know." So he said to the nurse: "Pull down the sheet." When she did Leo made a fist and belted the old man over the liver and the old man jumped and let out a cry and Leo turned to his assistant again and said: "He's got a sub-phrenic abscess. Drain him this afternoon." Then he turned to me and said: "Let's go to lunch."

Then after he abused that cop and we had a drink and some lunch we came back and he did a stomach resection and two hernias and then two pilonidal sinuses. He did everything under spinal anesthesia and he had those big orderlies who put the patient into position and then he'd do the spinal himself. That was what got them. He was the great advocate of the spinal and it got all the anesthetists and anesthesiologists. They thought he was a wild man and they tried to destroy everything he wrote and even my own anesthetists didn't believe it so at that A.M.A. meeting in Atlantic City I got them together. I remember the first one coming up to me and saying: "I understand you know Kastner." And I said: "That's right." And he said: "A few of us want to meet that sob." So I told Leo there were three or four who wanted to meet him and when we got down to that bar in the hotel that night there were eight of them, all holding professorships, and we all sat down at two tables pushed together at the back and I introduced Leo to them and they went at him. For two hours they went at him and at no time did he fail to come up with a case to neutralize whatever they said.

I remember, too, how at the end there was a string combo playing in the room, walking from table to table, and they were over in the corner by some potted palm trees playing to a young couple. The young guy was handing out dollar bills and finally when I guess he ran out of dollar bills the combo came by our table and Leo had just finished making a point and pulled out a five-dollar bill and handed it to the one with the violin. "Here," he said. "Let me borrow that for a minute." So the violinist took one look at Leo sitting there and looking like a gorilla and he said: "You won't break it, will you?" "No," Leo said and he took the violin and stuck it under his chin and began to play.

When he did, everything in that room stopped. I remember how that room had been full of noise, how we had to raise our voices to be heard, but when Leo started to play that gypsy music that room went completely silent. Even the bartenders stopped mixing drinks and everybody in that dark, smoky, crowded room was looking at and listening to Leo and when he finished and handed the violin back I remember how that whole room broke into applause and in five minutes I'll bet we had twenty drinks on that table.

That was Leo all right and it wasn't too many years after that when that horse killed him. It was a strange thing, but not ironic really when you come to think of it, that it was that horse, that horse that he always called the greatest animal in the world because it challenged him every time he rode it. It was astounding that it was that horse that finally won in what he called that contest they had between them, astounding that that big dumb animal finally threw and killed a man who was a genius or close to it because that's what he was. That was the only way you could explain him because when you first looked at his surgery it appeared so coarse it was appalling until you realized that somehow, by eliminating all the froth and lace and by reducing all the most complicated procedures to their simplest forms he had finally simplified and simplified until he was a kind of Cézanne of his time of surgery.

That's what he was, too, really, a kind of Cézanne of surgery without one wasted motion or hurried movement and the creator of a type of painting that you can't yourself produce or really even imitate. You can't do it or even imitate it and all you can do is borrow a move from it here and there when that move fits you and you can make it your own.

But the risks. When you think of the calculated risks he had to take and the hundreds of mistakes he must have made until he got it that way, got it down to its simplest forms, and that's what it was today, really, the calculated risk. It was the calculated risk and it should have worked but it's strange and this time it's ironic, too, that that was the term that that little Roberto Leon used in the office that night when I asked him about the smoking and he said: "That's what you call the calculated risk." That's what he said, exactly what he said, so on Roberto Leon I took the calculated risk. I took it because as Rob keeps saying he had no other chance and if I had it, that carcinoma like he had it, I'd want Rob to take it on me because there's no other out and because it's got to work, got to work because it worked on those three dogs and we'll do another one on Saturday and another and another and it'll be months or even a couple of years before we see it again, probably, but we'll see it again one of these days and when we do I know it'll work because it has to work because there's no reason why it shouldn't work and that's why when we see it again it'll work because it has to work and why I know it'll work.

10:43 A.M.

XVIII

So now if they'll let me, he was thinking, hanging his smock back in his locker and closing the door, I'll do Mr. Scheller. It's true that the O.R. is the only sanctuary we have and if they had let me in there at 8 I'd be closing him by now. I'd know by now if he's a vena cava case and by now we'd have tried that graft or we wouldn't and I'd know that by now, too. If it turns out that we do try that graft, he was thinking, walking to the phone, it'll take me better than three hours and Carrie will have to tell them to delay that mitral at University.

"This is Dr. Carter," he said into the phone. "Will you get Carrie McKeen at my office?"

"Yes, Doctor," the operator said. "She's on the line talking with Admissions. Shall I ring her on your public phone?"

"No," he said. "Thanks, but I'll try her again in a couple of minutes."

He went into the lavatory and heard the shower running and knew it was Frank Stanczyk. When he came out he took another cap, glazed-paper stiff with starch, out of the box on the window sill and opened it and fitted it on and tied it in back. He picked up another gauze mask, tightly rolled, and went back to the phone.

"Here she is now, Doctor," the operator said. "Thank you for waiting. Here's Dr. Carter."

"Matt?" Carrie McKeen said.

"Yes."

"For John's sake, why aren't you doing Mr. Scheller?"

"I'm going in right now."

"It's about time. What are you people doing over there this morning, anyway?"

"Loafing. Do me a favor and——"

"I've already done you a half-dozen favors this morning. Have you seen Mr. Benjamin Davies' daughter?"

"Yes. About a half-hour ago."

"Well, thank God! She was calling in here. What's the matter with her, anyway?"

"She's losing her father."

"That doesn't give her the right to abuse people."

"Listen," he said. "Call University and get that O.R. supervisor. Tell her I'm going to be delayed getting away from here and tell her to put that mitral stenosis back from 2 o'clock to 3. I want them to hold up the pre-op medication for an hour and——"

"That's that Mrs. Pappas."

"That's right. I'll be finished here at 3 and they can open at 3 and I'll be over there in fifteen minutes."

"All right, but what about patients? You've got patients at 5 o'clock."

"How many?"

"You've got three and Rob has three. You won't be back here before 6."

"I'll be there at 5:30. Is there anybody I don't have to see today?"

"There's Mr. Worthy."

"Who's he?"

"You remember old Mr. Worthy. John Worthy. You did a right upper lobe on him two years ago, that nice old man, and he's due at 5 for another six months' check-up, and there's——"

"I remember him. If you can get him on the phone tell him I'll be a half-hour late. I haven't got time to talk now, but if I get jammed up Rob can take one of mine."

"All right. I called Marion and told her you'd pick her up at 8. I ordered that dress shirt and they'll deliver it this afternoon, and——"

"Good," he said. "When it gets there, try it on and see how it looks."

"Oh, for John's sake, Matt," she said. "Go to work."

"I am," he said.

Walking down the hall, tying the bottom strings of the mask around his neck, he saw the foot of the bed coming off the elevator and then the whole of the bed, the white sheet up to the patient's neck. At the head of the bed, pushing it and steering it to make the turn, was Jimmy Wilson, short, stocky, his shoulders full in the white short-sleeved jacket and his skin almost black against the white.

"Here we go now," Jimmy Wilson was saying. "Here we just make this turn, and here come Dr. Carter, too."

"Good morning, James," he said. "Is this my patient?"

"That's right," Jimmy Wilson said. "This here's Mr. Scheller and I just tell him he a lucky man to have Dr. Carter."

"How are you this morning?" he said to Mr. Scheller and walking beside the bed.

"I don't know," Mr. Scheller said, looking up but not moving his head on the pillow.

"You're going to be all right," he said. "This is going to be a lot easier than you've been imagining."

"I don't know," Mr. Scheller said.

"That's what I tell Mr. Scheller," Jimmy Wilson said, positioning the bed against the wall opposite the door. "I tell him Dr. Carter can fix anybody. I tell him that when I get sick I'm gonna have Dr. Carter fix me, too, and then I won't worry."

"Thank you, James," he said. "You're still the best orderly we've ever had."

"I admire that," Jimmy said, smiling and nodding his head.

"Excuse me," he said to Mr. Scheller. "I'll be back in a second."

He opened the door to the O.R. and saw Darrow helping the anesthetist named Anne Morris wheel her machine to the head of the table. At the foot of the table the scrub nurse, her back to him, was sorting the instruments on the tray.

"You people about ready?" he said.

"In about two minutes, Doctor," the anesthetist named Anne Morris said.

"Who's that great scrub nurse?" he said.

"Mary Cleary, Doctor," she said, turning.

"I know," he said. "You doing all right?"

"I'll be ready when they are."

"Good," he said. "Where's Dr. Robinson?"

"He just started to scrub, sir," Darrow said.

"Good," he said.

He closed the door and turned back to the bed. Mr. Scheller, not moving and the sheet still up to his chin, was looking at the ceiling.

"How did you sleep last night?" he said to Mr. Scheller. He had turned down the sheet and taken Mr. Scheller's left hand and he had found the pulse.

"Not much," Mr. Scheller said. "I guess that pill they gave me didn't work."

"You slept more than you thought," he said.

He was counting the pulse. Even without a watch he wouldn't be off more than five beats but, more important than that, he could get the regularity and the strength of the pulsation.

"I don't know," Mr. Scheller said.

"You'd be surprised if you knew how much you slept," he said, thinking: His pulse is about 90 and not irregular and it's strong enough. That ten milligrams of morphine they gave him this morning is easing his tension a little but it's not exactly making him as bold as a bandit the way it does with some of them.

"That's fine," he said, releasing Mr. Scheller's wrist and pulling the sheet back up. "You're going to do just fine."

"That's what I tell Mr. Scheller," Jimmy Wilson said.

"Did you tell him you helped build this hospital?" he said, walking to the foot of the bed and picking up Mr. Scheller's charts.

"No, sir," Jimmy Wilson said.

"About five years ago," he said, trying to relax Mr. Scheller but starting to scan the charts, "we had a new wing built here and Jimmy Wilson was one of the builders."

"A mason's helper," Jimmy Wilson said. "I carry the bricks and the mortar."

"Then he decided he didn't want to leave us," he said. He was quickly following the line between the dots on the temperature chart and he saw that the temperature was 99 at 8 P.M. and 98.2 twelve hours later. "He likes it here."

"That's right," Jimmy Wilson said.

"So he's become our best orderly," he said. He had scanned the line between the circles on the respiration chart and noted they were between 18 and 22 a minute and normal.

"I admire that," Jimmy Wilson said.

"He's also our best boxer," he said, thinking: The white blood count at 8000 and the hemoglobin at 12 grams are normal. "In fact, he's our only boxer. He boxes in the Golden Gloves."

"Next year I win," Jimmy said.

"You always say that," he said.

Each year Jimmy Wilson would post on the bulletin board the same sign:

Sponcor Needed
Middleweight boxer requires sponcors
to enter Golden Gloves Turnament.
Signed Jimmy Wilson.

"Last year I make the finals here," Jimmy Wilson said.

Each year, because Jimmy Wilson was unable to stretch his pay check from Thursday to Thursday, he would sell his protective cup and ring shoes and robe, and so ten of them would chip in five dollars each to re-equip him.

"You don't eat right," he said to Jimmy Wilson but still checking Mr. Scheller's charts and thinking: The urinalysis is good with no blood cells or sugar or albumen and the bowel movements are normal and the blood pressure is all right at 140 over 80.

"I eat fine," Jimmy Wilson said.

"Too many jelly doughnuts," he said. He had finished scanning Mr. Scheller's charts and he placed them back at the foot of the bed.

"That's what I like," Jimmy Wilson said. "Jelly doughnuts."

"I've been looking at the results of your tests," he said to Mr. Scheller, walking around to the side of the bed. "They're all excellent, so everything's going to be all right."

"I just hope so," Mr. Scheller said, turning his head now and looking at him.

"It will all go just fine," he said. "Jimmy, here, will move you inside in a minute and I'll see you in there."

"Doctor?" Mr. Scheller said.

"Yes?"

"There's something I'd like to tell you."

I'd rather not hear it, he was thinking, but I will. If, at this time, they want to, you have to let them speak because it's better spoken.

"I've never been a very religious man," Mr. Scheller said.

"Oh?"

He heard this more often than those who spoke it knew. At first it flattered his ego, his hero image of himself, but after the first few times he came to realize that, as much as he wanted them to believe in him, it embarrassed him, this substitute faith in him that is forced by their fear of death.

"I've never been much for going to church," Mr. Scheller said.

"I understand."

"But I trust in you."

"I accept your trust," he said, taking Mr. Scheller's right hand in both of his and looking down at him. "Now please believe that you're going to be all right, because you are. When you're in there, they're just going to stick your arm with a needle, like they did the other day when we looked down inside your windpipe with a bronchoscope. That's all you're going to feel, and the next thing you know you'll be back in your room waiting to kid the nurses."

"I believe in you, Doctor," Mr. Scheller said.

"Good," he said.

He put Mr. Scheller's hand down on the sheet and heard the door open behind him. The floating nurse walked by him to the foot of the bed.

"Here we go now," Jimmy Wilson said, pulling his mask up.

"You're going to be all right," he said to Mr. Scheller. "Just remember that."

He turned then, as they started to maneuver the bed, and pulled his own mask up, knotting the two strings above his cap, and he walked to the next door and went in and walked to the sink next to Bob Robinson.

"You find Mrs. Scheller and her son?" Bob Robinson said, scrubbing.

"Yes," he said. "They were waiting for me."

He had taken a brush out of the holder and, with the foot pedal, he had squirted some of the Septisol onto the brush and into his left hand.

"You see Benjamin Davies' daughter?"

"Yes," he said. He had worked up a lather in the palm of his left hand and was brushing under the nails. "I explained it to her and her mother."

"Thank God," Bob Robinson said. "She's been raising the roof."

"I also told Mrs. Kirk's husband."

"I see him on TV," Rob said. "What's he like?"

"A fine man. He took it as well as anyone could."

"It's a damn shame," Rob said.

"He's decided he doesn't want her told, at least not now. They're buying a new house and he's going through with it so she won't suspect anything."

"It's a damn shame," Rob said, scrubbing.

"Bernie Waterman's doing fine," he said, squirting Septisol into his right hand and starting on the nails.

"You think we cured him?"

"I think so," he said. "I didn't have time for Anthony Trusco and Lynn Cummings."

"We doing her tomorrow?"

"That's right, and after we finish here I've got to get over to University for a mitral."

"I'll look in on her," Rob said, rinsing his hands and forearms. "I'll also see Trusco."

"I think he's curing himself. I looked at his new pictures last night and he's fifty per cent better."

A week before, when they had looked at Anthony Trusco's original X rays, his lungs had seemed pervaded by snowflakes. He had been running a temperature for two weeks and complaining of headaches and had a non-productive cough. When a skin test for tuberculosis came back negative the possibilities were that a cancer from an unidentified primary source had spread through his blood stream and filtered out through his lungs or that he had psittacosis, a virus spread by parrots, parakeets, and a number of other birds.

"I know," Rob was saying. "I compared the new ones with the old pictures this morning and half that blizzard in there has cleared."

"Ask him again if he hasn't been around a parrot or a parakeet," he said. "I once had an electrician who picked it up doing some rewiring in a pet store."

He was scrubbing the back of his left hand now and starting up the forearm. He had been doing this, scrubbing two and three times a day, for so long that he no longer had to set the timer. He had become as accustomed to the passage of five minutes as, he read once in Red Smith's column, Tommy Loughran became accustomed to the passage of three minutes and so was able to finish every round he boxed in his own corner.

"Trusco puts down flooring," Rob was saying, "linoleum and rubber tile and that kind of thing. I asked him about pet shops, but he says he hasn't worked in any."

"Has he been to a zoo?" he said.

Because he scrubbed so often, and for so long, and worked always in rubber gloves, his hands had become so soft that he was conscious of it when he shook hands with other men. In fact, it actually embarrassed him with men like Anthony Trusco.

"I asked him that," Rob was saying, "but he says not."

"Get him to think back again over any private homes or apartments he did where there might have been a bird."

"I will," Rob said. "This thing interests me."

"As long as he's winning, we won't change horses."

"You see Mr. Scheller in the hall?" Rob said.

"Yes."

"You think we've got another Roberto Leon?"

"We'll know in a half-hour," he said.

"I'd better get in there," Rob said, "and see how they're doing with him."

When he finished scrubbing he rinsed his forearms and hands, pushed the door of the operating room open with his right shoulder and, his hands up in front of him and palms toward himself, he walked across to the table with the sterile gowns and folded towels on it. He picked up a towel and dried his hands and arms and, as he did, the scrub nurse saw him and came over and shook out a gown. He slipped into it, and she pulled it around him and tied it in back. Then he opened one of the towels, ripped open the packet of powder, and powdered his hands. He picked up the left glove, carefully but automatically picking it up by the inside, where the gauntlet was folded down, and he slipped it on. He snapped on the right one, the soft smell of the small cloud of powder coming even through the mask, and then he pulled the gauntlet of the left glove up over the knitted wristlet of the gown and adjusted the right one.

Once he did not even know how to put on a pair of gloves. It was that first day when he assisted at that thyroid at General and he couldn't get the hemostats to open and he was shaking all over. It was that short, stout German surgeon with the silver-rimmed eyeglasses and the fat hands and he was shouting: "Off, off, off!" And then: "No, Doctor. No, no, no! It's not difficult! Hold them like this!" And all the time he, who wanted now to be a surgeon more than anything else in the world, was shaking like a leaf.

As he turned back now to the room he saw Mr. Scheller, the upper half of his body uncovered, thin and pale-skinned on his back on the table under the lights. He was already under the Pentothal Sodium, with the intra-tracheal tube down his windpipe and the anesthetist named Anne Morris taping it to the right cheek.

"Well, Orphan Annie," he said, "how are you doing?"

"Fine, Doctor," she said, looking over at him with those big blue eyes over the mask. "We're doing just fine."

"Good enough," he said.

Standing there, his gloved hands folded in front of him priestlike, he watched Darrow and Jimmy Wilson while they turned Mr. Scheller onto his left side, the left arm, the intravenous tube rising from it, out along the arm board. Darrow was sliding the flat metal grounding plate for the Bovie, the electric cautery machine, under Mr. Scheller's left hip.

"Now let's get that left leg bent," he said to Jimmy Wilson, "so he'll be nice and steady."

He had learned it in the war, early in Normandy, that if they bent the under leg up they wouldn't roll as much on the litters. He had learned it as soon as they hit Normandy and when the thirty litter bearers had all they could do to handle them because they had five hundred casualties the first night when they were hoping for no more than fifty, or just enough to keep everyone busy. Then they had lost one truck, coming in at Utah, but fortunately they had dispersed their instruments over three trucks, and whenever he thought of this he remembered that one German. He had always felt a special urge to take care of the prisoners, to show them that Americans are decent people, but that night, walking down the line of litters and coming to that one German, he had done no more than reach down and push his intestines in and walk on because he knew it was hopeless and he couldn't waste the time. As it was, he and the two others had operated for twenty-four hours straight, surprisingly not aware that they were tiring until, at the end, the hoarseness of their voices gave away their fatigue.

Now he watched the anesthetist put the pillow under Mr. Scheller's head and Jimmy Wilson fit the pillow up between the legs. Then the floating nurse and Jimmy Wilson were anchoring the body, pulling the wide adhesive tapes across the hip, crossing them at the hip, and sticking them to the sides of the table. When Darrow started to soap the right chest and back he walked over and looked again at the new set of X rays, at the shadow lying up there high in the right lung and immediately adjacent to the heart.

"Those are much sharper pictures than the ones he came in with," Bob Robinson was saying, walking up.

"That's right," he said. "These are good."

Two days before, when he had bronchoscoped Mr. Scheller, he had seen the growth coming out of the right upper lobe orifice, or opening, where the bronchus, or branch of the windpipe, enters that lobe of the lung. He had seen only the top of the growth sticking out because, viewed through a bronchoscope, a bronchial tumor is like an iceberg with most of it hidden from sight.

"You know something?" Rob was saying, looking more closely now at the lateral view. "The way it's not exactly in the mid-line but a little bit anterior to it, makes me think that if it hasn't invaded his superior vena cava already it's close to it."

"That's the way it looks," he said.

The tumor, in the light of the scope, had looked like cauliflower, although red instead of white, and when he took a small specimen of it with the biopsy forceps he knew that the odds were twenty to one that it was cancer. Twenty-four hours later he had seen the pathology report: "Bronchogenic carcinoma, squamous-cell type."

"Doctor," he said to Darrow now, "you're not trying to scrub my patient away are you? You wouldn't want me to have to go out and find a new one."

"No, sir," Darrow said, stopping and looking at him, the swab in the holder arrested in midair.

"That's fine. I think you can paint him now."

"I'll paint him," Bob Robinson said to Darrow. "You'll have to go out and do a fast second scrub on yourself."

"Thank you," Darrow said.

"Mary?" he said to the scrub nurse. "You've got that polyethylene tubing soaking?"

"Yes, Doctor."

"In three sizes?"

"Yes, sir."

"You're all right," he said. "You're a champion."

He watched, conscious of his growing impatience to begin, while Bob Robinson painted. He watched him dip into the pan of disinfectant and swab the whole area, the orange-pink merthiolate running down ahead of the swab and Rob spreading it evenly as he went.

"You know you're very good at painting?" he said. "I don't think I've ever seen you do it before and you're a regular Rembrandt."

"Thank you," Rob said, "but do you think I'll ever be a surgeon?"

"I wonder the same thing about myself," he said, and then to the anesthetist: "How's he doing?"

"Fine, Doctor."

"Excuse me, Doctor," the scrub nurse said, "but what size blades do you want?"

"I'll take medium," he said. "He doesn't seem like he's going to be too tough."

He saw Darrow come in from the scrub room and walk to the table against the wall and pick up a towel. He saw that Bob Robinson had finished the painting and that the floating nurse was moving the pan of disinfectant away.

"Good," he said. He walked up to the table and, realizing that it was a little low, he looked down and found the foot pedal and raised the table to just the right height so that, at the end, he would not feel it in his shoulders, in the deltoids.

Darrow, in his gown and gloves now, was moving in at his left and Bob Robinson was walking around to the other side of the table. To the right the scrub nurse had moved the instrument table up and had swung the instrument tray across on its stand, and when he reached across his chest with his left hand she pressed the scalpel into it.

"Now we always make our scratch," he said to Darrow, "the width of a hand below the scapula and halfway between the scapula and the spine. If you go too close to the scapula you interfere with the nerve supply, and this man's a painter. He needs all his muscles, particularly on this side."

"Yes, sir," Darrow said.

He had turned the scalpel over in his left hand and now with the back of it he made the scratch, just marking the skin, bringing it down in the Big C and shifting it to his right hand and finishing under the right breast. Then he made two small cross marks, intersecting the scratch line about twelve inches apart.

"So when we put him back together again," he said to Darrow, "we'll know where it goes."

"Yes, sir," Darrow said.

He placed the first towel and then the three others, as a frame, around the scratch. Where two of them intersected at the right breast he snapped on a towel clamp.

"We put this clamp here," he said to Darrow, "so that when we put in our decompression tube later we don't have to look all around for the right spot under the drapes."

"Yes, sir," Darrow said.

No, he was thinking, I wouldn't really want to be young like he is and starting out all over again. To me this body, now that the thinning, aging ugliness of it is about to be draped away, will become beautiful. He won't see it yet, but I will find beauty here in the miraculous, clean, functional, always-in-the-same-place orderliness of everything.

Over the whole body now he and Bob Robinson and Darrow were spreading the green thoracotomy sheet with the white-trimmed opening. At his left he clamped his corner of it at shoulder height to the empty intravenous stand and, when Bob Robinson had clamped his corner to the stand with the bottles of saline and reserve blood hanging from it, Mr. Scheller's head and the anesthetist bending over him were hidden from view. Then, to his right, he clamped a towel to the sheet and to the near corner of the instrument tray, and Bob Robinson did the same on his side.

The reason he won't find any beauty here, he was thinking, is that he remembers that under this sheet there lies a man and, not yet able to forget this, he thinks of pain. Only Rob and I really know that we are about to do all that can be done for this man and so we will find what he will not find until, all the observing and the assisting and waiting over, he is here with his own patient and they have agreed that this is the best, the only, bargain and he is on his own. Then he'll find it, if he's going to make a good surgeon, or perhaps he won't.

"Now we make a trough here," he said, placing two rolled towels upright in the fold of the drape in front of him. "That's so that any instruments that slide off his hip or thigh will slip in here instead of falling on the floor."

"Yes, sir," Darrow said.

"And this is our clothes line," he said, placing four lengths of gauze along the edge of the drape. "It keeps this gauze out of the middle of the instrument field. I've seen knives fly when they've been caught in the gauze."

"Yes, sir," Darrow said.

He moved back now to his left, and leaning over the drape, he looked down at the anesthetist, sitting on her stool next to the Stevenson respirator and the gas tank and bending over Mr. Scheller's head.

"Good-bye, Orphan Annie," he said. "I'll see you later."

"Good-bye, Doctor," she said, looking up at him.

"Is everybody ready?" he said.

"Right, Matt," Bob Robinson said, from the other side.

"You?" he said to the intern on his left.

"Yes, sir."

"Yes, Doctor," the scrub nurse said.

"What time is it?"

"It's 11:14, Doctor," the floating nurse said.

"Okay, let's go," he said, and he held out his right hand. "Knife."

XIX

The first knife he ever used was the bone-handled pocketknife that his father gave him. He was about nine years old, and for a long time he wore it on a chain and his father showed him how to skin rabbits with it until he became very good at it himself.

Now he felt the handle of the scalpel press into his hand and he closed on it. With one long, easy, I-have-done-this-three-thousand-times motion he made the long, curved cut. Following the pink-on-pink line of the scratch he applied just enough pressure to get through the skin and the fat to the fascia, the tough tissue over the muscles, and as he did he saw the pink-painted skin pull back and the yellow of the fat layer follow it and then the white fascia lying beneath.

One day, when he must have been about ten or eleven, he was walking out in the canyon east of town with the single-shot .22. It was about 3 o'clock in the afternoon and he saw the cottontail in the shadow of the gray volcanic rocks and he got it with the first shot. When he started to skin it, he found four young inside, and as he opened each sac there was a gasp. He didn't know then that these were the last breaths of life, so he carried the four unborn back the four miles, carefully wrapped in the skin and cradled in his hands. He put them on the warm asbestos covering on the top of the furnace in the basement, where his father found them that night and explained to him what he had done.

"You see, Doctor?" he said to Darrow now. "The bigger the incision you make, the more money you can charge. Do you believe that?"

"No, sir."

I'll have to loosen him up, he was thinking. During the early routine you have to keep them loose, these interns and Little Orphan Annie and Mary Cleary. You don't want them tired when you get to the critical part of the problem, so you have to keep thinking of ways to relax them.

"You'll note," he said, "that this patient has been very considerate of us. He has kept himself thin."

Across from him Bob Robinson was starting to clamp the stockinet material onto one edge of the wound, so he reached out and the scrub nurse handed him his. He clamped it to the skin along the outer edge and folded it back to cover the skin.

In the old days they all used linen skin towels, but in France when

they ran out of them, he borrowed the knitted stockinet that the or-
thopedic people used. How many amputations he did in those days he
never knew, but everybody was an orthopedist as well as a general surgeon anyway. Except when there was a big push on, they worked at
night because the wounded wouldn't come in until 4 or 5 o'clock in the
afternoon. Then they had to be separated by that triage system into the
walking wounded, the wounded, and the shock cases, so he'd sleep
until 4 o'clock. When he got up he'd look them over and have supper
and then he'd start about 9 and work until 7 in the morning. They wore
their operating gowns right over their field jackets, and when there was a
big push on like the break-through at St. Lo and during the Bulge
they'd work for twenty-four hours before they'd take a few hours' sleep.
If any good came out of it, it was the experience they got out of the
enormous volume they handled and the confidence they derived from
the blind faith that the poor kids had in them, and then a few little
things like that elastic stockinet that molds itself over the chest wall so
much better than the linen towels that now a lot of them use it.

"Where did you go to school, Doctor?" he said, smoothing down the
stockinet.

"Right here at the University," Darrow said.

"Good," he said. "Then you think a good deal of Dr. Winton."

"Yes, sir. I do."

In his own life, and before Pete Church, Leonard Furman was the first
of the big ones. The first operation he ever saw was that cyst that
Furman did on Jim McClain's sister. When, watching, he began
to feel weak, Furman noticed the sweat on his forehead and told the
nurse to take him out, but he saw it through and then fainted on the way
downstairs to tell Jim that his sister was all right and to play it as if it
were nothing.

"There's a bleeder," he said, spotting the small spurt where the vessel
had been severed. "He thinks he can hide, but I recognize him."

Sponging with the gauze in its holder in his left hand and taking the
hemostats, or scissor-action locking clamps, in his right, he clamped
the bleeders on his side while Bob Robinson worked the other. Going
into the chest, as Pete Church first taught him, is really just three cycles
of cutting and clamping and tying off—first down to the muscles, then
to the ribs and finally into the chest—and there would be perhaps a
hundred more of these small veins and arteries that they would cauterize
with the Bovie or tie.

"How's your car behaving?" Bob Robinson said to him.

"Fine," he said, "but I had to have the plugs replaced. Those German plugs won't take our high-octane gasoline."

"It serves you right," Bob Robinson said.

They were starting now to tie the first of the three hundred or more knots. A surgeon's knot is a square knot, but Pete Church's hands used to move so fast when he tied that, the first time he assisted him, he asked if he were really tying square knots or just grannies that tend to slip. Then Pete Church had taken him into the scrub room and right there, tying to one of the faucets, he had shown him how you put in two grannies and then the square knot to snug it down. He had shown him how you use the two middle fingers as a shuttle, instead of twisting the wrists. It is really a one-handed knot and after that he carried silk with him for months, practicing with it whenever he had a few minutes, tying thousands of knots around the round, chipped, white-enameled bed posts in his room and even practicing to tie blind inside an empty tennis-ball container as Alexis Carrel, who invented that perfusion pump with Charles Lindbergh to keep organs alive outside the body, said he used to practice inside a penny match box.

He held one of the clamps now on Bob Robinson's side while Bob Robinson passed the black silk thread behind it, slid it down, tied it, and knotted it twice more. Then Bob Robinson held for him while he tied.

"No, Doctor," he said as Darrow cut the first thread. "You're holding those scissors like a woman. Here."

When you are beginning you have to learn to pick up scissors all over again. He took the scissors from Darrow, and he showed him how to hold them, with the thumb and ring finger in the eyes of the scissors, the middle finger to the right side, and the index finger down the length of them as a pointer.

"And when you cut," he said, showing him, "you slide the scissors down to the knot, turn them up like this, and then cut. That cuts it the width of the scissor blade above the knot and you're in no danger of cutting the knot."

"I see," Darrow said.

"Also," he said, "that's how you cut blind. When you can't see the knot you just ride the scissors down the silk until you come to it, rotate, and cut."

"Yes, sir."

"Now you're ready for anything."

When they had finished the tying and discarded the clamps he sponged again along the walls of the cut. As he did he saw a small bleeder, close to the underlying fascia and at Bob Robinson's side.

"There's a sneaky one," he said.

"I've got it," Rob said, clamping it.

"Is this thing working?" he said, picking up the forceps of the Bovie and finding with his left foot the pedal under the table.

"Yes, sir," the floating nurse said. "I think it is."

"It's not working now," he said, touching it to the nose of the clamp as Bob Robinson held it. "What's it set at?"

"Forty, Doctor," the float said, bending over the dial on the Bovie.

"Move it up to forty-five," he said.

He touched the nose of the clamp again and saw the small blue-white flame and heard the small crackling sound. He saw the blackening beneath the clamp and then the slight odor of burning came to him.

"That does it," he said. "Knife."

He started at that auscultatory triangle where the trapezius and the latissimus dorsi, the shoulder and back or shrugging and rowing muscles, join and frame that perfect port through which, the week before, he had heard more clearly than anywhere else that squeaking-door, broken-reed sound in Mr. Scheller's chest. With the forceps in his left hand he picked up the fascia over the opening and he cut down through it. He discarded the forceps and, turning his left hand palm up, he slid the first two fingers into the opening and under the trapezius and the rhomboids, the muscles that connect the shoulder blade with the vertebrae and stabilize and elevate it. Spreading the fingers and moving them ahead of the scalpel, he made the incision back-handed and saw the clean snap-back of the muscles released by the cut. Then he shifted the scalpel to his left hand, inserted the two fingers of the right, spread them, and made the left-handed cut back-handed through the latissimus dorsi. With each cut, and certain of himself, he went all the way through the rhomboids, too, and down to the periosteum, the tissue covering the ribs as again, at the very beginning, Pete Church had given him the assurance to do when, like all beginners, he tended to be a scratcher.

"You notice that we don't divide the serratus anterior," he said, referring to the lifting muscle. "In fact, we go out of our way to preserve it by just liberating the back edge because this man is a house painter. If you save a patient but leave him a semi-cripple you've only won half the battle."

"Yes, sir," Darrow said. "I understand."

The trouble with scratching, he had often thought, is that you are never in command. You're like a water bug, always hovering on the surface. You don't seem to be able to get down in and run the operation and so it runs you until, finally, with experience, you master it, except that the born scratchers never do.

"Sponge," Bob Robinson said.

"Did you ever play football, Doctor?" he said to Darrow.

He had discarded the scalpel and was tying another bleeder for Bob Robinson. They would tie about two dozen of the major vessels here but the smaller ones had retracted into the muscles and would seal themselves off.

"No, sir," Darrow said. "I never played much, but I enjoy watching the pros on Sundays when I get a chance."

"Did you see that game on Sunday?" he said, watching Darrow hold the scissors properly now as he cut the tie.

"No, sir," Darrow said. "I was on duty."

"This is just like football," he said, holding a clamp while Bob Robinson tied behind it. "Say you're a halfback going wide. You have to have two speeds. That's what we have. These chest openings are automatic, so we just go along one-two-three at top speed."

"I understand," Darrow said.

Alex Johnson was the master of pace. Because of that TB that finally got to his spine and his kidneys, he had to save time and save himself and so he learned, and taught, how to race through the openings to get to the problem.

"Then when we get inside and see what the problem is we slow down," he said, sponging and flipping the sponge back onto the towel draped across the kick bucket on the floor behind him. "However, there's one difference. We always start out fast, but when you're a halfback on that wide play you start out at three-quarter speed. Then when the defensive man commits himself, you go into high. You give him that reserve burst and you're around him. Right?"

"Yes, sir."

When Alex Johnson got to the problem, however, he slowed to a walk. He became as meticulous as a brain surgeon, all that preciseness in his nature that revealed itself as he walked around his office straightening the pictures and squaring the chairs against the wall coming out again now at the table.

"That was a pretty good game on Sunday at that," Bob Robinson said. "I saw the second half."

The scrub nurse was wringing the saline solution out of a hot pack and Bob Robinson took it and placed the wet gauze over and around the exposed wall of the cut on his side. The next one he placed himself, and Bob Robinson hooked the curved end of the first retractor over the hot pack and around and under the shoulder blade. The second retractor he placed next to Rob's, and then he handed it to Darrow and waited as the two of them pulled back on the retractors and the opening began to widen.

"Oh come on, you guys, lift," he said. "You two should go to the gym more often. Let's pull that up there."

As they pulled harder now, he reached up and under the shoulder blade, once more the way Pete Church first showed him, and felt the serratus anterior muscle attached to the second rib. It is always conspicuous there, so you know at once where you are and don't have to fight your way up to the first rib and now, starting with the second rib and moving his fingers down over the ribs, he counted them slowly.

"Two, three, four, five," he counted, and he reached over and pulled the retractor for Bob Robinson while Rob reached up and counted.

"Right," Rob said.

"How are you, Orphan Annie?" he said.

"We're all right, Doctor," she said, her voice coming up over the drape. "His pulse is 86, and his pressure is 130 over 85."

"Good," he said. "Knife."

Over the fifth rib he made the cut, about ten inches long, through the periosteum, the tough, adherent covering of the rib. When he dropped the scalpel onto the towel at his right the scrub nurse handed him the periosteal elevator, which is badly named because what it really resembles is a dinner knife with its blunt end bent over.

"Good girl," he said. "You can scrub on my Olympic team any time."

The elevator is the one the Army developed in 1918 and that he has always used, and if you know how to use it correctly you can do it with just two basic moves. With the first move and back-handed he scraped the periosteum back from his incision and across the upper half of the rib. With the second move he scraped it down across the lower half. And, as he did, he saw the clean, almost bloodless gray-white arch of the rib emerge.

"Your hand must always lead this instrument," he said to Darrow. "If you were to push it and it slipped it could puncture the chest. As long as you're dragging it, you're in no danger."

He was going around the rib now, scraping in two quick moves the periosteum away from the nearer half of the under side of the rib. Then he did the other side, completely exposing the section of rib.

"Very nice, Matt," Bob Robinson said.

"Don't flatter me," he said, packing gauze under the rib at both ends of the exposed section to elevate it slightly. "You know it's just as easy as shelling peas. Rib cutter."

With the double-action cutter he severed the rib in the back and then in the front. He handed the cutter back and, with the other hand, gave the severed ten-inch portion of the rib to Darrow.

"If you need another rib," he said, "you can have this. Our man here will grow a new one in three months."

"No, thank you," Darrow said, turning the rib over, looking at it. He handed it to the scrub nurse and she placed it in a towel.

"Bone wax please. Then the rib cutter again."

He took the sterile beeswax and packed the two remaining ends of the rib to keep the marrow from oozing. Then he took the rib cutter once more and cracked the fourth and sixth ribs toward the back.

"I discovered," he said, explaining to Darrow, "that these ribs would crack under the rib spreader anyway, but in the wrong place. Now I crack them where I need the extra exposure in the back."

"Yes, sir."

It is like that Latin motto, he sometimes thought. From the old oxen the young learn to plow. There is nothing you can do about the pill pushers and the Great Jaffreys except wait for attrition to get rid of them, but you can teach these kids how to do it the right way and then there is always hope that they will be good.

"Now, Orphan Annie," he said, "you're going to have to work. You're going to have to breathe for this man, because I'm going to open the pleura."

"I'm ready, Doctor."

He knew she would be turning on the automatic respirator now, and he reached in and, with the slightly opened scissors, he split the inner periosteum and then the pleura, the soft, almost latex-like lining of the chest cavity. When he did, he heard it rushing in, the air destroying the chest vacuum but unable to collapse the lung because Orphan Annie, sitting there below the drape and watching her dials and feeling the pressure in the anesthetic bag with her hand, was maintaining Mr. Scheller's normal breathing. He could hear the tick-hiss-tick of the respirator.

"Rib spreader."

When he took the rib spreader and started to place it he had the feeling that something was loose. He turned the spreader over.

"Hey!" he said. "Where's the wing nut? There's no wing nut here."

"Oh," the scrub nurse said. "Oh, it's all right. It's right here."

"Why, Mary," he said. "I'm glad you're not fixing my car."

She handed him the nut and he put it on. He started to place the spreader but saw that the lung, expanding under the set pressure of the respirator would be in the way.

"Orphan Annie," he said. "Take five or six good breaths and then cut him off so we can get this spreader in."

"Yes, Doctor."

He waited then, until he saw the lung go down. When it did he placed the spreader where he wanted it, between the fourth and fifth ribs, and set it firmly. Then Bob Robinson gave the handle four turns and the opening began to enlarge.

"Fine," he said, releasing the spreader. "Keep cranking."

As Bob Robinson turned the handles, the sides of the spreader moved out and the rectangle framed by the steel of the spreader opened to about five inches by eleven.

"Okay, Orphan Annie," he said. "You can go back to normal now."

There within that rectangle now lay the lung, the pink and purple and black marbleized whole of it rising and almost filling the opening and then receding, the ebb and flow of it controlled by the machine as Orphan Annie resumed the rhythmic breathing.

"What time is it?" he said.

"It's 11:33, Doctor," the floating nurse said.

That's nineteen minutes, he thought. Sometimes you can open in twelve minutes, if he's a real skinny one and everybody is loose and doing his job.

"Orphan Annie?" he said. "How much blood has he had?"

"Only about 120 c.c.s, Doctor."

That's about right for going in, he was thinking, and now she wants to continue that normal breathing but that lung is in our way.

"Can you drop your pressure a little?" he said. "I want you to collapse the lung a little so we can see what's wrong with our man."

"Yes, Doctor."

"Lung forceps," he said. "Two of them."

He positioned them on the lung. Then he handed them across to Bob Robinson, and Bob Robinson pulled the lung toward himself.

"Fine. That does it."

This, now, was what it was all about. He reached in with his left hand and, with the rest of them watching in silence and even Orphan Annie half standing and looking down over the end of the drape but still reaching down and feeling the pressure bag, he moved his left hand under the lung and then slowly up toward what, until this moment, had been first just a succession of symptoms and then a light shadow on an X ray.

He felt the lung, normal and pliable, and then through the so-thinness of the glove he felt his fingers come to the edges of it, the beginning of the hardness, the spreading patch. He was above the root of the lung and he could just get his index finger between the root and the hardened mass above it. Then he reached in with both hands and traced its outlines between them and cornered it.

"Tilt the table toward me, please," he said to the floating nurse, withdrawing his hands and waiting while she bent under the table and turned the handle. "That's enough. That's fine."

He took the two forceps from Bob Robinson and pulled the lung toward his own side. Then, reaching in with his right hand and moving back the under portion of the lung, he could see the grayish-white cancerous growth spreading onto the superior vena cava. It covered about a half-inch and extended off the vena cava to the pericardium, the thin covering over the heart.

"You were right," he said to Bob Robinson.

"Right?" Rob said.

"About a half-inch of the superior vena cava is invaded and it's on the pericardium, too."

"Roberto Leon?" Rob said.

"Almost an exact duplicate," he said. "Take a look for yourself."

And it is, really, almost an exact duplicate, he was thinking, holding the lung back and waiting for Rob. For months I have seen it again and again in my mind and now it is no longer just in my mind but right here on the table.

"He's got it on there, all right," Bob Robinson was saying. "He's a ringer for Roberto Leon."

"I want to check his liver," he said, handing the forceps back to Rob.

He reached down to the diaphragm and through it the liver felt good. It was soft and smooth and he knew that it was free of the disease.

"His liver is fine," he said.

He was looking over the rest of the pleura now. He was searching for other signs of spread of the disease but he found none.

"This is a patient," he said, for Darrow and Orphan Annie and Mary Cleary, "who was afraid he had cancer of the lung, so for months he tried to forget it. He thought that, if he could forget it, it would go away, and now he not only has cancer of the lung but it has extended onto his superior vena cava and his pericardium."

So when I get inside the pericardium, he was thinking, I may find I can scrape the cancer right off the vena cava. Then I won't have to re-move a section of it and use the pulmonary artery for a graft to replace it and he won't be Roberto Leon at all.

"Toothed forceps," he said, "and a knife with a number eleven blade."

"Forceps here, too," Bob Robinson said.

They placed the forceps about a quarter of an inch apart and about an inch from the cancer and picked up the pericardium. With the scalpel and between the forceps he cut a half-inch incision through the peri-cardium.

"Scissors."

Inserting the scissors into the opening and staying well outside the cancerous area he made a curving cut around it. Then he lifted it, the heart beating there in the opening, and saw that the cancer had extended through the pericardium and was visible on the interior surface. Above, where the pericardium becomes a sheath over and around the superior vena cava, he saw that the normal space between the sheath and the superior vena cava no longer existed, but had been obliterated by the disease. He released the pericardial flap and, with the forceps, picked up the sheath in the free area above the cancer. He made another open-ing, entered it with the scissors, and dissected down until he could go no further, until he had run into another dead end where again the cancer plaque was adhering to the vena cava.

"We're not going to peel this one," he said, handing the forceps to Bob Robinson. "The cancer hasn't completely encircled the vena cava, but it's adhering on three walls. Take a look."

So it really is Roberto Leon at that, he was thinking, standing there with his hands clasped priestlike in front of him and waiting for Rob. If I do anything, if I take that lung, I've got to take that section of the vena cava and do that graft. If I try it he may die right here on this table, but if I don't, if I just close this chest and send him back to that wife and that son he won't have much more than six weeks or two months at the most and that's it, just as plain as that and right now.

"I guess I was right at that," Bob Robinson said, straightening up.

"You were. Now I want this table tilted back again. I want to look at the right pulmonary artery."

It is the large blood vessel carrying the dark venous blood from the heart to the right lung, and running behind the superior vena cava. As he opened, from the back, the sheath covering the artery, it dissected so easily that he knew that it was not cancerous and could serve as the graft for the vena cava. Then he checked the superior pulmonary vein and found it also free.

"The artery is fine," he said looking at Bob Robinson. "What do you say now?"

"Well," Rob said, looking back at him. "I say his system can stand it and I say we've been waiting for this and we're ready for it and we can do it."

At times like this, he had often thought, the only thing to do is to see yourself as the patient. If I'm ever like this, I hope to heaven they don't just sew me up again and send me back. If they do lose me, all they have to lose is a little off their reputations while I lose my life, but still I want that chance.

"So I say yes," Rob was saying, waiting for him, "because we have to give him a chance to see which way he goes."

"If we don't give him that chance we know which way he'll go," he said, "so I say yes, too."

He had known he would say it, but he had needed to think it all out once more and to take that last breather. Now, having said it, having committed himself, he felt the small ground-spring of anticipation rising in him, the small welling of excitement that at the beginning was a part of every operation until, after so many years, he had done so many that now only rarely, only in the tough ones, was he aware of it.

"Now if you'll hold this lung forceps," he said to Darrow, "Dr. Robinson will hold the other and you people will keep this lung out of my way."

He started to dissect the tissue around the tubelike bronchus, freeing it. As he did, he isolated the bronchial arteries, the small blood vessels bringing blood to the bronchial tubes.

"In going around the bronchus," he said for Darrow, "you point your instrument always toward the trachea and not the artery. If you should break into the artery you're in trouble because you can't see for the blood and besides, with this patient, we want to use the right pulmonary artery later for a graft on the vena cava."

"Yes, sir," Darrow said.

As he isolated the smaller vessels now he clamped them. Then he divided them and, with Bob Robinson holding the clamps, he tied them off and held the sutures up as Darrow cut them.

"Now two right angle clamps," he said. "Now, Orphan Annie, I want this lung to collapse a little once more because I'm going to divide his bronchus."

With Bob Robinson and Darrow holding the lung out of the way he placed the first clamp, cutting off the air to the lung, on the tubular bronchus about a half-inch from where it branches off the trachea, or windpipe. He placed the second a half-inch from it and, with one cut, he went through the cartilaginous arch and the membranous floor.

"The bronchus is divided," he said. "Now I'm going for the right pulmonary artery, and I want the full length of it."

He reached around to the front and depressed the artery. Bob Robinson reached in and put his right hand under the aorta, the main trunk of the arterial system, and between it and the artery, and pulled the aorta up.

"Fine, Rob," he said, seeing the artery, pinkish-gray, starting at the main pulmonary artery and running behind the aorta and the adjacent vena cava to the lung. "What's his heart doing now, Orphan Annie?"

While you are in there, it had occurred to him once, you are almost one with the patient. You are so much a part of a man who is really a stranger to you that, like the beat of a musician's foot, your head moves a little with the rhythm of the patient's heart, and he had felt it miss just that once.

"His pulse is 100, Doctor. His pressure is 120 over 80."

"Good."

Going around to the back again he finished the isolation of the artery that he had started earlier, dissecting the weblike tissue around it, as close as possible to its origin at the main pulmonary artery. He placed the second one about a quarter-inch from it and, holding the two of them in his left hand and with the scalpel in his right hand, he cut between them and watched the end retract to the first clamp but leave a cuff.

"Four-o silk with an atromatic needle," he said. "I'll need eight of them."

Taking the curved needle in the scissor-action, locking-clamp needle holder he put the first of the eight interrupted, or individual, sutures in the cuff of the artery. Then, estimating his spacing, he started to put in the others, rotating his hand and the needle with each.

"The tendency is to pull the needle straight," he said to Darrow, "but if you pull it on the curve of the needle the hole in the artery will be no bigger than the needle. If you sew up a blood vessel and see it leaking you'll know what you did wrong. Right?"

"Right, sir," Darrow said.

When he had finished he waited for Darrow to cut the threads. Then, using a running stitch, and placing the needle each time between the other eight, he completed the closure and removed the clamp.

"No leaks," he said. "It must be the great help I'm getting today."

"No doubt about it," Bob Robinson said.

He isolated then the superior and inferior pulmonary veins, the two of them returning the blood from the upper and lower lobes of the right lung and converging in a Y just before they enter the heart. Then he clamped them, cut them and tied them.

"Scissors."

Continuing the incision he had made earlier in the pericardium, the covering over the heart, he cut around the cancer plaque on the superior vena cava. He reached over and took the lung forceps, from Bob Robinson and handed it to Darrow, who was holding the other.

"Hold these in both hands, Doctor," he said. "Now lift. Lift hard."

As Darrow lifted the lung came out. Darrow stood there, holding it, looking at it and then at him.

"You see, Doctor?" he said to Darrow. "You came here wanting to be a surgeon, and you've just performed your first pneumonectomy. You've removed a lung."

"Well, hardly," Darrow said, "but thanks anyway."

"I'll take it," he said, "and Mary, make some room on your instrument table so I can get the pulmonary artery off it."

On the table he cut the artery at the point near the lung where it divides into its branches. With the forceps he passed it to the scrub nurse.

"Now take good care of this," he said, "and I'm not kidding. Wrap it in a saline sponge and don't drop it. This is our only chance, so if anything happens to it we're sunk."

"Yes, Doctor."

"We lost a little blood here," Bob Robinson was saying, examining the empty chest cavity. "Tonsil sucker."

He handed Bob Robinson the metal suction tube used in tonsillectomies and waited while he drained the area. Then he started to remove the first of the chain of lymph nodes, the steppingstones at which cancer stops as it spreads through the lymphatic channels. They are about the size and shape of small kidney beans, and as he took them he saw that those that had been closest to the lung were speckled white with cancer but that the ones beyond, near the trachea and the main bronchus going to the left lung, were a normal black.

"The adjacent ones are diseased," he said, "but we're running into a little luck after that. They look fine."

"Do you want these to go to Pathology, Doctor?" she said.

"Yes," he said, passing her another, "and I want this one and two others I'll give you from here marked tracheal bifurcation nodes and put in a separate bottle."

"Yes, sir."

"Now look at that," he heard someone say behind him. "I wonder if he knows what he's doing."

"Who's that?" he said, recognizing Maury Rand's voice. "Maury?"

"Yes, sir," Maury Rand said. "I guess he knows what he's doing."

"Mark this one peri-esophageal node," he said to the scrub nurse, and then for Maury Rand: "Listen. I'd be almost out of here by now, but I have a patient who didn't want to believe he had carcinoma, so while he was trying to wish it away it spread not only to his pericardium but also to his superior vena cava."

"Don't complain to me," Maury Rand said. "You wanted to be a chest surgeon."

"I'm not complaining," he said.

He had washed out the chest cavity with saline solution. He was waiting now while Bob Robinson drained it with the tonsil sucker.

"Knife," he said to the scrub nurse, "and have your steel-wire sutures ready with those long forceps. This is a bad bronchus to close because the cartilage of the wall has almost turned to bone."

"I don't think I care to stay to see this," Maury Rand said.

"Good-bye," he said, and then: "Orphan Annie?"

"Yes, Doctor."

"I'll let you take ten breaths for our patient and then stop."

"All right."

"Stop."

He cut a half-inch off the satin-white toughness of the tubelike, horseshoe-shaped bronchus to get beyond where the clamp had crushed the tissue and to permit him to make the closure flush with the trachea, or windpipe. As he made the cut he left the floor of the bronchus extending out slightly like a tongue to allow for the recoil, and then he forced the curved needle and the first suture through the middle of the roof and the floor and pulled the floor up tight. He knotted the wire three times and took the sponge stick, the clamp with the gauze, and pressed it over the opening.

"Now you can take ten more breaths," he said. With the gauze he was blocking the contaminated air from the mouth and pharynx from getting into his field, and he could count the breaths by the rhythmic gurgle of the moisture in the trachea. "Okay?"

"Yes, Doctor."

He put the eight other sutures in the same way. He spaced them evenly so that each would carry the same load, stopping after each for Orphan Annie.

"All right," he said, finally. "The bronchus is closed. Saline wash, please."

Now he would test it. Now he would see if he had really closed it so that none of that contaminated air could possibly get into this chest, and he took the pan of saline from the scrub nurse and, tipping the pan, he poured the solution into the open chest until it covered the stitches against the trachea.

"Now see if you can make it leak, Orphan Annie," he said. "I want you to push hard on your bag. You ready to push?"

"Yes, Doctor."

"All right, push. Push hard. Are you pushing, Annie?"

He watched the surface of the saline solution above the stiches. There were no bubbles.

"I'm pushing hard, Doctor," he heard her say.

"Okay," he said. "You can stop. Good girl."

He looked at the clock on the wall. It was 12:21.

"I think," he said, "that at this point he should have had two transfusions. Am I right, Orphan Annie?"

"He's just finishing his second, Doctor."

"How is he?"

"He's all right, Doctor. His blood pressure is 110 over 80."

When Bob Robinson and Darrow had finished draining the area with the tonsil suckers he began to isolate the superior vena cava. He was liberating it from its bed, the vein as big around as his thumb, thin-walled and the blueish-black of its used blood showing through, draining back to the heart.

"Now, Mary," he was saying, "I want you to have ready the largest of those three pieces of polyethylene tubing you've had soaking, the one about the size of my ring finger."

"Yes, Doctor."

"And where's our good float?"

"Right here, Doctor," the floating nurse said. She was kneeling, opening the used blood-stained gauze sponges and spreading them, to be counted on the drape on the floor in the corner.

"I want you to go out and get a pack of matches. You and I are going to light a camp fire in the scrub room."

"Yes, sir."

"There's a bleeder, Matt," Bob Robinson said. "I'll get it."

"And Mary?"

"Yes, sir."

"I'll want you to have your two lengths of umbilical tape ready and

those two lengths of the small tubing. Also your four-o silk with atromatic needles, twelve of them."

"Yes, Doctor."

He had finished freeing the vena cava, and when he looked up the
floating nurse was coming back from the scrub room. She held up a
pack of matches and he nodded.

"Now let me have that tubing, Mary."

That cancer involves a half-inch, he was thinking, taking the forceps
with the tubing in it, so I'll resect an inch. That will give me a quarter-
inch margin on either side and if I make the tube about three inches
long I'll have enough room to snare it and it won't be so long that we'll
have trouble getting it out.

"Scissors," he said, and with the forceps holding the tube in his left
hand he cut through it.

"All right," he said to the floating nurse. "Let's go."

She held the door to the scrub room open. He walked through, holding the tube in the forceps, and waited for her to let it swing closed
again.

"Now just light a match," he said, "and hold it steady."

When she had lighted the match and held it out to him, he rotated
one end of the tube just above the flame. As he turned it he saw the
end swell and flare up and out into an even, encircling collar.

"Very good," he said, withdrawing the tube. "Now blow out that
match and light another one."

"Yes, sir."

"Good girl," he said when he had completed the flared flange at the
other end. "You've just won your merit badge for outdoor camping."

"Thank you, Doctor," she said.

So this is it now, he was thinking, as she opened the door for him.
What it all comes down to now is just six minutes, at the most, just
those two three-minute intervals, and we can do it because we've got
those dogs to prove it and because I know we can do it.

"Now, Mary," he said, the others watching him, "let me have that
right pulmonary artery you've been taking such good care of."

"Yes, sir."

"What we're going to do now," he said, fitting the section of pulmonary artery over the three-inch length of flexible, translucent tubing,
"is this. We're going to put two clamps on the superior vena cava which
will give Orphan Annie a little trouble. We're going to open the vena
cava between them, slide in this plastic tube with the artery, snare the
vena cava around the ends of the tube, and remove the clamps. Then,

with the tubing serving as a temporary conduit so that the blood can drain through it, we're going to resect an inch of the vena cava, including the cancer, and put in the first sutures to make this graft. After that we'll clamp him again to annoy Orphan Annie, remove the tube, close our final sutures, and unclamp him. Clear, Annie?"

"Yes, sir."

"His blood pressure still all right?"

"Yes, sir."

"Now you know it's going to fall and he's going to turn blue when we restrict the blood from returning to the heart, but we won't keep him clamped for more than three minutes at either time. If I'm any good it'll be less."

"I understand."

"Now I've got another job for you," he said, turning to the floating nurse. "You're the timekeeper. When I tell you, I want you to watch that clock. Once I say: 'Go!' I want you to call out to me at the end of each minute. Call out: 'One minute! Two minutes! Three minutes!' I don't think we'll get to three, but if we do you call it out. Clear?"

"Yes, Doctor."

"And, once we start, don't take your eyes off the clock."

"No, sir."

"Now you hold this, Doctor," he said to Darrow, passing him the forceps holding the tubing with the sleeve of artery over it. "I'll take it from you when I want it."

"Yes, sir."

"Now let me have the umbilical tape," he said to the scrub nurse, "and then one of those smaller tubes and a small clamp."

It is like a thin white shoe string and he placed the first tourniquet-like snare around the vena cava close to the heart. He wrapped it around twice, loosely, and did the same for the second snare, three inches above the first and above the cancer plaque.

"I'm leaving them loose enough," he said to Bob Robinson, "so you can shift them as much as you have to before you snare them down."

"Good," Bob Robinson said, holding the two vascular clamps, one in either hand.

"Everybody set now?"

"Right, Matt," Bob Robinson said.

"Yes, Doctor."

"Scissors," he said. "Watch that clock. Go!"

He watched Bob Robinson put the first clamp across the vena cava above the upper snare. He watched him place the second below the lower snare and close to the heart, and then, pinching the superior vena cava above the cancer between his thumb and his index finger, he made the first cut with the scissors halfway across it, about a quarter of an inch above the cancer plaque. Then he pinched below the growth and made another cut but again going just halfway to leave the remaining portion as a floor on which he could slide in the polyethylene tubing. Then he made the longitudinal cut between the other two just outside the edge of the cancer.

"All right," he said, and then to Darrow: "I'll take that now."

With the forceps holding the polyethylene tubing and its artery in the middle, he slid the upper end into the opening in the vena cava and pushed it up until he felt it meet the upper clamp. Then, bending the tubing a little, he worked the lower end into the opening and straightened the tube and slid it down toward the heart.

"One minute, Doctor."

"Thank you."

"Take it down a little more, Matt," Bob Robinson said.

"Okay," he said, lining it up with the lower snare and thinking: We're doing fine. If I can just keep this lined up in position for this snare we'll do fine.

"It's good up here, Matt," Bob Robinson said.

"Then snare it, and I'll get this one," he said. He had to slide the umbilical tape up slightly to position it and then he pulled up on the snare, tightening the vena cava under it around the plastic tubing just within the flange at his end.

"Snared here," he said, removing the vascular clamp across the vena cava below the tube. "Unclamp him up there."

"Got it," Bob Robinson said.

"Two minutes, Doctor."

"Good," he said. "You can forget the clock now until I need you again."

"Very nice, Matt," Bob Robinson said. "Just about two minutes flat."

"Orphan Annie?" he said. "Our patient get blue?"

"Yes, Doctor."

"What's his pressure now?" he said. He was completing the dissection around the vena cava, above and below the growth.

"It dropped to 90, but it's beginning to come back up."

"His color improving?"

"Yes, Doctor."

"Here's our troublemaker," he said. Holding the severed one-inch section of the vena cava in the forceps, he turned it over, looking at it, and then handed it to the scrub nurse. "Now I'll need some three-o silk for two traction sutures."

He placed the first traction suture through the superior vena cava near the lower cut, tied it and passed the two long threads to Bob Robinson. Halfway around from the first and toward Bob Robinson's side he placed the second, tied it and handed the threads in their snap to Darrow.

"Just hold these loosely for me now," he said, and then to the scrub nurse: "That four-o silk and atromatic needle."

Now this is where we lost before, he was thinking, watching the vena cava rotate, its bottom side exposed as Bob Robinson pulled on his traction suture. It was right here, while I was doing these lower stitches that the tube popped out above and we had to reclamp and I lost Mr. Roberto Leon.

"You'll keep an eye on that upper snare, Rob?"

"I'm watching it. It's fine."

He started his first stitch through the vena cava and picked up with the needle the lower end of the sleeve of artery. Using a running stitch and sewing toward the under side he went a quarter of the way around and then passed the thread under the vena cava and picked it up on the other side.

"It's fine, Matt," Bob Robinson said.

"Good," he said, and then to Darrow: "I'll take that traction suture."

Pulling evenly, he saw the vena cava rotate the other way, toward himself and Darrow. He turned it until he could see the last bottom stitch he had put in.

"Just keep that same traction on," he said, handing the threads with the snap on them to Darrow.

"Yes, sir."

He completed the sewing of the bottom side. He took the traction suture from Darrow, allowed the vena cava to revert to its normal position, finished sewing across the upper side and tied it.

"Very good, Matt," Bob Robinson said, cutting the thread.

"Thank you, my friend."

He did the same at the top of the graft, except that he used the running stitch along the under side only. On the upper half he put in eight interrupted, or individual, stitches, pulling the threads all up together, putting a snap on them but leaving them loose, the polyethylene tubing showing between the stitches in the gap between the vena cava and the artery.

"A wipe for Dr. Carter," he heard Bob Robinson say.

He waited, aware for the first time now that he was sweating, while the floating nurse wiped his brow with the gauze.

"Thank you," he said. "How's he doing now, Orphan Annie?"

"All right, Doctor. His pressure's up to 110 over 80 now."

"Good," he said, "but now I've got to give you trouble again. We're going to clamp him once more to complete this graft. We were two minutes doing the first half, so we should be under two this time."

"Yes, Doctor."

"Is my timekeeper ready again?"

"Yes, Doctor," the floating nurse said.

"Now, when I say: 'Go!' you'll count off the minutes again."

"Yes, Doctor."

"Everybody else ready?"

"Right, Matt."

"Yes, Doctor."

"Vascular clamp," he said. "Watch the clock. All right. Go!"

He placed the clamp on the vena cava above the upper snare. He loosened the upper snare and discarded it and saw Bob Robinson had removed the lower one.

"Good," he said. "Now pinch it. Forceps."

He watched Bob Robinson pinch, between the thumb and forefinger of his left hand, the vena cava around the polyethylene tubing near the lower end and at the entrance to the heart. It was the way they had rehearsed it four times in the dog lab, Rob to pinch it hard enough to restrict any heavy back-flow of blood from the heart, but still permitting him, as he himself worked from the other end, to force the lower end just inside the entrance to the heart and down low enough to expose the upper end in the open upper suture line and extract it.

"Let up just a little," he said.

"Enough?"

"Good."

Sliding the tube down, forcing it ahead of his fingers as he squeezed the vena cava above it, he could see its upper end now at the loose upper suture line. With the forceps between two of the ties and grasping the top of the tube he withdrew it, some blood coming with it, but the blood stopping when Bob Robinson placed the lower clamp across the vena cava close to the heart. Then he picked up the snap holding the eight single sutures and pulled them up tight.

He removed the snap and started to tie the three knots on the first of the eight. He put in the first knot, felt it give a little under the second and put in the third. As he tied them he passed the long ends to Darrow.

"Just hold these," he said. "We'll cut them all together."

"One minute, Doctor."

"Good."

He did them all like that, putting in the three knots, passing them to Darrow. When he had finished seven he straightened up.

"Okay," he said. "Unclamp him below."

When Bob Robinson removed the clamp close to the heart he saw the vena cava fill up from below, then the bubbles of blood in the opening around the last loose suture as the rising blood forced the air out ahead of it. As the blood started to come he pulled the last suture up, tied it three times, and saw only the small leakage around the suture line.

"Got it," Bob Robinson said, reaching above and removing the upper clamp, the blood starting to drain now through the vena cava, through the graft and into the heart.

"Two minutes, Doctor."

"Oh," he said. "Thank you. I forgot to make the grand announcement. The graft is completed."

"That was nice, Matt," Bob Robinson said, cutting the sutures above the knots. "That couldn't have been more than a minute and fifty seconds."

"How's our patient, Orphan Annie?"

"His pressure is coming back, Doctor. It was down to 90 again."

"Color improving?"

"Yes, Doctor."

He placed the white strips of Surgicel over the suture lines at the top of the graft and then at the bottom. It would seal off the small bleeding around the needle holes and, finally be absorbed by the body.

"That's a beautiful graft, Matt," Bob Robinson said.

"It looks good to me, too," he said, examining it, and then to Darrow: "You understand that we had to use the patient's right pulmonary artery because the body tends to reject a foreign graft in the veins and when they've been tried in the past the blood has drained so slowly through the vena cava that they've been ineffective."

"I understand, sir."

"Now we've got to patch that pericardium."

With the index finger of his right hand he reached between the chest wall and the pleura adhering to it. Freeing the pleura, smooth and more fragile than the heart's own natural covering that he would repair, he cut a rectangle approximately the size of the opening he had made in the pericardium when he had removed the growth. This patch, translucent and not unlike the latex of his gloves, he spread on the towel to his left and in front of Darrow. Into each of the four corners of it he looped a silk thread, and holding the patch up by the top threads, the bottom threads dangling, he laid it over the opening with the bare heart beating in it, now covering the heart.

"Now Dr. Robinson will just keep a little tension on it," he said, passing the two top threads to Rob. Then he took the bottom threads and adjusted the patch. He sewed the four corners, then stitched the bottom and the other three sides.

"Any good tailor would be appalled by the crudeness of this," he said for Darrow, "but it will keep the heart from herniating out through the opening, and that's what it's for."

He had lost one that way about ten years before. It was that white-haired old man whose son had brought him all the way from Ireland. The old man had never spent a night away from his wife since they were married. He had never been out of his own country before and it was the spring of the year. The old man had charmed them all with his smile and his old country expressions and his laughter, and when he had lost him, that morning he would never forget, he had walked the son down to the end of that fourth floor and they had stood, each with one foot up on that radiator by that low window with the rod across it, and he had tried to explain it. The son had taken it with his face set and nodding, and then they had shaken hands and the son had left. Alone, he had stood there for a long time, looking up the river, alive in the sunlight. Across the avenue the trees were just coming to bud, and he had thought of how green they say Ireland is in the spring and then, perhaps for the last time, he had felt tears in his eyes.

"Besides," he said to Darrow, "in a few days this patch will grow right into place."

"I understand, sir."

"That's that," he said, and to Bob Robinson: "You care to put the tube in?"

"Any time," Bob Robinson said. "Let's lift this stockinet."

He released the clamp holding the stockinet and, lifting the stockinet, he watched Rob take his bearings from the marker clip he had put on the skin towels during draping and make his stab wound between the fourth and third ribs. He watched him tunnel up with the long, curved Carmault clamp and over the top of the second rib into the chest, then feed a corner of one end of the tube into the clamp inside the chest and pull the tube out.

"This is just a decompression tube," he said to Darrow. "We place it at the top of the chest so that, as the body fluid fills the chest, it can be unclamped occasionally to let the air out. We'll remove it in about thirty-six hours, and after several weeks that fluid will form a semi-solid jelly in there."

"Yes, sir."

"Now we're going back to that serial dilution of bacteria you learned in first year bacteriology," he said, and then to the scrub nurse: "Let me have that pan of saline."

"Yes, sir."

"Let's say there are ten million bacteria in there," he said, tipping the pan and pouring the saline into the chest. "Now you people suction this out and there'll be only ten thousand left. Then we'll fill the chest again, suction that out and we'll have only a thousand. The third time we'll be down to ten, and the fourth time to two lonely survivors. Right?"

"Yes, sir."

"Who's throwing things around here?" he said, hearing the bottle land in the plastic waste basket behind him.

"I am, Doctor," the scrub nurse said. "It's just a saline bottle."

"You mad at me, or something?"

"No, sir."

"All right," he said, after they had drained the chest with the tonsil suckers for the fourth time. "Now I'll shake this antibiotic powder in here to kill those last two bacteria, and if Dr. Darrow thinks that any organisms are still alive in that environment, I want him to speak up."

"I'd say you've got them, sir," Darrow said.

"How's our sponge count?"

"The sponge count is correct, Doctor," the floating nurse said.

"Then let's crank him closed."

It's 2:29, he thought, looking at the clock, and that's not bad. We can close in twenty minutes, and I can see Mrs. Scheller and her son and be out of here by 3. They won't be opening Mrs. Pappas until 3, so I'll be there in plenty of time.

He watched Bob Robinson turn the handle of the rib spreader and take it out. He watched him examine the walls of the incision for any bleeders and then put in the rib approximator, hooking one prong at each end behind the fourth and sixth ribs on either side of the opening left by the missing fifth rib. He watched him turn the handle and bring it abnormally close together in the center to get the ends as close as possible.

"Now we can go back to our one-two-three," he said to Darrow. "Your two-o silk, Mary."

Sewing through the intercostal muscles he brought together the edges of the periosteum that would regenerate the new rib. Then he restored the other muscles to their normal position, with the needle holder in his right hand casting the loose thread toward Rob as you would a trout fly, sewing through the tough fascia above and below each muscle and just catching a piece of the muscle, picking up the needle on the other side in such a way that, when he passed the empty needle to the scrub nurse, she could rethread it without having to unclamp the needle holder and reposition it, sewing the next interrupted stitch while Bob Robinson, the sutures always landing right in front of him, tied the previous one.

"And now we reconstruct our auscultatory triangle," he said to Darrow, who was cutting the ties for Rob. "There isn't any lung to listen to any more, but it's still a landmark for our reconstruction."

"Yes, sir."

"Orphan Annie? Can we have that right arm?"

"Yes, sir."

"Good," he said, seeing the shoulder move back toward normal, and then to Darrow: "Now, if you know your anatomy and the mechanics involved here you don't have to be a tackle for the Packers or the Giants to hold up this shoulder."

He showed him how, by placing the middle finger of the left hand on the acromion process, the bone running along the top of the shoulder, he could pull the shoulder up without moving the whole mass of the upper chest. Then he sewed the rhomboids and started on the trapezius muscles.

"You've scrubbed with a number of doctors in this hospital," he said to Darrow, "so you've seen cancer in a variety of organs."

"That's right, sir."

"In the male over forty, what's the most frequent cancer of any organ?"

"Well," Darrow said, "I was going to say cancer of the prostate or the stomach."

"They're both close," he said, sewing the latissimus dorsi now, "but the answer is cancer of the lung."

"Yes, sir."

"And you know that cancer of the lung is a great mimic."

"Yes, sir."

"So what other diseases cause the symptoms this patient had: pain in the chest, although in his case it was high in the shoulder, blood in the sputum, loss of appetite, loss of weight?"

"Well, TB and pneumonia."

"That's right," he said. "You can relax on that shoulder now."

He did the front edge of the latissimus dorsi, casting toward Bob Robinson, putting in the fifteen stitches. He had completed the triangle, and he waited while Bob Robinson removed the clamps and the stocki-net, leaving only the drapes and, beneath them, the four skin towels framing the incision. Then, casting again and sewing through the fascia in the fat layer, he brought it together with thirty interrupted stitches.

"Your four-o silk, Mary."

With a straight needle, matching the cross-marks he had made across the first scratch almost three and a half hours before, he put in the first stitch and pulled the merthiolate-painted skin together. Bob Robinson matched the other marks, and the two of them, each starting from his own end, put in the final stitches, sewing and tying at half-inch intervals, closing the wound.

"No," he said, as Darrow reached in and cut the threads close to the knot of the first tie. "We cut all the ties at once and about a half-inch from the knots so there's no chance of them coming undone."

When they had finished and Darrow had cut the ties he waited while Bob Robinson washed off the incision with a saline sponge and covered the wound with a towel. They removed the drapes and the skin towels, and he watched Bob Robinson swab the wound with the yellow-ish-brown tincture of benzoin to assist the adhesion of the tape and to protect the skin.

"Dr. Robinson likes to put it on the sutures, too," he said to Darrow, "so that if there are any organisms running around they'll get their feet stuck and be unable to reproduce."

He placed the gauze, four thicknesses of it, covering the long, curved wound. He held it there while Bob Robinson pressed down the four-inch-wide elastic adhesive tape at the upper end, stretched it, pressed it down over the gauze and bordering skin and, letting up on the stretching, terminated it at the lower end under the right breast.

"Rob," he said, "you're a gentleman. You've made me look good all morning, or is it afternoon?"

"It's 2:35, Doctor," the floating nurse said.

"Any time at all, Matt," Bob Robinson said. "It was a pleasure, and I think we really did something today."

"Orphan Annie?" he said. "How is he now?"

"He's all right, Doctor. His pulse is 82. His blood pressure is 120 over 80."

"I have to get over to University," he said to Bob Robinson. "I'll check on him before I leave and see Mrs. Scheller and her son if they're here. If you'll look in on our other people I'll be back to the office by 5:30."

"Sure, Matt."

"Will you dictate the op-note?"

"It'll be a pleasure."

"Thank you, all," he said, "Dr. Darrow and Orphan Annie and Mary and my good fire maker and timekeeper."

"You're welcome, Doctor."

The floating nurse was untying his gown and he slipped out of it and left it in her hands. He tossed the rubber gloves to her and pushed the door open. In the hall he slipped the mask down and untied it from around his neck, thinking: I should know her name. It's no good not being able to call them by their names and it used to be that I'd hear them once and remember them but it isn't that way any more.

2:38 P.M.

XX

The locker room appeared empty, but as he started to undress he heard voices coming over the top of the row of lockers. He stripped out of his scrub suit and threw the shirt and trousers with the cap and mask into the canvas hamper.

"I don't care what Ribicoff says," he heard one of the voices he did not recognize say, "and I don't care what Kennedy says, either. The moment anyone tries to tell me what patients I can treat or how many I can treat I'm getting out of the profession. I've been at this too long to . . ."

He took his money out of his left sock and reached into his locker and put it in his wallet. He took his watch out of the other sock and put it on his wrist.

"Of course they're not admitting to it now," the voice was saying, "but give them an inch and they'll take . . ."

He dressed, aware for the first time, of a slight discomfort in his trapezius muscles, high in his shoulders. It was not the over-all tiredness he had known after Roberto Leon, after they had worked so hard for those six and a half hours and then lost, but just that small ache that he felt more often now in recent years.

In fact I'd like to go right back in there and do another one, he was thinking. It worked beautifully, and I wish Stan or Bronson had seen it. That Darrow doesn't really know what he saw because he doesn't know how this thing has been licking us all for years, but there's no reason why, if we can get a clean artery like that, we can't do it every time. We know we can do it now, and if Mr. Scheller comes back like he should, if he doesn't fall off a scaffold or get hit by a cab in the next couple of months, I'll do a paper on it for the *Journal*. The trouble with doing a paper is that these days everybody is writing and nobody's reading, but this one is worth it and I'll do it.

"So ask anybody in England," the voice coming over the lockers was saying. "Oh, I know there are some kids just out of school who like the security and the regular hours, but you ask any of the good ones how they like it and they'll tell you . . ."

He had finished dressing and he walked out into the hall. He stopped at the nurses' station and waited for Sally Wheeler to finish talking on the phone.

"Oh, it's you," she said, turning from the phone. "That was your patient's son. He's up in the room, waiting for news."

"Call him back, will you?" he said. "Tell him I'll see him in the lounge up there in two minutes. I just want to check on his father in the recovery room."

"I understand you did very well, a real tricky one."

"I missed you, Sally, but I'll see you in the Bahamas."

"After today," she said, "I'll need some kind of vacation."

There were four of them in the recovery room, Mr. Scheller closest to the door. He was lying on his back, the sheet up to his neck, the head of the bed elevated in the semi-Fowler's position to encourage the flow through the graft, the intravenous tube running to his left arm from the suspended bottle of five per cent glucose in water.

"Is he awake yet?" he said to the nurse.

"Not yet, Doctor. He's starting to move but he hasn't really responded yet."

"How's his blood pressure?"

"Fine. He's 120 over 80."

He lifted the sheet and picked up Mr. Scheller's right hand. He found the pulse was strong enough and regular enough and he saw that, while the skin color was still pale, the beds of the finger nails and lips were pink. He ran his thumb below the Adam's apple and into the sternal notch, that V at the top of the breast bone and, feeling the trachea, the windpipe, still perfectly centered he knew that the heart had not shifted.

"Will you feel in here once in a while?" he said to the nurse. "I just want you to check occasionally that the trachea is remaining in the midline."

"Yes, Doctor."

"Thank you."

"You're welcome, Doctor."

He walked to the elevator, waited for it, and then rode up to the sixth floor. As he stepped off the elevator he saw Mr. Scheller's son waiting for him right there and looking right at him.

"I'm sorry, Doctor," the young man said, "but I couldn't wait. I . . ."

"That's all right," he said, smiling. "Your father's doing fine."

"God bless you, Doctor," the young man said, the tears coming into his eyes, but the young man smiling and shaking hands. "God bless you always."

"That's all right."

"Will you tell my mother now? It's been a long wait for her."

"Certainly."

The young man walked, hurrying, ahead of him to the lounge. Mrs. Scheller, in the dark blue dress and holding her handbag, was standing waiting for them, and when she saw them the tears started into her eyes, too.

"But the doctor says he's fine, Mom," the son said. "He says he's all right."

"That's right," he said, smiling and taking Mrs. Scheller's hand. "We got it all out, and he's in the recovery room now. Pretty soon they'll be bringing him back here to his own room."

"May God bless you, Doctor," she was saying.

"After they bring him back," he said, "you'll be able to see him for a few minutes. Of course, he'll be pretty sleepy."

"God bless you again, Doctor," Mrs. Scheller said, still crying and still holding his hand.

"Thank you," he said. "He's going to be all right."

So that's that, he was thinking, riding down in the elevator, and it's the way you always dreamed it would be and the way it is sometimes.

You always did want to be a hero and when you win them it's great and it's impossible to even imagine anything else like it in this world.

In the surgeon's lounge he snapped off the light button next to his name and he walked to the door and out onto the street. He looked up at the sky, as gray as it had been in the morning, and he walked to his car.

As he drove down the block, starting to relax, it came to him that he had had nothing to eat or drink since the coffee and the cake with Mary MacGowan almost six hours before and that he was hungry. With the heart at University and then the office he would not get another chance until they sat down at that party, and he would stop at the hot-dog cart near the river as he used to do regularly before the old man who ran it died during the summer from whatever it was.

When he stopped at the second light he saw the cart with the orange and green umbrella at the opposite corner. The young man who took the old man's place was serving a customer, with a couple of others waiting, in their work clothes and out of one of the warehouses or, perhaps, off the docks.

The light changed and he drove across the intersection. He turned the car across the street and up onto the apron and stopped it next to the cart, the front bumper almost touching the corrugated steel door of the warehouse. He had done it many times just like this, while the old man was still alive, and he turned off the motor and found he had no change and that the smallest bill he had was a ten. He waited until the young man, seeing him, walked over.

"What's yours, Mac?" the young man said.

"Let me have a hot dog with mustard," he said, handing him the bill, "and a Coke."

"One with mustard and a Coke," the young man said. He had turned and had started back toward the cart, but he stopped and turned around again and handed back the bill. "I ain't got change of a ten."

"But I haven't anything smaller," he said, "and I want to eat."

"I already told you," the young man said, looking at him again and shrugging.

"All right," he said. "You hold the ten. I'll be back in a couple of days to get the change. I trust you."

"I don't wanna be responsible for it," the young man said, turning his back on him again and walking back to the wagon.

He waited while the young man served another customer. He waited for him to look at him again.

"Look," he said, finally, the others eating their hot dogs and watching this now. "Are you going to give me something to eat or not?"

"I told you I ain't got the change, Mac," the young man said, and then he looked at the others and shrugged. "I already told him that."

It was 2:55 P.M.